ELEMENTAL THIEF

Also by Rachel Morgan

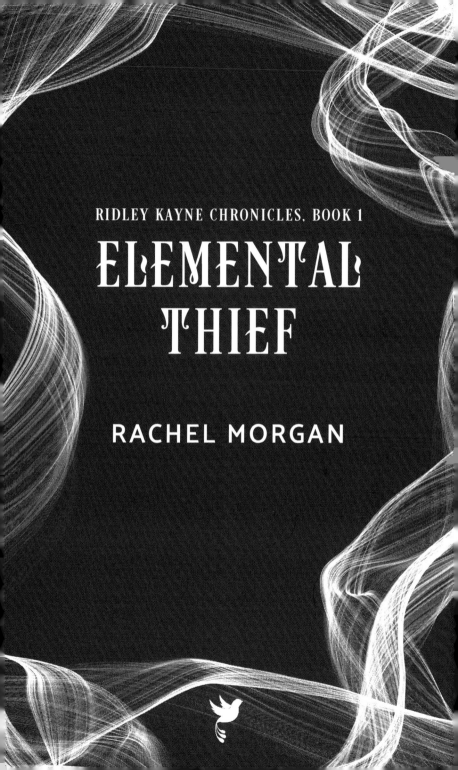

RIDLEY KAYNE CHRONICLES, BOOK 1

ELEMENTAL
THIEF

RACHEL MORGAN

ISBN 978-0-6399436-3-3

www.rachel-morgan.com

CHAPTER 1

THE DARK AFTERNOON SKY crackled with magic as Ridley Kayne crept across the penthouse apartment she was about to rob. She kept her hood up and her head angled away from the cameras, hiding both her face and her distinctive white-blond hair. Years had passed since she was last at the top of Aura Tower, but not much had changed. The open-plan space with its high ceilings and gleaming surfaces was still decorated with uncomfortable-looking furniture, exotic art, and the Davenports' private collection of ancient artifacts. That last bit was where Ridley's interest lay, so she was relieved to see the Davenports hadn't grown tired of showing off their most priceless possessions.

She tiptoed past glass cases containing centuries-old urns, hand-painted beads, and items fashioned from rusted metal and carved bone. It was a wonder no one had robbed this collection before, especially since the items were now infinitely more valuable than they'd been before the Cataclysm destroyed most of the world's history. Then again, Ridley thought as she paused before a porcelain vase to breathe in the unusual scent of fresh flowers, it was probably impossible for anyone who didn't possess her exact skill set to get in and out of this apartment undetected. No doubt the richest family in Lumina City thought they were untouchable way up here on the two-hundredth floor.

She exhaled and continued moving, marveling at how quiet it was up here. The sounds that usually accompanied her jobs—the revving of car engines, the ads on billboard screens, the buzz of scanner drones—were almost nonexistent at the top of the city's tallest building. All Ridley could hear through the floor-to-ceiling windows was the wind and the faint hiss and crack of magic in the storm clouds. She turned near the grand piano, her eyes moving from one artifact to the next—some familiar; others new to her—as she searched for one in particular. Her gaze skimmed across a coffee table, a rug, and up to the paintings on the opposite wall.

And finally, she spotted it. On a pedestal positioned between two paintings stood a solid gold figurine with a ring of tiny green stones around its neck. It was enclosed within a glass box, but that was no problem for Ridley. She headed straight for it, wondering how much time would pass before the Davenports noticed it was—

At the sound of a lock clicking, Ridley froze. Her gaze snapped toward the pair of entrance doors. Then, without hesitating a moment longer, she darted forward and slipped around the corner into the passageway that led to the bedrooms. Her heart thumped uncomfortably as she pictured the doors swinging open. A moment later, they closed. Someone muttered something in a voice too quiet for Ridley to tell whether the owner was male or female. She knew what the muttering was about though. A shrill beep should have pierced the air the moment the door opened, but Ridley had disabled the apartment's entire security system as soon as she'd arrived, and so the newcomer was greeted by silence.

The staccato click of heels against the polished floor met Ridley's ears. So it wasn't Mr. Davenport who was home, and it wasn't the Davenports' son—not that Ridley would ever have expected Archer Davenport to walk in; he'd left Lumina City more than a year ago and hadn't been back since. That left—

"Mom, you forgot the alarm again," a voice groaned.

Delilah Davenport. She wasn't supposed to be home yet. Ridley was almost certain she had a dance class on Thursday afternoons. "Well I just got home, and it wasn't on," Lilah continued, presumably speaking into her commscreen. "And neither is the smart home system, it would seem. Probably needs an update." Ridley heard a tap and a beep and then—

"Good evening, Delilah," a feminine voice purred.

"There we go," Lilah muttered as Ridley smirked. She'd disabled the home automation system along with the security. The last thing she needed when attempting a heist was a robotic voice greeting her and offering her a drink or asking what music she wanted to listen to.

"What can I get for you this—"

"Nothing, thanks," Lilah snapped in a loud voice. "Yes, I know it isn't six yet," she continued in a quieter tone, the clean click of her heels moving toward the other side of the living area. "Irina wasn't feeling well, so she ended the lesson early."

Ridley tilted her head to the side until she could see Lilah. The girl had one arm wrapped around her waist and her commscreen pressed to her ear as she faced the window. Ridley followed her gaze to the view outside. Heavy clouds blotted out so much of the sky that street lamps across the city were already on. From way up here, at the top of Lumina City's tallest building, she could see beyond the many twinkling lights and the ten-story-high wall to the wastelands that surrounded the city in every direction. Flashes of magic illuminated the overgrown remains of buildings and roads, but other than that, the train was the only other source of light out there. It wound through the darkness like a bright silver snake with its arxium metal casing lit up. Ridley followed it with her eyes, imagining the walled city hundreds of miles away at the other end.

"That's fine," Lilah said to her mother, snapping Ridley's attention back to the inside of the apartment. "I'm sure he won't mind. He saw you and Dad last night." She paused, and Ridley bit her lip as she considered her next move. "Yes, the two of us can just order something. We'll be fine, Mom."

Lilah ended the call, and Ridley pulled her head back before the other girl could turn and see her. Footsteps moved across the room toward the passageway. Ridley pushed away from the wall and ran for the nearest door. She slipped past it and pressed herself against the wall inside the next room—and realized her mistake immediately. She'd assumed this was still a guest bedroom, but the pink and purple items furnishing the space and the clothes draped across almost every surface clearly marked it as Lilah's. With no time to duck back out, Ridley ran for the walk-in closet.

She could have used other means to conceal herself, but this was her second job for the day and she was growing tired. Making her way unseen into two apartments and disarming two security systems had taken a lot out of her. And she still had to escape Aura Tower, which would take almost as much effort as breaking in. Exhausting herself before she managed to get out wasn't a good idea.

She reached the closet and pulled the doors shut just as Lilah entered the bedroom, raising her voice to tell the lights to switch on. Ridley forced herself to breathe slowly as she leaned forward and peered between the slats. Lilah tossed her purse onto the bed and told the large, sleek screen sitting on her desk to wake up and find her favorite streaming celebrity news channel. Several moments later, the cheerful voices of two women and a man filled the room as they discussed the fashion that had graced the red carpet at a recent charity event. Ridley shut her eyes for a moment and pushed aside the familiar pang in her chest at the mention of several well-known designers. Stupid celebrity news. Did Lilah really have to choose *now* to watch this trash?

Ridley opened her eyes to discover that Lilah wasn't, in fact, watching her favorite celebrity news channel. She sat on her bed with two laptops open in front of her. As her fingers sped across one keyboard and then the other, Ridley smiled.

Seeing the over-the-top wealth of the people she stole from always helped assuage her guilt. Not that she felt all that bad to begin with. People like the Davenports had far more than they could ever need. Ridley was only doing her bit to right the scales by taking from them.

Lilah scooped her glossy brown hair behind one ear, then shut both laptops and stood. She placed one in the bottom drawer of her dresser beneath several layers of clothing, and the other behind a pile of books at the top of a bookshelf. *Interesting*, Ridley thought, but Lilah was now crossing the room, which meant Ridley had far more urgent matters to pay attention to. If Lilah opened the closet, Ridley would have no choice but to—

But Lilah headed straight past Ridley's hiding spot and into her en-suite bathroom. Ridley exhaled and raised her hand to the closet door, listening carefully. The shower turned on. Steam drifted lazily into the bedroom. Ridley counted to ten, and when Lilah still hadn't reappeared, she pushed the closet open, shut the doors silently behind her, and hurried from the room. Less than a minute later, with the gold figurine in her hand and the glass box sitting undisturbed on its pedestal, she left the apartment the same untraceable way she'd entered.

No one called out to her as she made her way across the marble floor of Aura Tower's foyer two hundred stories below, but she waited until she was out of the building and across the street before allowing herself to relax. She zipped up her jacket, tucked the figurine inside, and breathed more easily. She'd done it.

She turned a corner, believing no one was watching as a gust of wind blew her hood back and tangled the strands of her pale hair. Ten minutes later, in an empty side street behind several overflowing garbage bins, she assumed no one witnessed the quick exchange in which the figurine moved from her hand to someone else's and a thick envelope found its way into a pocket inside her jacket.

But after making two planned stops at two different rundown apartment buildings and noticing the same shadowy figure outside each one, Ridley began to grow suspicious. So she headed away from home instead of toward it. She took another three turns into three random streets before finally confirming her fear: Someone was following her.

CHAPTER 2

THE MAN FOLLOWING RIDLEY wore a vintage fedora hat, and his hands were pushed deep into the pockets of his dark maroon coat. He must have seen the envelope Ezra handed to her, must have seen the cash she took a few seconds to count before slipping the envelope inside her jacket. He would also have seen her stopping at the two apartment blocks, but what he *wouldn't* have seen were the two new envelopes she'd left on two different kitchen tables, each filled with half the money Ezra had given her. Ridley had nothing left on her now, but the man in the maroon coat didn't know that.

She mentally kicked herself as she tried not to change her pace. She and Ezra, the dealer she sold her stolen items to, were always so careful about the meeting spots they chose. How had someone seen them? But perhaps, Ridley wondered as she turned yet another corner and increased her pace ever so slightly, this wasn't a coincidence. She wasn't the type to get paranoid, but this job hadn't exactly been of the regular variety. Ezra rarely received specific requests from clients.

Ridley stole things—jewelry, art, pre-Cataclysm collectibles—Ezra presented them to whoever might be interested, and hopefully the items would sell. It wasn't every day that one of those clients came back to him and said, *Get me this item from Alastair Davenport's private collection of ancient relics.* Which meant someone *knew* before she even broke into the Davenports' apartment that it would happen. And if that someone hadn't been careful with his information ...

"Dammit," she muttered as specks of rain landed on her head and shoulders. A glance at the store window to her right told her the man was gaining on her. Perhaps he knew she'd noticed him and decided there was little point in keeping his distance now. Or maybe he didn't know, but either way, it was time she stopped pretending she was oblivious.

She sped up, heading straight for the subway entrance up ahead. If she wasn't so tired already, she would have disappeared another way, but she knew if she tried *that* particular method right now, she'd end up with the kind of migraine that felt like a screwdriver piercing her eyeballs. Besides, at this time of day it would be easy to lose the man among the crowds down in the subway.

She reached the subway entrance and the scanner that arched over it. Her pulse quickened, as it did every time she approached a scanner, but it beeped happily as she passed beneath it, the round bulb above her head flashing green for a second as it detected her AI2. She hurried down the steps, dodging between people and raising her fingers out of habit to brush the two small scars on her neck just behind her left ear.

The first scar came from her first amulet, embedded beneath her skin at birth. The old-fashioned term 'amulet' always conjured up images of crudely molded arxium charms hanging from necklaces and bracelets, the way people wore their protection centuries ago before someone decided to place a charm beneath the skin instead. These days, the amulet was a flat piece of silvery arxium metal the size of Ridley's pinkie nail. Its anti-magic properties—the same properties that made arxium a necessary component of the wasteland trains and the wall surrounding Lumina City—prevented anyone from using magic against her.

She got her second scar at roughly the same time everyone else did: after the Cataclysm when the use of magic was banned worldwide. Just in case anyone planned to ignore that law—anyone stupid enough to risk pulling on the wild elemental magic that now covered most of the earth—an additional law was put in place dictating that everyone receive a second amulet, the Arxium Implant 2. With this second amulet beneath the skin, it was impossible to pull magic from the environment and use it.

Ridley reached the bottom of the steps and pushed forward through the throng of people. Muffled music thumped from a nearby pair of headphones while somewhere overhead, an intercom beeped and a voice announced a delay in one of the subway lines. Instead of moving with the crowd toward the turnstile, Ridley weaved her way to the restroom. Seconds later, she was inside, holding the door slightly ajar and watching through the sliver of space for the man in the maroon coat. She spotted him as he reached the final step and began struggling to push his way through the crowd toward the turnstile.

"Ohmygosh, and they caught her, like, *right* in front of my apartment building!"

Ridley glanced over her shoulder as she became aware that she wasn't alone in the restroom. Two girls leaned against the wall beside the hand dryer, peering at something on a commscreen. A video, she realized as a tinny female voice reached her ears: "... finally tracked her down and arrested her earlier this afternoon." Ridley returned her gaze to the man who was heading straight for the turnstile and about to give her a chance to sneak back up to the street.

"What an idiot," one girl said. "She had to know she'd end up dead."

"I know, right? One-way ticket to the death penalty."

"Well, yeah, either that or from magic blowing up in her face. Like that chick on top of the Haddison Building earlier this year."

At the word 'magic,' Ridley's attention snapped back to the two girls.

"Serena Adams?" the second girl replied.

"Yeah, her. Why don't people *learn* when they see things like that? No, they have to go and experiment and put everyone else's lives in danger."

"Shh," the other girl said, and pointed at the commscreen.

"All we can confirm at this point," the voice from the video continued, "is that her AI2 was removed sometime within the last few days, allowing her to pull magic from the environment, a crime that has been punishable by death for close to a decade now. The woman, whose name we have yet to confirm, is an employee of Capita Farms on the edge of the city. It was the farm's proximity to the arxium wall that alerted several of the woman's colleagues to the fact that elemental magic was being used: The magic rebounded upon making contact with the wall's arxium plating, first causing minor damage to a solar panel, then followed minutes later by a small explosion that destroyed a section of a wheat field."

As the newscaster continued speaking, Ridley touched the scars behind her ear yet again, hesitating as her eyes followed the man in the maroon coat. But as much as she wanted to know more about this woman who'd just got herself arrested, Ridley had more important things to worry about right now. She pulled the door open enough to stick her head out and watched the man finally push through the turnstile and rush forward without looking back. She ducked out of the restroom and walked the other way, back to the stairs and up to the street.

Raindrops—a little larger than before—pattered down around her. Ridley tugged her jacket off, turned it inside out to reveal the light blue lining, and pulled it back on. After covering her head with the hood once more, she shoved her hands into her pockets and walked as quickly as she could without running. In the back of her mind, she mapped out the quickest way home—a two-block walk, a bus ride, and another quick walk—but she kept most of her attention directed behind her.

With every corner she turned, her eyes darted back over her shoulder. Still no maroon coat or fedora hat in sight.

The bus she caught carried her fifteen minutes away from the city center. She survived the annoying kid kicking the back of her seat while singing rude variations on the old 'roses are red, magic is blue' poem and got hastily to her feet as soon as the bus neared the first Demmer District stop. She climbed off, jumped over a puddle, and skirted the soggy trash blocking the drain. Demmer wasn't exactly the slum of the city—the bus would have had to continue for another five minutes or so to reach that part of town—but it certainly wasn't an area anyone from the glitzy skyscraper district would frequent.

Ridley crossed the street as the bus grumbled and groaned and pulled away from the stop. She turned a corner—and that was when the bolt of magic flashed downward. It struck a pole half a block ahead of her, rebounded off the bent pole in multiple zigzagging flashes, and hit the road, cracking the tar and sending a small shock wave through the ground. Ridley stumbled back against a laundromat window, her heart jumping into high speed as the last spark of magic cracked a garbage bin in half and vanished. Her first thought was that it must have come from the storm brewing overhead. The many arxium panels—flat bus-sized pieces of arxium metal hovering a little higher than the city's tallest building—were supposed to reflect atmospheric magic away from the earth. But the large spaces that existed between the panels made it easy for stray magic to find its way through during particularly volatile storms. It was startling to witness firsthand, but it wasn't unheard of.

Then Ridley's gaze moved beyond the fissure in the road. She saw flashing blue and red lights and a car screeching to a stop. A woman raced in front of the car, then leaped over the cracked road. Something blue and wispy rose away from her hands and arms, streaming behind her as she ran. Shouts and gunshots echoed between the buildings, and Ridley realized suddenly that the magic wasn't from the storm above. The magic was pulled from right here in the city. Pulled by the woman fleeing past her. Ridley flattened herself against the laundromat window, her thoughts tumbling wildly over one another. Was this the same woman the police had arrested earlier? Had she somehow escaped? Would the magic she'd pulled end up destroying the entire street and everyone in it?

Before running around the corner and out of view, the woman grabbed hold of a lamppost and swung around to face the cops racing toward her. Her hands came together, then appeared to claw at something invisible in the air. Just beyond her fingertips, magic appeared in glowing blue wisps. With precise, hurried movements—movements Ridley hadn't seen anyone use in years—the woman scooped at the magic. Her palms touched, her hands twisted, then her arms moved apart in a sweeping motion as her fingers traced patterns too fast for Ridley to follow. The wisps coalesced, formed a bubble, then exploded outward in a brilliant blue flash.

Ridley ducked down, squeezing her eyes shut and throwing her arms up to shield her face. The light vanished almost instantly. She blinked and tried to peer closer, both afraid and curious. Surely the woman had intended to create more than just a flash? Her hands or fingers must have made the wrong movement, produced the wrong conjuration. Ridley watched as the woman pulled desperately at the air a second time.

Crack.

Ridley flinched as the woman jerked backward. She seemed to sway a moment, then half-fell, half-slumped to the road. Her head hit the tar and the faint blue wisps drifted away just as three uniformed men gripping guns reached her motionless body.

Ridley didn't wait to see what happened next. As the rain began to fall harder, she pushed away from the window and ran.

CHAPTER 3

RIDLEY DID HER BEST to think of *anything* except the dead woman as she ran all the way home: The smell of rain, the slap of her shoes against the pavements, the spray of water every time she hit a puddle. By the time she reached Kayne's Antiques, her throat burned and she was completely out of breath. She leaned her forehead against the glass door for several moments, allowing her heart rate to slow and making one last effort to shove the image of that still body from her mind.

As thunder rumbled overhead, she inhaled deeply and pushed open the door into the antique store. The familiar chime of the bell above the door greeted her ears, tinkling again as the door eased shut behind her. "Hey, Dad," she called to the man sitting behind the heavily carved oak desk on the far side of the store.

He looked up and peered at her through his jeweler's glasses. "Oh, sweetie, you're home." He tilted the magnifier lenses upward and smiled. "How was tutoring?"

"Same as usual," she answered, shrugging out of her wet jacket. It wasn't a lie. She *had* been at the tutoring center before sneaking into the apartment of one of her students to retrieve the stolen pearls she'd overheard him bragging about. It was only after that quick and easy robbery that she'd taken a detour to Aura Tower. *Busy day*, she thought to herself, breathing out a long sigh. "Did you eat lunch?" she asked as she slipped between the displays of teapots, clocks, books, and other old objects. Maverick Kayne tended to forget about meals when he was fully absorbed in his work—which appeared to be the case right now, given the numerous minuscule watch pieces and tiny tools spread across his work surface. "I left something in the fridge for you, remember?" Ridley walked around the counter with the antique cash register and stopped beside her father's desk.

"Uh ..." His eyebrows, flecked with gray, pinched together. He twisted his wedding ring around his fourth finger. "Yes. I did have lunch. Oh, and you don't need to worry about doing anything for dinner. Shen brought something over from his mom."

"Hey," Shen said at the sound of his name. Ridley looked up and found him standing in the doorway that led to the back rooms, his hand raised in a half wave and his straight black hair almost touching the doorframe above him. "I left the dish on your stove upstairs."

"Hi, stranger," Ridley said, her face breaking into a smile. "Didn't see you at the rock wall this morning. Did you end up having to work?"

"Yeah." Shen slouched against the doorframe. It was a bad habit of his from years of being self-conscious about his height. "Sorry about that. Mom needed help. Is Meera doing any better?"

"Well, I don't think she hates it anymore, so that's progress."

"Great." Shen brightened. "It's only taken us, what, five years to convince her to give indoor climbing a go?"

"Approximately. But she still says, and I quote, 'This is one of the stupidest sports ever.'" Ridley rolled her eyes and leaned her hip against the side of Dad's desk. "Anyway, thanks for bringing dinner over. I could have come and picked it up."

"And saved me the looooong walk across the road from our shop to yours?"

"Yes. That long and arduous walk."

"It's a strenuous one indeed," Shen said with a long-suffering sigh.

"I don't know how your short legs ever make the journey."

"It's a mystery. I should be winded and out of breath right now."

"You two," Dad muttered without looking up at them, and they both started laughing. Shen and his family lived across the road above the Chinese takeout shop his parents owned. Mrs. Lin had been sending food over at least once a week since Ridley and her father moved in above Kayne's Antiques after the Cataclysm. Ridley and Shen had been friends almost as long.

"Well, tell your mom thanks." Ridley held up her hand, and Shen high-fived her as he walked past.

"Sure. See you and Meera at rock climbing tomorrow

afternoon. Unless," he added as he reached the front door and looked back, "you guys have tutoring again?"

"No, today was the last class." Ridley scooped her damp hair away from her neck—being careful not to pull the silver chain she always wore—and ran her fingers through the tangled ends, trying to separate them. "The center figured they'd let the kids relax for their last four days of summer break."

"How kind of them." The bell chimed as Shen opened the door. He lifted the hood of his raincoat. "'Kay, see you tomorrow then."

"See ya." Giving up on the tangles, Ridley turned to face Dad and found him watching her. "What?"

"Are *you* planning to relax over the next four days, or will you be spending all your time obsessively climbing indoor rocks?"

She spread her arms out, palms up. "What's wrong with obsessively climbing indoor rocks? It's exercise. A full-body workout for both strength and cardio."

Dad sighed and tilted the magnifier lenses back down over his eyes. "Yes. You've quoted the promotional pamphlet to me before. But how about you spend a little time *outside*?" he suggested as he picked up one of his tiny tools. "You know, relaxing and enjoying the last few days of summer?"

Ridley snorted. "Ah, yes, summer. Rain only half thc time instead of rain and snow all the time. Temperatures *almost* warm enough for me to remove my jacket."

"You forgot the bit about working on your tan," Dad added without looking up.

A small smile touched her lips as she looked at the picture frame standing beside a coffee mug of pens and pencils on the desk. "And you forgot to remind me to be grateful we're alive and that Lumina City survived the Cataclysm. That's what you usually say at this point in the conversation."

Dad still didn't look up, but Ridley could see his smile. "After nine summers repeating this dialogue, I figured it might be time for you to say that bit."

Ridley put on her chirpiest sing-song voice. "I'm grateful we're alive and that Lumina City survived the Cataclysm."

"Like you mean it?"

She sighed, her fake smile slipping. "I do mean it. I really do. I'm beyond grateful we were protected." An image of the erratic flashes of magic bouncing back and forth across the street earlier crossed her mind before she continued. "It's just ... what's the point in spending time outside when the sun barely manages to make its way through the clouds and magic, and when it does, it's hardly warm enough to be enjoyable? It's nothing like the old summers."

Ridley was eight years old at the time of the Cataclysm, old enough to remember now what summer was like before that fateful day. The day of the GSMC, the Global Simultaneous Magic-Energy Conversion. That was the day thousands of magicists around the world had tried to harness more energy from the elements than they'd ever harnessed before using thousands of simultaneous conjurations—and instead ended up destroying most of civilization. Magic, wild and powerful, had erupted across the earth, ripping through anything and everything that wasn't protected by arxium. And those cities that had been labeled paranoid—the cities that had 'wasted money' putting thousands of hovering arxium panels in place to reflect magic away on the off chance that something *might* one day go wrong—were the only places that survived.

Ridley's home, Lumina City, had been one of those places. She was fine. Dad was fine. But her mother had been out there, on the road, traveling back from visiting Ridley's grandparents where they lived in a small town several hours away. A town that had no arxium protection. Ridley used to fantasize about her mother returning one day. Perhaps she'd been inside someone's arxium bunker and not on the road. Perhaps she was busy battling through the wastelands, making her way back to Ridley and Dad. But in her heart, she knew it wasn't possible. Her mother had called from the road mere minutes before the explosion that changed everything. Ridley had spoken to her.

After the Cataclysm, Dad's business had gone under—every fashion accessory and jewelry item he'd crafted using magic had been rounded up by a new government task force and destroyed—and within the space of a few months, after Dad settled all their debts, he and Ridley found themselves left with nothing but a small amount of savings and Grandpa's antique store. Dad had inherited it several years earlier when Grandpa died, and someone had been managing it since then. Dad took over management of the store—he couldn't afford to pay someone else to do it—and added 'watch repairs and jewelry design' to the sign in the window. He didn't get many customers though. True antiques were valuable, but the name Kayne scared people off. It was risky doing business with someone whose primary income used to be generated by magic. Who knew if Maverick Kayne might secretly use magic to create a pair of earrings or get a watch to start ticking again? What if the antiques he sold were actually created by some conjuration he did whenever the scanner drones weren't flying overhead?

Ridley knew about the rumors because she'd heard them. She'd listened intently as she sat on uncomfortable couches waiting for Dad while he went to interview after interview, trying to find a new job in a post-Cataclysm world where no one needed the skills he possessed. She quickly learned that no one would ever give him work. It took Dad a little longer to come to the same conclusion.

And so Ridley and her father remained in the small apartment above Kayne's Antiques, and nothing—especially summer—was ever the same again.

"I know it's not like the old summers," Dad said, pulling her from the memory of hot sand, icy lemonade, and the smell of sunscreen. "But it's the only summer you're getting, so I suggest you enjoy the last of it."

"Dad," she said, pressing her palms down on the desk and leaning closer to him. "If anyone should spend some time outside, it's you. You're in here *all* the time."

"That isn't true. I'm not in here during your shifts."

"And how many of those do I have? Not nearly enough. You need to give me more so you can have time to—"

"Sweetie, it's fine." Dad finally removed the jewelers glasses and smiled at her. Though wrinkles creased his brow from too much frowning and his hair was now more gray than black, his eyes were still as blue as Ridley's. "I know how hard you have to work to keep your scholarship. And there's all your extra-murals. I'm not going to pile any more onto your shoulders than I have to."

Guilt shifted uncomfortably in the pit of Ridley's stomach. She was hardly the perfect child Dad thought she was. Sure, she committed hours of her life to tutoring underprivileged kids, and it was something she genuinely enjoyed, but the fact that it would look great on her application to join The Rosman Foundation after graduation was the main reason she'd started tutoring. And indoor climbing was a good way to stay fit and healthy, but the skills she'd learned definitely came in handy when breaking in and out of certain buildings. "What about *your* shoulders?" she pressed, pushing her ulterior motives to the back of her mind where they belonged.

"My shoulders are just fine, Riddles. Even if they're not *physically* as strong as yours."

Ridley knew there was little point in arguing with him. It had never worked before. "Well, can I at least close up for you today?" she asked, looking at the cuckoo clock on the wall. "You can finish that watch tomorrow. Go upstairs and read a book or something until closing time. Or take a walk around the block. Get some rain and fresh air. I mean, you know—" she rolled her eyes "—air that's fresher than the centuries-old air inside this place."

Dad leaned back and stretched his arms out to the side. "Maybe," he mumbled around a yawn. He opened one of the desk drawers, pulled out his cracked secondhand commscreen, and scrolled through a few notifications. He exhaled slowly. "Yes, okay." He pushed his chair back and stood. "I'll take a walk. Even if it's just around the apartment upstairs. I've probably been sitting for too long." He slid the commscreen into his back pocket and pulled Ridley into a hug. "You should stop trying to take care of me, you know?"

She smiled and squeezed her arms tighter around him. "Never."

He chuckled against her hair, then stepped away. "Oh, and, uh ... Don't touch anything on the work area."

"Dad. I know by now not to touch anything on the work area."

"I know, I know. Just reminding you."

"I might tidy up *around* the work area," she added, "but I absolutely will not touch the work area."

"Thanks, Riddles." With a final smile, Dad turned away and walked through to the back rooms.

Ridley sat in Dad's chair, then shifted to the side as she felt something hard in her back pocket. She remembered the string of pearls and pulled it free, making a mental note to return it to the tutoring center coordinator's office the next time she was there. She imagined the look of relief on the woman's face when she discovered it—and the disbelief on her student's face when he got home tonight and realized the pearls he'd stolen were gone. *Hypocrite*, she imagined he would say to her if he knew what she spent many of her nights doing. *You steal, so why can't I?* "There's a difference," she whispered.

She removed her commscreen from inside her jacket. The only notification on the screen was a message from Meera saying she could barely lift her arms after all the climbing Ridley had made her do that morning. Ridley smiled to herself as she set the commscreen down and began tidying the outer areas of Dad's desk. Next to all the antique pieces in the store, the commscreen looked completely out of place. That and her state-of-the-art laptop and commpad were the most modern—and most expensive—pieces of tech in the whole building. They were part of her scholarship package, and the school gave her a new version of each at the start of every year. Ridley thought it was unnecessary, but she didn't complain. She generally passed the older versions on to Shen or someone else in his family.

After pausing at the picture frame to brush her thumb over the photo of her six-year-old self sitting between her mother and father, Ridley continued straightening the surrounding objects. She returned pencils to the coffee mug, gathered up blank note paper that hadn't been scribbled on, and closed the little carved wooden box her mom had given her dad years ago. Her fingers traced the tree carving on the lid as her thoughts returned to the woman who'd died only a few blocks from here for the crime of using magic.

Ridley wondered if she'd been a trained magicist before the Cataclysm. Her movements had seemed more intricate than those required for average, everyday conjurations. But she could have taught herself if she had a copy of one of the old magicist texts. All the paper editions had been gathered up and burned after the anti-magic laws were passed, but it had been impossible for the government to control the deletion of every single electronic text that explained the use of magic.

The bell above the front door rang out again, startling Ridley from her thoughts. She straightened, looked up, and her heart almost stopped at the sight of the girl who stood there smiling sweetly at her.

Delilah Davenport.

CHAPTER 4

RIDLEY WIPED THE SHOCK from her face and replaced it with an innocent smile. "Lilah. How nice to see you here. It's been ... what? Ten years?"

On the far side of the room, Lilah Davenport's gaze slid slowly from one display case to the next. "Probably more."

"I'm surprised you remembered how to get here," Ridley added, knowing she should keep her mouth shut and finding herself utterly unable to follow her own good instincts.

"I didn't," Lilah said. She waved her commscreen at Ridley as she stalked between the tables and cabinets. "Some tiny corner of the net seemed to remember this place still exists and showed the car where to go."

"Lovely," Ridley said, her overly fake smile stretching wider as she forced herself to keep her fists hidden behind the desk. She knew she should be afraid right now. Her mind should be racing back over the events of the afternoon, working furiously to figure out whether there was any possibility of a camera in the Davenports' apartment having seen her face. But all Ridley felt was heat in her veins and a heavy pulse pounding in her ears.

Lilah looked over her shoulder at the door, then turned her frown back to the table of candlestick holders and tea-spoons in front of her. She was dressed more casually now than when Ridley had seen her earlier, but even in jeans and a sweater she managed to look glamorous. Perhaps it was her perpetually glossy hair. Or her perfect posture. Or—

The bell over the door jangled again. Ridley looked toward it, and her jaw just about hit her chest. "Oh, there you are," Li-lah said to her brother. "I thought you were right behind me."

The door swung closed behind Archer Davenport as he wandered past an eighty-eight-year-old wrought iron side table toward Lilah, his gaze traveling lazily across the store's contents. "Just checking the takeout options in this area. How do you feel about Chinese?"

"From this part of town?" Lilah wrinkled her nose. Ridley might have thrown something at her if shock wasn't still root-ing her to the spot.

Archer shrugged. "Yeah, why not? It's not exactly the Ju-long Bar, but how bad can it be?" He finally deigned to look across the room at Ridley. With a small nod, he said, "Hey," before looking away.

Which was actually quite something, Ridley had to admit. He'd barely spoken a word to her since the Cataclysm. *Where have you been?* she almost blurted out. It was the question ev-eryone would ask the moment they realized he'd returned. Archer had left Lumina City at the beginning of last summer as soon as he'd graduated high school, and it seemed not even his friends knew where he'd gone. The most popular rumor was that he'd run off to get away from his overbearing parents so he could continue his partying playboy lifestyle in peace. Ridley saw a few holes in that theory, but in truth, she was just as clueless as everyone else.

"Fine, whatever," Lilah said. "We can get Chinese here. Anyway." She turned to face Ridley as if they'd been in the middle of a conversation when Archer walked in. "It's our mother's birthday tomorrow, and with everything that's—" She cut herself off, her expression faltering for only a moment before she smoothly went on. "We both forgot. I was just going to pop out to Voletti's quickly, but Archer reminded me that Mom already has all the scarves she could possibly want and that we should get something different. He remembered she likes quaint old things." She looked around, her eyes landing on a midnight blue masquerade mask that definitely wasn't an antique, though it was almost as old as Ridley, and added, "I told him this place was always more of a secondhand shop than a genuine antique store, but he didn't listen. So here we are."

Ridley nodded slowly, focusing more on Lilah's story than on her barely disguised insult. It *might* be true that it was Mrs. Davenport's birthday tomorrow. Or the real reason that Lilah and Archer had come all the way to the butt end of Demmer District could be that they'd noticed the missing figurine and taken a close look at their home's security footage. Was Lilah waiting for the perfect moment to reveal that she knew exactly what Ridley had done? If so, she was taking her sweet time. She walked slowly through the store, humming quietly as Archer stood with his arms crossed, reading something on his commscreen.

"Did you see this?" he asked Lilah, unfolding his arms and pointing the commscreen to face her. She moved closer as he added, "They arrested her, but she escaped and lost control of all the magic she'd managed to pull."

"Yeah, I saw," Lilah said, peering at the screen. "No doubt the magic would have killed her if that bullet hadn't. Reminded me of what's-her-name who went to Wallace."

"Serena," Archer said, slipping the commscreen back into his pocket.

"Yeah, Serena Adams." Lilah sighed and picked up a solid brass nutcracker. "If people want to be stupid and break the law, then that's what happens. I just wish they'd go do it somewhere it won't affect the rest of us. What *is* this?" She frowned at the nutcracker, which was essentially two metal clowns joined by a hinge. Pretty much useless these days considering how rare nuts were. "It's, like, the weirdest thing I've ever seen."

"Mmm," Archer said, looking at the nutcracker for only a moment before his gaze moved onward. "Mom wouldn't like it."

Ridley couldn't help staring as the two of them stood side by side. They were so alike—dark hair, dark eyes, the confidence that came with their wealth and status—and she hated them equally in that moment. She opened her mouth to tell them she was about to close the store and that they'd have to find their last-minute gift elsewhere, but a creak from the floorboards upstairs reminded her that Dad would never turn customers away, no matter how he felt about them. His pride might once have been more important to him than the bills he needed to pay, but that had changed after his savings finally ran out and their electricity was cut off for the first time.

"How about this music box?" Ridley found herself saying, shoving down her own pride as her feet carried her around the side of the desk. She picked up a small wooden box with a flower-shaped mother-of-pearl inlay decorating the lid. "It's almost a hundred and twenty years old. The lid has been chipped on the corner here, and part of the mother-of-pearl inlay is gone, but it's in otherwise excellent condition. My father fixed the cylinder mechanism so it still makes music."

"Sure, let's take a look," Archer said.

As Ridley carried the box to them, some part of her mind wondered if Lilah had been waiting for her to come closer. Maybe she wanted Ridley to be right in front of her when she stared into her eyes and told Ridley she knew exactly what she'd done. But Lilah said nothing as Ridley set the box down beside the nutcracker, opened the lid, and twisted the small metal ring on the side of the box to wind up the mechanism. The metal cylinder with its tiny spikes began to turn, and a sweet but somewhat uneven melody filled the room.

"It sounds a bit ... off," Lilah said.

Archer tilted his head. "True, but it has an old-world charm to it."

Ridley nodded, doing her best to keep her smile glued to

her face. *Do it for Dad*, she reminded herself silently. *For Dad. For Dad. For—*

"Why hasn't this item been sold already?" Archer asked, lifting the music box carefully as it continued to play its tune. "It must be quite valuable if it's so old. Surely someone else has wanted to purchase it by now."

Ridley sucked in a deep breath, wishing she didn't have to explain this bit. "We don't get a great many customers here. People know who Maverick Kayne was before the Cataclysm. They're afraid magic might be hiding inside everything in this shop, or that all the antiques are fake and have been aged with magic, or something crazy like that."

Lilah frowned as the music box's mechanism wound down, playing its last few notes slower and slower until it came to a stop. "How do we know this item is genuine?"

Ridley sighed. "We have files for everything." She gestured over her shoulder to the back rooms. "You can look at the paperwork if you want. Find out when and how my grandfather acquired this music box."

"Paperwork can be faked," Lilah said.

For Dad, Ridley repeated silently, clamping her jaw shut so she wouldn't tell Lilah exactly where she could stick her fake paperwork.

"I believe it's real," Archer said. "And I like it. I think Mom will like it too. We'll take it," he told Ridley, and she couldn't help wondering how many times he'd said those words before. Classic cars, expensive watches, rare vintage Champagne. *We'll take it* rolled so easily off the tongue for someone as wealthy as Archer Davenport.

Ridley took the music box from Archer—telling herself not to feel weird as her fingers accidentally brushed his—and closed the lid before heading for the counter and the antique cash register. The Davenports followed. Ridley slid the slim gray PayLX pad toward them, then pulled a few sheets of tissue paper from beneath the counter. Even as she began wrapping the music box, she kept waiting. Waiting for the moment Lilah would slam her fist down on the counter and shout, "I know it was you! You broke in and stole that figurine! Admit it!" But Lilah said nothing as Ridley lowered the packaged music box into a Kayne's Antiques bag. She silently placed her commscreen on top of the PayLX pad, her gold-polished nails glinting in the light. There was a pause as they all waited for the transaction to go through. Ridley glanced up, found Archer watching her, and looked down again.

The PayLX pad beeped. Lilah clasped her commscreen in one hand and lifted the Kayne's Antiques bag in the other. "Thanks," she said. And without another word, she and Archer left the shop.

It was only as the door shut behind them that Ridley finally relaxed and allowed herself to believe it really was a coincidence that two Davenports had walked into her store little more than an hour after she'd robbed them. She leaned against the counter and let out a long breath. "So weird," she murmured.

Then she crossed the room and locked the front door. After switching off all the lamps around the store, she walked into the office at the back. She passed the staircase that led up to Grandpa's old apartment, checked the back door was locked, and slid the bolt across. But as she turned away, movement caught her eye from outside the small window beside the door. She stepped back a little so she wouldn't be seen as she looked out and found—

Archer. And the man in the maroon coat. Speaking to one another.

"What on *earth*?" Ridley whispered. The stranger looked her way, and Ridley pulled her head back further. She waited for several heart-pattering seconds, then inched her head forward again. Something moved at the open end of the alley, and her eyes flicked toward it: A running figure, a blond head turned back for a moment. Her breath caught in her throat as her gaze whipped back to Archer and the stranger—just as the latter slumped to the ground, a dark patch blooming across his shirt around a glowing knife protruding from his chest.

His hands lay still at his sides.

Blood spread slowly away from his body.

The wisps of glowing magic around the knife disappeared.

Then a woman's scream ripped through the quiet evening, and Ridley looked across the alley to where Mrs. Longbourne from the shoe shop stood at her back door. Her husband joined her a second later. Then Shen's father and another man appeared at the open end of the alley where, only moments before, Ridley had seen someone running away.

She didn't wait to see anyone else. She didn't wait to let anyone see that *she* was also watching. She raced up the stairs as Dad shouted her name. "It's okay, I'm fine." She didn't stop as she reached the top step, but instead ran across the small living area. After skidding on the handwoven rug, she landed on her knees on the couch and leaned over the back of it to pull the curtain aside a few inches.

"What's going on?" Dad asked. "What happened?" A moment later, he joined Ridley on the couch and peered over her head through the gap.

"I think ... I think someone was just murdered."

"*What?* Wait, is that ..."

"Archer Davenport," Ridley filled in as Dad's voice trailed off. Where was Lilah though? Ridley couldn't see her anywhere in the alley.

Tense silence filled the small apartment as Ridley and Dad watched the activity below. Someone must have called the police, because it wasn't long before there were flashing lights and screeching tires and uniformed men and women running toward Archer. "Careful," Dad said as he drew back slightly. "If anyone looks up—"

"I know," Ridley said, pulling the two curtains together until only a crack of space remained between them. She and Dad had always done their best to avoid police attention, and tonight was no different. Neither of them wanted to be questioned as witnesses.

Through the narrow gap between the curtains, Ridley and Dad watched as Archer was dragged away by two police officers. "How very strange," Dad murmured. "He's been gone for so long, and when he shows up out of the blue ... *this* happens."

Ridley nodded. She didn't mention that Archer had been downstairs just minutes before she saw him in the alley. She didn't mention that the man in the maroon coat had been following her earlier. And she didn't mention the person she'd seen running from the alley. She didn't know what was coincidence and what wasn't, and there was no point in freaking Dad out. But there was one thing that *would* be public knowledge soon enough, so she didn't bother keeping it to herself.

"It was magic, Dad," she whispered. "Magic killed that man."

CHAPTER 5

"*ARCHER DAVENPORT?*" RIDLEY'S friend Meera repeated the following morning as they sat together on the couch in Meera's family's living room. "Seriously? What was he doing behind your building?"

"He was probably lost," Ridley said, hugging one of the threadbare cushions to her chest. "I mean, it's a long way from the top of Aura Tower to a back alley in Demmer District. Easy for a rich boy to take a wrong turn and lose his way." Her tone was light, but Meera's question was the same one that had been plaguing Ridley's mind as she tried to fall asleep the night before.

What was Archer doing in that alley?

Had he ended up there by chance? Wrong place, wrong time? Or did he actually know the man who'd been following Ridley earlier that afternoon? She kept thinking back on the few seconds she'd seen them standing together. They'd been speaking, she was sure of it, but she hadn't seen enough to be able to tell if they knew each other.

"Okay—so—wait." Meera sat up straighter, looped her

long black hair behind her ears, and pushed her owl-like glasses up her nose. "Archer Davenport was in your store, and then you saw him in the alley behind your building talking to some stranger seconds before that stranger ended up dead—killed by a knife with *magic* on it. And now Archer, who can't have performed any magical conjuration himself because it's been confirmed he still has both his amulets, has been charged with the murder."

"Yes. Mrs. Longbourne said she saw the stranger, the knife in his chest, and Archer standing right in front of him. No one else." Ridley frowned. "Haven't you looked at the social feeds today? Or the news?"

"No! Anika's got some educational documentary on." Meera gestured to their old TV, where the ocean from a time before the Cataclysm moved across the screen while a soothing British voice spoke about whales and dolphins and other species on the brink of extinction. "And she's not even watching it," Meera groaned, climbing off the couch and picking up the remote from beside her eleven-year-old sister. Anika lay on her stomach on the floor, her chin propped up on her palms as she read a book. Meera exited the documentary and opened a news app. She started scrolling through the various recent stories.

"Well, it's not like you need to see it now that I've told you all about it," Ridley pointed out.

"True." Meera lowered the remote. "So ..." She shook her head again, as if still trying to wrap it around everything Ridley had just told her. "Wow. Alastair Davenport must be furious.

It can't be good for the public image when your son winds up accused of killing someone and getting involved with magic. Though why you'd need to put magic on a knife that you're about to stab someone with, I have no idea. Wait—" Her hand flew out and smacked down on Ridley's knee as her eyes widened. "Do you think they'll give Archer the death penalty for this? I mean, he couldn't have pulled the magic himself, so at least he didn't break that law, but the crime is magic-related."

"I don't know. I doubt it. Someone else without an AI2 must have applied the magic to the knife and given it to Archer. That isn't enough to earn Archer the death penalty, is it? And no one actually saw him stab the man, so I'm sure that charge won't stick for long."

"But it must have been him, right? Who else could have done it if he was the only one there?"

"Yeah ..." Ridley said slowly. But there *was* someone else who could have done it: the blond figure she'd seen running from the scene. She hadn't mentioned that bit to Meera. She was ninety-nine percent certain she recognized the guy, but she didn't want to start a rumor if it *might* not be true.

"This is crazy," Meera continued. "Archer Davenport, charged with both murder and possession of an illegal magical item. And he just got back," she added, as if this somehow made it worse. She tilted her head. "When did he get back?"

Ridley lifted her shoulders. "No idea. Probably very recently, since none of us saw anything about him on the social feeds until this morning."

"And you said Lilah was there too?"

"In the store, yes, but I didn't see her near the alley. Maybe she was waiting for the food."

"The food?"

"I heard them saying they were getting Chinese."

"From Shen's place?" Meera's expression suggested that of all the things Ridley had told her so far, this was the strangest.

Ridley breathed in deeply—inhaling the spices wafting through the air from whatever was cooking in the kitchen—and sighed. "I don't know. I assume so."

"Wow. *Never* in a million years would I have pictured Delilah Davenport inside the Lins' place."

"Who's Delilah Davenport?" Anika asked, looking up from her book. "That name sounds familiar."

"Nobody you know," Meera said, waving away her sister's question. "So did Archer say where he's been for the past year and a bit? Or why he's back now?"

Ridley leaned her elbow against the back of the couch and rested her cheek against her palm. "Sure, yeah, we sat down over a cup of tea and chatted all about what he's been up to since he left."

Meera grabbed one of the smaller cushions and threw it at Ridley. "I mean, like, did you *overhear* anything interesting?"

Laughing, Ridley threw the cushion back at Meera. "No, I didn't overhear anything interesting."

"But you agree that this is all super weird, right?"

"Yes, definitely. Either that or a crazy bunch of coincidences."

"Oh, and what about the fact that the guy who died was

following you earlier in the day? How did he figure out where you live if you managed to lose him in the subway? And why was he following you in the first place?"

Ridley shook her head. "Don't know." She was fairly certain he'd been following her because of the envelope of cash, but she couldn't tell Meera that. Meera knew nothing about that particular extra-curricular activity of Ridley's. Nobody except Ezra knew what she did in her spare time, and that was only because she needed someone to sell the things she stole. What bothered Ridley more than the fact that someone wanted her money was the fact that he'd managed to follow her home after she'd been convinced she'd lost him. Was she losing her touch?

"Is this what you guys are talking about?" Anika asked, pointing to the TV where the story about the unidentified man murdered by a magic-laced knife had popped up in the queue of scrolling stories.

"Yes, that must be it," Meera said. She pointed the remote at the TV and clicked on the story. A still image of the alley behind Ridley's apartment appeared alongside a male news presenter's head, and the same words Ridley had heard numerous times already began playing. After relating the incident, the news presenter explained that the deceased victim, who had no scars behind his ear, let alone any arxium implants, had not yet been identified.

"No amulets?" Anika said. "But that's not possible. He's, like, grown up. Wouldn't the drones have caught him by now?"

Ridley shrugged as she played with the silver chain

around her neck. "He must have managed to stay away from the drones somehow. Or found a way to fool them."

"A witness reported seeing magic on the blade," the presenter continued, "and police who were at the scene have confirmed that the nature of the wound was consistent with the type of conjuration meant to ensure a quick death."

"A quick death," Anika repeated in a whisper. "I didn't know there was a conjuration for that."

"Yeah, you probably shouldn't be listening to this," Meera muttered, pointing the remote at the TV again and exiting the news story. "You can carry on reading your book."

"Fiiiiine." Anika returned her gaze to the book on the floor in front of her, and Ridley leaned forward to get a closer look at what she was reading. Larger than a novel, with curling page corners and dirty smudges along the fore edge of the book, it could only be one thing. "You're reading a *textbook* right now?" she asked. "You know school doesn't start for another few days, right?"

"Uh huh," Anika answered absently as she turned another page.

Ridley looked at Meera, who sighed. "She's an overachiever."

"Like you?" Ridley asked with a grin.

"And like *you*." Meera shoved Ridley with her foot. "She's hoping to get into Wallace next year on scholarship."

"Don't bother, Anika," Ridley told the younger girl. "Wallace Academy is full of stuck-up rich kids. You'll have way more fun down the road at Park High. Ask Shen. He finished last year, but he always said he enjoyed it there."

Anika looked up. "*You* guys are at Wallace."

"Yes, but we're part of a very small group of completely awesome, non-snobby, non-rich kids."

"And by 'small,' she means the two of us," Meera added with a laugh. Wallace Academy was where Meera and Ridley had met, when they both began seventh grade at the prestigious school situated two blocks away from Aura Tower. Being the only two scholarship students in their year and feeling very much on the outside, they naturally gravitated toward each other, forming a fast friendship early on.

Anika frowned as she pushed her glasses—almost exactly the same as Meera's—up her nose. "I know you're joking. You and Meera wouldn't have worked so hard to keep your scholarships at Wallace if it wasn't the only way for people like us to have a better future. So I'm going to keep working until I get in. And right now I'm learning all about the way things used to be before magic turned wild, like all the magi-tech stuff, and it would be a lot easier for me—" she glared at Meera "—if you would just *tell* me what it was like, since you're old enough to remember."

Meera shifted against the cushions, straightening ever so slightly. "I don't need to tell you what it was like. Whatever you need to know is in that textbook. And don't spend too much time on that section. You don't want your teachers to think you're showing an inappropriate interest in magic."

"My interest isn't *inappropriate*," Anika argued, wrinkling her nose. "It's academic. I want to know as much as I possibly can before I get to the scholarship exam in a few months."

"So read the textbook," Meera replied. "And every other textbook I gave you. You'll be fine."

"It wasn't particularly exciting," Ridley said to Anika. "You only think it was that way because it's forbidden now. But back then, it was just an ordinary part of life. Just another subject to study at school. Some people were good at it and ended up specializing as magicists so they could learn how to transform magic into an energy source and how to create all that magi-tech stuff you're reading about. And everyone else just did basic, everyday conjurations."

"Ridley!" Meera hissed. She'd already grabbed her comm-screen while Ridley was talking and shoved it under the nearest cushion. "You know people can land themselves in serious trouble for showing too much interest. Our commscreens are probably listening to us right now, getting ready to send this conversation straight to the government."

"You know you're completely paranoid, right?"

"I'm not paranoid." Meera pulled her commscreen out and held it near her mouth as she added, "Magic is *bad*. It's a danger, a threat to our society, and we have no interest in the way it used to be incorporated into our lives."

"I know it's bad *now*," Anika said, "and I definitely don't want to pull it or manipulate it or anything. I just figured that if I know *more* than what's in the textbooks, then I'll have a better chance of—"

"Hey, girls," Mrs. Singh said, hurrying into the living room with a bag over her shoulder and her staff access tag hanging around her neck. "I'm off to the hospital."

"Now?" Meera asked. "Isn't your next shift only supposed to start this evening?"

"Yes, but Helen's sick. I'm filling in for her."

Meera pushed herself to the edge of the couch and stood. "Mom …"

"It's fine, honey." Mrs. Singh crouched down and kissed Anika's cheek. "Extra shifts are good, remember?"

"Not when you're supposed to be catching up on sleep," Meera reminded her. Mrs. Singh was a hospital laboratory technician, and it seemed to Ridley that she was almost always working more than was healthy.

"It's fine," Mrs. Singh repeated, but Meera stood and took her mother's arm.

"Can we talk?" she asked quietly, pulling Mrs. Singh toward the kitchen.

Ridley met Anika's gaze. A beat of silence passed. Then Ridley grinned, shoved Meera's commscreen back under a cushion, and lowered herself to the floor beside Anika. The younger girl tugged at the blanket she was lying on and draped the free half over her head and Ridley's. Once they were enclosed within their makeshift tent, Anika focused on Ridley with shining eyes and said, "It can't have been *that* ordinary. Magic can do amazing, unexplainable things. Even the everyday things must have been cool."

"They were," Ridley said. "We just didn't realize it because that's the way life had always been for everyone. No one ever thought there'd come a time when we *couldn't* pull magic and use it."

"But some people *did* think that, didn't they? You told me before that there were always some who didn't trust magic. They said it was too unstable and shouldn't be used as an energy source."

Ridley nodded. This wasn't the first secret conversation she'd had with Anika about magic. The girl was just as studious as her older sister, but she lacked Meera's fear of the law. She was thrilled by the stories Ridley told her of the way things used to be. "Yeah, there were always a few extremists trying to get the rest of the world to agree with them, especially after the GSMC was proposed," Ridley said, "but hardly anyone took them seriously. Obviously a whole bunch of people in positions of power decided we should be *careful*, which is how we ended up with arxium panels hovering over certain cities, but even most of those people were still happy to enjoy the benefits of magic."

"And the walls covered in arxium weren't built around cities until *after* the Cataclysm," Anika said, "so I guess they didn't think we needed to be *that* careful."

"Correct. The only reason some cities survived was because of the panels."

"Oh, I had a question about the panels. They're high up, higher than the tallest buildings, obviously, but not *many thousands* of feet high. So sometimes clouds form lower than the panels, right? That's what this book is saying. So what stops the magic that's in those clouds from also being below the panels?"

"The cloud level might be lower sometimes, but the actual magic doesn't usually get past the panels," Ridley explained. "It stays higher up at the top of the clouds. And the panels have these small sections that are *not* made of arxium that use the magic up there to generate enough power to keep the panels hovering. It's quite clever."

"Oh yes, there's this whole section about the hover tech and how it manipulates the magic up there to do something that keeps the panels from being blown around when the wind is super—" Anika stopped at the sound of footsteps.

"Next time," Ridley whispered before throwing the blanket off and scrambling back toward the couch. She climbed back onto it and pushed her hair out of her face—and met Meera's confused gaze across the room.

"Everything okay?" Meera asked, her eyes moving back and forth between her sister and her friend.

"Yep," Ridley said. "Just explaining a few important things to Anika. I think she understands now."

"All right. Cool." Meera crossed the room and plopped onto the couch with a sigh. "Mom's gone to the hospital. She asked if we can look after Anika and Triven until my dad gets home."

"Okay. Sure. I'll just let Shen know we can't meet him this afternoon."

Meera nodded. "He'll understand. He always does." It wasn't the first time she'd been forced to cancel plans to look after her younger siblings, and she was right that Shen would understand. He often had to do the same thing.

"So," Meera said, sitting up and tucking her legs beneath her. "Let's talk about Derek. Have you heard from him again?"

Ridley blinked at the sudden change of subject. She forced her mind away from her two best friends' family responsibilities and turned it to Derek for the first time in days. What with planning the Davenport job, and then the murder outside her back door, there hadn't been much time recently to think about boys. "Uh, no, I haven't heard a thing," she told Meera. "I asked for another week, so he's giving me another week."

"And this week ends …"

"Um … tomorrow? Maybe the next day?"

"Ridley! If you're so uninterested in the guy that you can't even remember what you told him, then—"

"I *do* remember what I told him," Ridley insisted. "I just forgot what day it is. Today's Thursday, right? And I told him … Saturday." She nodded. "Yes, I said Saturday, because I wanted to make a decision before the Wallace dinner."

"It's just a date, Rid," Meera reminded her. "Why do you have to think so hard about it? Either you're interested in the guy or you're not."

"I am interested, it's just … well, he's one of them. You know, the entitled rich kids who look down on people like us."

"Well clearly *he* doesn't look down on you or he wouldn't have asked you out. Come on." Meera poked Ridley's leg. "You guys spent all that time together researching solar vehicles—"

"That was your project actually. We were doing battery electric buses. Way more useful in a post-Cataclysm world than a solar vehicle."

"Whatever. You spent a lot of time together, and he obviously decided you're worth pursuing."

"Pursuing?" Ridley deadpanned. "Seriously? Nobody our age says that."

"Stop avoiding the subject. You need to decide before *tomorrow* night, not Saturday night."

"Tomorrow night? I thought the Wallace dinner was on Saturday."

"It is, but Elise's thing is tomorrow. I'm pretty sure Derek will be there, so just tell him then."

"Oh. Yeah. Elise's party." Ridley twisted a strand of hair around her finger. "Are we going to that? It's always so awkward."

"I know, but it's tradition. And it's our last time. Our last end-of-summer bash. If we don't go through the awkwardness one last time, we'll someday regret it."

Ridley rolled her eyes. "I highly doubt that, but yeah. I guess we should go. I'll message Derek." She lifted her commscreen from a side table and typed a quick message to Derek, asking if they could talk at Elise's party.

"Meera?" Anika said. "Look. It's about the guy in Ridley's alley." Ridley sent the message, then looked up. Anika was pointing at the TV where a new story surrounded by a flashing red border had popped up at the top of the news app. The words 'Breaking News' were stamped across it.

Meera rummaged among the cushions until she found the remote, then pointed it at the TV and selected the story. The same news presenter's voice filled the room once more.

"... that new footage has been released from a hidden surveillance camera at the scene."

"What hidden surveillance camera?" Ridley muttered. "There's no camera in our alley."

"Well, he did say it was *hidden*," Meera pointed out. "Maybe it was one of the drones?"

"... which reveals," the man continued as an image of Archer being pushed into a police vehicle filled the screen, "that another person was present at the time of the murder."

Ridley breathed out as a weight lifted from her shoulders. At least she no longer had to feel guilty about keeping this knowledge to herself. There had been two rich kids in her alley last night, and the police could figure out which one of them had been responsible for the murder.

"Wait," Meera said, leaning forward as a different still image, slightly grainy, appeared on the screen. "Wait, wait, wait. Holy freakin' crap. Is that ..."

Ridley gripped the arm of the couch, ice shooting through her veins at the sight of the person she most certainly had *not* seen in the alley behind her building last night.

"We can now reveal to you," the news presenter announced, "that this person was a young man named Shen Lin."

CHAPTER 6

RIDLEY'S BLOOD POUNDED in her ears as she headed straight for Aura Tower. Her shoes smacked the pavements, her hands curled into fists, and she was in danger of grinding her teeth away completely as she marched past block after block toward the Opal Quarter, the most affluent part of the city center. The bus had wound up in a traffic jam about halfway there, and Ridley couldn't handle sitting still knowing she could walk faster than the bus could drive.

The grimy streets and graffitied walls gave way to glass structures that grew ever taller as she neared the center of town. Gigantic screens on the sides of buildings flashed brightly colored advertisements and reminder messages prompting people to visit their nearest clinic or hospital if they suspected a problem with either of their arxium implants. Ridley saw none of it; the screens had become part of the background years ago. Instead, she focused on the words repeating endlessly in her brain—*A young man named Shen Lin*—as her fury simmered.

When she reached Aura Tower, she slipped past the reception desk in the foyer, ignored the elevator reserved exclusively for the penthouse level, and made her way into one of the others. Archer wasn't at home right now. Ridley had scrolled through the various social feeds after getting onto the bus and spotted three different photos of him eating lunch at De-Luxe on the hundred and fiftieth floor. Apparently he'd been released in record time once the police confirmed that this new evidence now pointed to Shen. It seemed it hadn't taken long for Archer to resume his normal life.

Ridley's anger mounted as the elevator soared upward. It slowed, stopped, and she marched out onto the hundred-and-fiftieth floor of Aura Tower. She crossed the indoor park that took up half this level, forcing herself to uncurl her fists as two young children watched her with worried expressions.

She reached the other side of the park, stepping onto glossy tiles once more, and stopped in front of the glass sliding doors of De-Luxe. It didn't take long for her to spot Archer. He was sitting with his mother and sister on the far side of the restaurant at one of the tables positioned for the best panoramic view of the city. *Filthy liars*, Ridley thought as she glared at them. She wondered how much they'd paid their lawyers to fabricate this so-called 'new footage' that supposedly showed Shen stabbing the unknown victim. She was about to march in and confront all three of them when Mrs. Davenport and Lilah stood and headed toward the ladies' room.

Well. That was even better. Ridley would confront the murderer on his own. He'd have no one to hide behind. She walked forward. The glass doors slid silently apart, and the hostess looked up, her welcoming smile already in place. Ridley strode right past her. "Oh, excuse me, you can't just—"

Ignoring the woman, Ridley weaved her way between the tables and slid without pause into the chair opposite Archer. "I can't believe you're letting someone else go to jail for you," she snarled.

"Ridley?" Archer looked around, as if someone might be standing nearby to explain her sudden appearance. All he saw was the anxious hostess, hovering at a respectable distance.

Ridley gripped the edge of the table, leaned forward, and said, "I saw what happened. Shen was nowhere near that alley. You know he didn't kill that man."

Archer nodded to the hostess, who gave him a relieved smile before turning away. Then he faced Ridley. "If you saw what happened," he said calmly, "then you know it wasn't me either."

"Really? And how do I know that? I know I saw someone else running away, but I didn't see whether you did it or he did it."

"Well it wasn't me, so—"

"Then why haven't you said anything?"

"Do you know who it was that ran?" Archer countered. "Did you see his face?"

"Yes." Ridley gritted her teeth. "I saw Lawrence Madson's pasty face."

"Then you know why I haven't said anything. He's untouchable."

"No one is untouchable if they've murdered someone!"

Ridley hissed. But as the words flew from her tongue, she had to wonder if they were true. If Archer's lawyers could get him out of this mess, then Lawrence's lawyers could do the same.

Archer leaned back and looked around, probably to check whether anyone had noticed the hostile girl sitting across from him. Or perhaps to see whether his allies—his mommy and sister—were on their way back yet. "Just stay out of this, Ridley."

"I can't stay out of this. My friend is currently in jail because you and *your* friend have enough money to do whatever the hell you want."

"Lawrence Madson is not my friend," Archer growled, fixing his gaze on Ridley once more.

"Then tell the truth about him being there!"

Archer crossed his arms, his momentary anger disappearing behind a polished veneer of composure. "I have other things to worry about right now. Other things that are, believe it or not, more important than this. So if you saw what happened and you so badly want the police to know the truth, then how about you tell them yourself."

Ridley gaped for a moment, then shut her mouth as she drew herself a little taller. "Fine. Maybe I will, if you're not going to do the right thing."

He made a sweeping gesture with his hand, as if to say, *Be my guest.*

She couldn't help it. Her mouth fell open again. "You're seriously just going to stand by while your lawyers tell lies for you and an innocent guy goes to jail?"

With his jaw set, Archer said, "Looks like it, doesn't it."

She shook her head. "You're unbelievable."

"Yes," he muttered, his dark gaze focusing somewhere on the table between them. "It would appear that I am."

Ridley pushed herself abruptly to her feet, causing a fork to slip off the side of a plate and the slim vase at the center of the table to wobble. She had plenty of other questions. *What were you doing in the alley? What did that man say to you before he died? Do you have any clue what Lawrence Madson was doing there?* But she couldn't trust herself to stay here a moment longer without launching across the table and attacking Archer. As satisfying as that might be, it wouldn't help Shen, and it might even land her in a cell next to him. Dad would be furious.

She marched away from the table and back toward the sliding doors. They parted for her, and she continued forward without a glance at anyone else. Tears stung her eyes as she crossed the park, but she pressed her lips together and blinked until they were gone. Fortunately, she didn't have to wait long for an elevator. Within seconds, one of them opened, revealing an empty interior. She hurried inside and shut her eyes until the doors slid closed.

She was alone in here. Completely alone. She knew for a fact that the Aura Tower elevators had no interior cameras. Cameras were trained on the *outside* of every elevator on every floor, but there'd never been anything inside. The Aura Tower residents wanted security, but they also wanted privacy. Which meant it didn't matter what she did in the time it took the elevator to reach the ground floor. No one could see her.

And so she let go of her tightly wound control. Breathing out long and slow, she looked down at her hands. Vibrant blue pulsed through her veins, visible through her translucent skin. She raised her eyes to the mirror on the opposite side of the elevator, and there it was, staring back at her: the reason she would never go anywhere near the police, despite what she'd told Archer.

Magic.

Bright and brilliant and blue, it glowed in her eyes and shimmered beneath her skin. It rushed through her blood, flickering visibly in her veins. The same magic that existed in the elements. The same magic that *should not* exist within her own body—and yet somehow always had.

She exhaled and watched the blue glow rise beyond the surface of her skin. In the space of a heartbeat, it became like the air itself, enveloping her in complete nothingness. And by the time the elevator doors opened on the ground floor and Ridley moved forward, it appeared to the confused security guard standing nearby that no one was there.

CHAPTER 7

RIDLEY WAS FIVE YEARS old when she discovered she was a complete freak. She'd been watching the flames in the giant fireplace of her old home, completely mesmerized. Of course, she'd known that fire was dangerous and she shouldn't touch it, but she'd held her hands close to the warmth, imagining what it would be like if it were possible to actually hold fire.

Then all of a sudden, her hands were made of fire. She was so terrified it took her several moments to realize she wasn't in pain. The flames had vanished then, leaving her hands looking normal—except for the glowing blue light that pulsed through her veins. Her parents had raced into the lounge after hearing her scream, but they didn't seem surprised when she showed them her blue hands. They explained it was magic. Magic she didn't have to pull from the elements like everyone else did. Magic that somehow existed *inside* her.

"The scar behind your ear is just a scar," her mother told her. "There's no amulet embedded beneath your skin." That explanation hadn't done much to help Ridley's fear. Even at age five she'd known she was supposed to be protected from outside magical influence. With no arxium implant, anyone could do anything to her, couldn't they?

Dad had quickly added that she was protected by her own magic. A special doctor had told them this when Ridley was born. Back then, before the Cataclysm, magic hadn't been outlawed yet, but her parents insisted she keep her magic a secret. She wasn't like other people, and they didn't want anyone taking her away and experimenting on her. She'd done her best to obey them, and the only time someone had ever come close to finding out was when she'd accidentally used her own magic at a friend's house. Fortunately, no one had seen her glowing blue skin.

At school, she learned to pull magic from the elements the same way everyone else did. She memorized the movements for basic conjurations exactly the way her teacher taught her. But sometimes, when she was alone at home, she didn't bother pulling. She used her own magic along with the required hand and finger motions to pick up the TV remote or heat the kettle. It was just easier.

Then the Cataclysm happened. Mom and millions of other people died. And almost overnight, magic-use became a forbidden practice. The law for the second arxium implant was put in place, and scanner drones swarmed the air above the streets. Dad took both implants that should have been embedded beneath Ridley's skin—the new AI2, and the AI1 they'd secretly removed when she was barely days old and her magic was reacting horribly to the arxium—and rolled each into a tiny cylinder so they could slide onto a chain. He put the chain around Ridley's neck and told her never to take it off. He also told her never to use her magic ever again, but his warning wasn't necessary. She knew what had killed her mother. She knew what had ripped her world out from beneath her feet.

Magic. It was a wild, destructive thing, and back then, she'd hated it with an intensity that threatened to erupt into actual flames. So she pushed it deep down within her, and it didn't surface again until two years later. That was the day things changed again.

That was the day she became a thief.

Still appearing to be made of air, Ridley crossed the foyer of Aura Tower. No one looked in her direction as she exited through the grand entranceway. It seemed darker outside than when she'd entered Aura Tower, which probably meant another storm was getting ready to drop a buttload of rain on the city. She glanced up at the threatening clouds and the white lightning and blue magic flickering within them. If she looked hard enough, she could *just* make out some of the panels hovering way above the city beneath the clouds. Close enough together that combined, they would reflect most magic away, but far enough apart to allow sunlight to shine through—on the rare occasion when the clouds parted.

Ridley passed another opulent apartment building, slightly smaller than Aura Tower, then Wallace Academy on the next block. She walked several more blocks down the road and waited until she was inside one of the stalls of a cafe restroom before rolling her shoulders, relaxing, and pulling her magic back inside her body. She examined her hands—normal—before leaving the stall and stopping in front of the mirror to check her eyes—also normal.

Back out on the street, she walked with her arms crossed tightly over her chest and her jaw clenched. She had to do *something* about Shen, she just wasn't sure what. She couldn't go to the police with her eyewitness account. She couldn't risk them discovering that the scars behind her ear hid no amulets, and that her body was basically a vessel of the most illegal substance on earth. But she refused to let her friend remain imprisoned for life for something he hadn't done. After all, he was the first person she'd ever stolen for. There was no way she wouldn't help him now.

She clenched her fists tighter beneath her arms as she stalked toward the bus stop, remembering her very first theft. She'd been ten at the time, and she and Dad had lived above Kayne's Antiques for almost two years. Shen, her friend for most of that time, had contracted some kind of sickness that required expensive treatment. He'd been to the local clinic, but they sent him home when it became clear his parents couldn't afford to treat him.

Ridley and Dad had visited Shen at home. Dad gave Mr. Lin some money and said he wished he had more to give. Mr. Lin tried to give it back, but Dad wouldn't let him. Ridley had been hopeful then. She thought maybe the money Dad had given the Lins would be enough for Shen's treatment. But she'd watched Dad closely as they left, and her hope withered. He blinked tears away and hugged Ridley tightly against his side, reminding her repeatedly how much he loved her. And Ridley had understood for the first time that her friend might actually die.

A day later, as Shen lay in bed across the street growing weaker, Ridley had gone with Dad to meet someone in the Opal Quarter. A potential buyer who was interested in an Art Deco emerald brooch from Kayne's Antiques but who couldn't be bothered to come to Demmer District. The three of them sat together on white loungers beneath umbrellas on a deck at Cafe Riviere while Dad showed the brooch to the client and Ridley tried to hold back tears every time she thought about Shen.

The woman—Ridley didn't remember her name, though she recognized her from their old life when Dad was respected and well-known among the upper class of Lumina City— ended the conversation quickly by telling Dad she didn't believe the brooch was genuine. After complaining about her time being wasted by a con artist and a cheap forgery, she opened her purse and placed her commscreen inside. That was when Ridley saw the fat wad of cash within.

At that moment, the injustice of the world hit Ridley squarcly in the chest. How could some people have so little that they couldn't pay for medical treatment, while someone else could probably buy a whole clinic with the petty cash in their purse? She made the decision right then to take that money. She knew it was wrong, but she didn't care. In fact, in some ways, thinking about stealing that money felt *right*. It would save her friend's life. What could be so wrong about that?

The woman stood, pulling the purse's leather strap onto her shoulder, and Ridley knew the only way to get her hands on that money without getting caught was with magic. It was a thought that terrified her. Nature's magic had become wild and deadly, an entity not to be trusted. What if the magic inside her body was just as uncontrollable? She didn't know, but Shen was dying and the woman was walking away and Ridley was running out of time.

"Wait!" Dad called out to the woman. He stood and hurried after her. "The brooch is genuine. It was verified by an expert when my father acquired it. I have the paperwork."

The woman stopped and turned back toward Dad, and Ridley didn't hesitate any longer. She pulled her sleeves down to conceal the blue light pulsing across her skin, then hid her hands beneath the edge of the side table between the loungers. Her hands formed the quick movements for a conjuration she hadn't done in years. A conjuration that would send her magic into the air in an invisible form that could lift, carry, move. As the woman said something about no longer trusting Dad, a strong gust of wind whipped past and flipped the top of her purse open. The woman shrieked as her skirt blew up. She clutched at the billowing folds as Ridley's magic wrapped around the bundle of notes and lifted the money from the purse. Serviettes flew off a nearby table as the money dropped to the floor and disappeared beneath the overhanging edges of a tablecloth.

The freak gust of air vanished, the woman spun around, and everyone in the restaurant looked up to see what all the commotion was about. Dad, his face burning with embarrassment, gestured to Ridley and hissed, "Come on. We're leaving now." She'd jumped up from the lounger, then mumbled something about needing to tie her shoelaces. As a waiter demanded to know what Dad had done to upset one of the restaurant's most valued customers, Ridley's hand shot beneath the table, grabbed the money, and pushed it into her pocket. She stood, took hold of Dad's hand, and huddled against his side, keeping her gaze fixed on the floor.

Dad managed to keep his temper to himself until they were out of the restaurant. Then he spent the whole of their journey home grumbling about how fickle people were and how they blindly followed everyone else instead of coming up with their own opinions. Ridley kept quiet and listened while trying to ignore the stolen money that felt hot and heavy in her pocket.

She knew where the Lins hid their spare key, so that night after Dad fell asleep, she snuck out of their home, across the street, and into the Lins' apartment. She left the money next to the kettle in the kitchen where Mrs. Lin would see it when she made tea the next morning. Which was exactly what happened.

And so Shen had received the treatment he needed. Ridley never told anyone what she'd done, but the idea that she could help other people in the same way she'd helped Shen stuck with her for a long time until eventually she stole again for someone else. Then again and again, always from people who had far too much to start off with, and always to help someone who had almost nothing. Part of her hated the fact that she relied on the same power that was responsible for killing her mother. But she told herself this power was different. Her magic wasn't the same as the magic out there in the wastelands. The cruel, destructive power that had ripped away so much life. Her magic was *good*. And so she continued to use it.

But as she strode down the street now, she knew in the back of her mind that she couldn't keep breaking the law to help people. Eventually she'd have to 'grow up' and find a more legitimate method of balancing the scales. Which was why she hoped to end up at The Rosman Foundation after graduation. It was a private organization dedicated to helping those who'd lost everything after the Cataclysm. Even now, a decade later, there were still thousands who needed help getting their lives back on track. But the foundation didn't hire anyone who hadn't at least finished school, so for now, stealing was the only way Ridley could make a difference. And if she had to break the law again to help her friend, she wouldn't hesitate. The law certainly wasn't going to do anything to help him.

She slowed to a halt at the bus stop and squinted at the schedule and the digital clock above it, calculating how long she had to wait. Only a few minutes, if there were no delays. She looked around as the emotive tones of the world anthem reached her ears over the sounds of vehicles and drones, and saw a large screen across the road on the side of an office building. It was playing one of those cheesy, uplifting high-lights reels from the Secretary-General's first speech after the global unification vote.

Ridley clenched her jaw as her hands balled into fists be-neath her arms. Seriously? Almost ten years on, and they had nothing better to throw up there than ads and that same stu-pid speech that was supposed to make everyone feel better about most of their world being obliterated? It was the last thing she wanted to listen to when she'd just been harshly re-minded of how unfair the world truly was.

Archer Davenport and Lawrence Madson had both been in that alley last night, and one of them was a murderer. *That's* what she needed to focus on now. She needed to figure out how to get whoever was guilty to admit what he'd done. She pressed her forefingers to her temples, trying to ignore the SG's magnified voice, but now that she'd noticed it, she couldn't block it out.

"... toxic oceans, unclean air, hundreds of species going extinct every day. We humans faced extinction too. Our world would not have lasted forever beneath the burden our species placed upon it. We started wars over resources. We were kill-ing our world while killing off each other."

"Remind us just how much the world sucked," Ridley muttered, "then tell us how wonderful everything's going to be now."

Sure enough, perfectly timed with the climax in the anthem, the SG's voice rang out: "But now we have hope! We will rise from the ashes of our grief. We will build our surviving cities into shining beacons of hope, and one day, when the magic has settled, we will take back our world."

Ridley snorted. This speech was almost ten years old and magic wasn't any closer to 'settling.' She doubted anyone truly believed it ever would. The video went on to show brief clips of all the improvements that had been made to the surviving cities in the years since the Cataclysm, but fortunately, the sound bites from the SG's speech had ended.

Ridley leaned against the bus schedule board and turned her thoughts back to Archer and Lawrence. They would never admit what had happened, at least not to her or to the cops. But maybe one of them would talk in private. To a family member or a friend. And if someone—or some*thing*—happened to overhear one of those conversations, then perhaps—

Ridley's train of thought derailed as she noticed her commscreen vibrating in her pocket. She took it out and realized she'd missed several calls and text messages from Meera, the first from about twenty minutes after she'd stormed out of Meera's home to confront Archer.

Meera: Where'd you run off to in such a hurry?
Meera: Hey, are you at the police station? Are you telling them you didn't see Shen anywhere in the alley?
Meera: Man, I really want to hurt the whole Davenport family right now. I guess when you have enough money, you can do whatever the heck you want.

Meera: Spoke to Mrs. Lin. She said Shen was out last night delivering a meal at the time of the murder. But the murder happened during the fifteen minutes after he did the delivery and before he returned home, so apparently that means he has no alibi :-(

Meera: Hey, call me when you get a chance, okay? I want to know what's happening.

Meera: Okay I'm freaking out now. Shen isn't a minor, so he's going to end up with a life sentence for murder. And that's the BEST case scenario. What if they think he's been doing something with magic even though he has his amulets? What if he gets the DEATH SENTENCE?!!!!

Ridley tapped the voice call button and raised her comm-screen to her ear. As the dial tone sounded, she turned away from the other people waiting for the bus. Meera answered within seconds. "Ohmygosh thank goodness. Where *are* you? What's going on?"

"I'm—at a bus stop," Ridley said, deciding mid-sentence not to go into detail about confronting Archer. She could tell Meera later. "But you need to just calm down, okay? Shen's not going to get the death penalty. No one can prove that he did anything with magic. And I'm sure someone will figure out soon that this new video footage—whatever it shows—is fake. I mean, they have an eye witness who said she saw Archer and the victim and no one else. Surely they have to listen to her as well."

Meera let out a shaky breath. "Look, all I know is that rich people can make their problems go away, and Archer Davenport—or his dad, at least—is one of the wealthiest people left on the planet. So if that family has decided they want to frame Shen for this murder, then I don't see it going any other way."

"Meera, breathe," Ridley told her friend as a bus turned a corner and moved toward the stop. "This is far from over. I'm going to do whatever I can to prove Shen's innocence."

"What do you mean? What can you possibly do that would—"

"I won't see you this afternoon, okay? There's somewhere I need to be."

"Ridley—"

"Chat later, okay? And please stop panicking. Everything's going to be all right."

Ridley ended the call before Meera could ask any more questions. Sliding the commscreen back into her pocket, she climbed onto the bus. As she sat and looked out at an advertisement for the TransAt Train on the giant screen across the road, she smiled to herself. *He's untouchable*, Archer had said about Lawrence Madson, but that wasn't true. Perhaps no one else could get to him, but Ridley could. She could walk right into his home, just like she'd walked into the Davenports' home.

She faced forward as she began mentally planning her next break-in. A break-in that would be even riskier than breaking into the Davenports' apartment. A target every sensible fiber of her being told her to stay well away from: the residence of Mayor Madson.

CHAPTER 8

JUDE MADSON HAD BEEN mayor of Lumina City for almost three years. His son Lawrence—a snotty rich kid the same as all the other snotty rich kids—graduated a few years ahead of Ridley at Wallace Academy. He showed up on tabloid covers every now and then, usually striding confidently into one of Lumina City's glamorous night clubs with some celebrity on his arm, or sitting astride one of his vintage motorcycles. Or, most recently, reclining at ease at the city's most expensive restaurant after surviving an attempt on his life. Ridley never opened any of the tabloids, so she had no idea what Lawrence actually did with his life these days—aside from fleeing dodgy alleys in unsavory parts of the city. *That*, she decided, would have made a great tabloid cover if she'd managed to capture it on her commscreen's camera. But she hadn't, which was why she needed to do some investigating on her own.

And so, several hours after confronting Archer—and after sending a message to Dad to tell him she might be late for dinner—Ridley found herself outside the imposing front gate of the Madsons' home. They lived on one of the largest properties near the edge of the city, alongside the Silvin River. Beyond the trees on the other side of the river, the orchards and farmlands began. And beyond that, of course, was the wall. The mayor had an apartment in the city center as well, but Ridley knew his family didn't spend much time there. Lawrence had always liked to boast about his large riverside home, the closest thing one could get to a country estate these days.

Rain pattered onto the road around her, but Ridley couldn't feel it. She was wrapped in magic made of air, and the effect was that the rain seemed to fall *through* her. It was a strange concept, but she'd long since stopped trying to make sense of her freakish power. Wasn't that part of what made it *magic*? The fact that it didn't make sense? Wasn't that why so many people throughout the ages had argued against its use as an energy source?

She breathed in—savoring the scent of wet earth that was so rare in most parts of the city—and let the breeze carry her up and over the gate. That was the great thing about using air to conceal herself: she could move wherever it moved. On the other side of the gate, the air carried her past the guardhouse and along the driveway toward the stately home. Then up and up and through an open window on the second story. It was actually surprisingly easy. She'd expected the most protected man in the city to have a home that was harder to break into.

She landed in a bathroom. Fluffy white towels hung over rails, and the jetted bath seemed big enough to fill Ridley's entire bedroom. She left the bathroom behind and moved into a passageway. Instead of letting herself become visible again,

she clung tightly to her magic. The house should be empty—
she'd waited until a sleek black car left the property, carrying
both the mayor and his son—but she didn't know if an alarm
system would be triggered if she let herself materialize, or if
hidden cameras were installed somewhere. The idea of getting caught here seemed even worse than getting caught at the
Davenports' place. This was the *mayor's* house, after all. Besides, she'd spent most of the afternoon at home finding out
where he lived and planning how to get there, so she wasn't
tired yet from overuse of magic. *May as well stay hidden*, she
thought to herself.

She moved through the various rooms upstairs until eventually finding the bedroom that must belong to Lawrence.
Framed motorcycle posters decorated the walls, a bookshelf
displayed the small trophy he'd won at a public speaking competition, and the open doors to the walk-in closet revealed
men's gym shoes on the floor and a few items of clothing
beside them. Now all Ridley had to do was hide one of the
two small listening devices currently residing in her back
pocket. She'd met Ezra in a cinema just before coming here
and swapped them for a pair of stolen earrings she hadn't
yet given him. She reached behind her, but with hands that
seemed to be made of air—and a pocket that didn't seem to
exist either—it proved impossible to get hold of one of the
listening devices.

So she finally let go of her magic, quickly pulling her hood
up the moment she was visible—just in case someone walked
in and saw her before she managed to disappear again. Then

she removed one of the two bugs from her pocket. After looking around for the best place to hide it, she chose the back of one of the bedside tables.

Her magic concealed her as air once more, and she moved on to explore the rest of the house. She needed to choose another spot to hide the second bug. The problem was, in a house this large, private conversations could happen anywhere. She passed through a dining room, then a wide passageway with frameless glass doors that looked out onto the garden. Rain drummed down onto a deck, and beyond that was a swimming pool and neatly mown grass with strange, unidentifiable white sculptures positioned here and there.

She paused inside a large study, wondering if Lawrence might sit there with his father and confide in him about exactly what had happened in the alley. She had no way of knowing for sure, but it didn't seem like he had that kind of relationship with his father. Perhaps he would tell his mother instead. In the news clips Ridley sometimes saw, it seemed like he was closer to her. Though perhaps that was only because the two of them generally had to stand back to let the mayor take the limelight.

Ridley continued through a second door that led out of the study and into the next room, which turned out to be a large lounge. Though she knew she shouldn't be wasting time, her curiosity got the better of her and she stopped by the fireplace to examine the framed photos on the mantelpiece. They chronicled Lawrence's perfect life from the time he was a toddler, through his school years, all the way to his Wallace

Academy graduation, where he stood with a group of his friends. They all had their arms around each other, smiling and laughing as some of them tossed their caps into the air. Ridley almost moved on before noticing the girl on the far right of the group. Serena Adams. The girl who'd had a promising future as a dancer before earning herself the unfortunate title of The Girl Who Blew Herself Up With Magic On Top Of The Haddison Building. She must have been a friend of Lawrence's—something he would no doubt deny if anyone asked him now. Ridley was surprised the Madsons hadn't replaced this photo with a different one. No one wanted to be connected to Serena Adams in any way after it turned out she'd been using magic.

At the sound of a faint hiss, Ridley froze. She twisted in the air and looked behind her, but there was no one there. She waited, her invisible heart pounding, but there was no noise other than the tick of the clock above the mantelpiece and the steady thrum of rain outside. She breathed in deeply to calm herself and noticed a new scent in the air. Something citrus. An air freshener? Was that the hiss she'd heard? She almost laughed as she imagined herself panicking over nothing more than an automatic air freshener.

But then ... her head began to spin. Nausea hit her at the same time her throat started closing. She gasped and felt herself stumbling, catching hold of the edge of an armchair—with a hand that was very much visible. She tried to push her magic outward, but the dizziness grew worse. When pain rocketed through her skull and the right side of her body, she realized she'd hit the floor. She lay there gasping, struggling to stay conscious, watching the ceiling and the side of the armchair shift in and out of focus, until everything eventually dissolved into darkness.

Ridley woke suddenly, sucking in a breath and blinking as her heart raced. Nausea and dizziness still plagued her, but her breathing felt almost normal. She pushed herself up into a sitting position, waiting a moment for the room to stop spinning before she looked around at the clock over the mantelpiece. She wasn't sure of the exact time she'd entered the Madsons' home, but she calculated she'd been lying on the floor, completely exposed, for at least fifteen minutes.

"Crap," she whispered. She tried her magic again, but the attempt filled her with such nausea she had to lean her head against the armchair as she breathed deeply and slowly. She opened her eyes as the nausea lessened, and that was when she noticed the light in the study next door. The floorboards creaked as a wheeled chair moved.

"Thank you," Lawrence Madson said. "I'll inform him when he gets home."

Double crap. Ridley scrambled on hands and knees toward the largest couch. What was Lawrence doing home? Hadn't he left earlier with his father? Or was that someone else she'd seen in the car with the mayor? Not that it mattered right now. Lawrence's footsteps were moving toward the study door, and

Ridley was only halfway behind the couch, and—

"Sound system, on," Lawrence said as he entered the lounge.

Ridley pulled both feet behind the couch and crouched as low as she could, holding her breath. Then she flinched as a speaker beeped somewhere nearby. A moment later, the haunting tones of a woman's voice accompanied by melancholy piano chords reached her ears. She hoped Lawrence would return to the study, but instead he crossed to Ridley's side of the room—*Triple crap!*—and stood at the glass doors, looking out at the garden. If he turned to his left, there was no way he could possibly miss Ridley.

She held her breath and decided to move instead of trying her magic again. She inched backward on her butt and the heels of her hands, hoping to make it around the other side of the couch before Lawrence turned.

Then the old-fashioned *ding dong* of a doorbell rang out through the house.

Ridley froze.

Lawrence looked over his shoulder—the shoulder pointed away from Ridley—and turned. He crossed the room without looking in her direction, leaving Ridley wilting with relief. She pushed herself up and peeked over the top of the couch. She couldn't see through to the entrance hall from her position, but she heard Lawrence open the door. She heard the pause before he said, "Davenport? What a surprise."

CHAPTER 9

LAWRENCE MADSON IS not my friend. That's what Archer told Ridley, so why was he here? Could he possibly be trying to do the right thing? Was he here to convince Lawrence to go to the police? Whatever the reason, Ridley couldn't help smiling at her luck. She might be stuck behind a couch and unable to use her magic without feeling ill, but the one person she needed Lawrence to talk to had just arrived. All the two of them needed to do now was take a seat in the living room, have a chat about last night, and *not* discover that she was hiding there.

"I'm glad I caught you at home," she heard Archer say. "I thought you might be out with your father."

"How fortunate for you that I'm not," Lawrence answered. His tone was civil, but Ridley wouldn't have described it as warm. It seemed Archer may have been telling the truth about them not being friends. They definitely knew each other though.

"I was surprised to hear you'd returned home," Lawrence said as the front door closed. "Enlightening trip?"

"Indeed. Most illuminating."

"I look forward to hearing more about it."

"I'm sure you do," Archer answered, his voice growing louder as the two of them moved closer to the living room. Ridley ducked down again behind the couch, but then Archer added, "Why don't we speak in your father's study?" and their footsteps moved past the lounge door.

Ridley rolled her eyes. She needed them to have their conversation *here* where the second listening device could pick up everything they said. She removed it from her pocket as Lawrence and Archer headed into the mayor's study through the other door rather than through the lounge. At least they weren't too far away. If she could get the bug closer to the door, perhaps it would be able to record everything they said.

She scooted forward a little and looked around the side of the couch, then pulled her head back immediately. The door connecting the lounge and study stood wide open, and Archer, sitting in a chair on one side of the mayor's desk, was in full view. Ridley clenched one fist and pressed it against her mouth as she considered her options. She could crawl unseen around the back of the couch, but if she tried to sneak out either side and Archer happened to look this way, he'd definitely see her. She couldn't get any closer to the study.

"You must have made some very good friends over there in France." Lawrence's voice reached Ridley's ears above the music as she pulled out her commscreen, switched on the voice recorder app, and placed it on the floor right at the edge of the couch beside the listening device. "So good," Lawrence continued, "that when one of those friends shows up in Lumina City, I find you huddling together with him in an alley."

"I'm not sure I'd use the word 'huddling,'" Archer said. "And believe me, I was as surprised to find him there as you were."

"Is that so? You didn't, perhaps, arrange to meet him there?"

"No. I was accompanying my sister to visit her friend nearby."

Ridley almost laughed out loud at that. *Friend?* It may have been true once upon a time, but that was many years ago.

"I find it most interesting that you were in the area too," Archer continued. "Perhaps *you* had arranged to meet him?"

Lawrence laughed. "I'm not sure why you find it interesting. I began following him as soon as we were alerted to his presence in the city. I wanted to see who he was looking for. In case it was someone like him."

"Well, as you know, I'm nothing like him. And I was about to relieve him of the information he was carrying—in as *subtle* a manner as possible—when you charged in and caused a scene."

A floorboard creaked. Something tapped the desk. "So sorry," Lawrence said, not sounding in the least bit apologetic. "Did I make things a little difficult for you, leaving you behind at the scene of a murder? How embarrassing for your family."

"The incident is of little importance to my family. What's important is the information that man was carrying. The information he was about to give me. I'm here to retrieve it."

Lawrence snickered. "Finders keepers."

Ridley tilted her head just far enough to see Archer cross his arms. "Have you opened the envelope?"

"Of course I have. You would, wouldn't you?"

"And?"

"Letters. All the same, and none of them addressed to anyone in particular. Very interesting contents, however."

After several moments of silence, Archer said, "I assume you don't plan to elaborate on these contents?"

"You assume correctly."

Archer exhaled sharply. "You're certain they're not addressed to anyone?"

"I'm not blind, Davenport. Like I said, there are no names."

At that, Archer's eyes flicked toward the door, and Ridley pulled her head back swiftly. She waited, holding her breath, but Archer's chair didn't scrape backward. He didn't walk into the living room, and he didn't call out 'who's there?' Instead, he said, "You'll bring the envelope to the next meeting, then?"

"Of course." A chair wheeled across the floor, and Ridley pictured Lawrence standing. "But until then, it will remain in my possession. Sorry you wasted your time coming all the way over here. You should have called first. I would have told you not to bother."

Chair legs scraped the floor, and Archer said, "Don't worry about it. I was in the neighborhood."

They walked out of the mayor's study, and in the quiet between two different tracks of whatever album was playing, Ridley thought she heard the same faint hiss she'd heard earlier. She still had no idea what caused the sound, or if it was related to the intense nausea and dizziness that had made her pass out, but she couldn't risk looking now. Her hand hesitated near her commscreen as Lawrence showed Archer to the front door. The door shut. Lawrence crossed the hallway. Ridley waited, barely breathing, but his footsteps grew fainter and disappeared.

Still, Ridley waited. But after a minute or so when Lawrence still hadn't returned, she ended the commscreen recording and switched off the listening device. She needed to leave. She had no idea if either of her devices had recorded anything useful, but she wouldn't be able to find out until she got out of here. After returning the devices to her pocket and peeking over the top of the couch once more, she stood and tiptoed to the edge of the room. Perhaps it was the act of standing after crouching down for a while, but by the time she reached the wall and pressed her back against it, her nausea had returned in full force. She tried breathing deeply, but that only seemed to make it worse. She leaned forward, hands pressing into her knees as she breathed deeply and silently repeated, *Don't pass out, don't pass out.*

At the edge of her gaze, a shadow moved. She saw shoes, dark pants, and she sucked in a breath and straightened hurriedly as a dark figure moved toward her. "Why are you still here?"

She blinked through her dizziness at the dark eyes glaring at her. "Archer?"

"You need to get out of here."

"How did you—"

"He's dangerous, okay?" Archer hissed, grabbing her by the arm and pulling her toward the glass sliding door, which, she now noticed, was partially open. "So whatever you were planning to do here this evening, don't. Just leave."

She tugged free of his grip, which sent her head spinning again. "Not until you tell me what *you're* doing here." Swallowing down her nausea and pulling herself a little straighter, she tried to regain some of her usual confidence. "Looks like you and Lawrence are quite close. I had no idea the two of you knew each other so well."

"I guess looks can be deceiving then, can't they?" His eyes traveled across her face. "After all, you look like a straight A scholarship student on the outside. No one would ever guess you're an expert at breaking and entering."

"I don't see any breaking, do you?" she retorted. "And how did you even know I was here?"

"Because I was doing my own sneaking around," he snapped, trying again to move her toward the door. "Hoping to get that envelope back. And I'd probably have it by now if I hadn't come across you passed out on the living room floor and had to improvise to keep you from getting yourself caught."

Ridley's confidence wavered. "You ... you saw that?"

"Yes, I found you here on the floor. I tried to wake you, but I heard Lawrence coming. I left through a window. Went back around to the front and rang the doorbell. Now you've cost me valuable time I could have spent searching for the envelope."

"What envelope?"

"You know, the envelope from last night. The big yellow one." Archer frowned. "You said you saw what happened. You said—" He shook his head. "You know what? Just leave. Forget about all of this."

"What envelope, Archer? What letters was Lawrence talking about? Why was that man outside my—"

Footsteps sounded from the direction of the hallway. As Ridley shot a glance across the room, Archer gripped both her shoulders and pushed her out onto the deck. "You need to stop asking questions." Then he slid the door shut and locked it. He disappeared into Mayor Madson's study, leaving Ridley staring through the glass with dozens of questions on the tip of her tongue and nausea churning her stomach. She blinked, remembered she needed to remain hidden, and hurried away through the rain before Lawrence returned to the lounge and found her standing there on his deck.

CHAPTER 10

RIDLEY WOKE THE NEXT morning and lay in sleepy bliss for about three seconds before reality and its disappointments crashed down on her. She remembered that one of her best friends was in jail. She remembered hiding behind the Madsons' poolhouse the night before until she could use her magic without feeling ill. She remembered replaying the commscreen recording when she got home, only to find that she could barely hear anything Archer and Lawrence had said over the sound of the music. She'd then downloaded the recording from the listening device, and though she could hear some of the words, most of the conversation wasn't clear enough to make sense.

She opened her eyes and stared at the damp stains and peeling paint on her ceiling, acknowledging once again that she had nothing that could help Shen, and that she'd come away from the Madsons' with more questions than answers. At least she'd raided the toy box beneath her bed—the toy box that contained all the cash that hadn't yet found its way to a worthy cause—and put everything into an envelope for the Lins. She'd crept into their kitchen late last night and left it by the kettle, in the same place she'd left an envelope years ago when Shen was sick. If all else failed and she couldn't find a way to prove her friend's innocence, the Lins could at least afford a good lawyer to defend him.

A quiet buzzing sound alerted her to a notification on her commscreen. She rolled onto her side and reached for it on the edge of her desk. The two messages at the top of the screen were from Meera, but just below them sat one from Derek, sent late last night.

Derek: Great, see you at Elise's then!

Ridley draped one arm across her eyes and groaned. She'd forgotten about Elise's party, just like she'd forgotten she'd asked Derek if they could meet there to talk. She shifted her arm enough to see Meera's message.

Meera: I'm thinking of not going tonight. I don't think I can have fun while Shen's stuck in jail.
Meera: And you never called me back yesterday. What's going on? What were you doing?

Ridley pushed herself up and swung her legs over the edge of the bed. She tucked her long white hair behind her ear and stared at her commscreen for a while, wondering what to say to Meera. Wondering what to do about Shen. She opened a news app on her commscreen and scrolled idly through it, stopping when she reached the story about the murdered man in her alley. A photo accompanied the story. A still image from the supposed 'footage' that proved Shen had been at the scene along with Archer Davenport and the unidentified victim.

"Hang on," Ridley whispered. Yesterday she'd assumed there was no hidden surveillance footage to begin with. No news channel had shown it, and Ridley believed it was all a big lie. But the grainy photo she was currently looking at included the stranger in his maroon coat with his hat in one hand, Archer wearing the same clothes he'd had on yesterday, and Shen. *Not* wearing the raincoat she'd seen him in yesterday. Which meant part of the footage was genuine and Shen had somehow been pasted in. And if part of it was genuine, then the original version—*without* Shen pasted into it—must exist somewhere.

Her heart raced as an idea began to take shape. She tapped the small photo of Meera's face, selected the voice call option, and brought her commscreen to her ear. "Ridley!" Meera said, answering after two rings. "Finally. What happened yesterday? Where'd you go?"

"I think we should go to the party tonight," Ridley said, ignoring Meera's questions. "There's someone I need to speak to. Someone who might be able to help Shen."

That evening, Ridley entered Aura Tower in a far more orthodox manner than she had several nights before: by stopping at the reception desk with Meera to check her name off Elise's guest list, and then waiting in front of one of the elevators. What made the experience so surreal though, was having Dad beside her.

His arm came up around Ridley's back, nudging her forward as the elevator doors parted. She walked forward, feeling a strange sort of lightheadedness. It had been easy while sneaking in here the other night to remain indifferent to this place. To pretend the tall tower with its shiny floors, restaurants, indoor parks, and glamorous apartments had no impact on her. But stepping into the elevator with Dad at her side brought on a sense of familiarity so powerful that, for a moment, Ridley could hardly believe more than nine years had passed since the two of them had lived here.

It had been a gorgeous home, up on the hundred and fifty-second floor. Ridley and her parents moved in when she was four years old, and she'd always taken the place for granted. Then the Cataclysm happened, Dad lost everything, and after moving into the tiny apartment above Kayne's Antiques, Ridley ended up at the public elementary school most of the other kids in Demmer District attended. Dad said Wallace Academy was off the table—no way could he possibly afford it—so Ridley worked her young butt off and received one of the few scholarships Wallace Academy offered for students entering middle school. Stupidly, she'd thought her life would return to something a little like normal then. She would see all her old friends again. They would accept her because she was a Wallace student. She would hang out in Lilah's penthouse most afternoons and pretend she was still one of the city's elite.

That didn't happen. Her friends all followed Lilah's lead and continued to ignore her. And so the only time Ridley entered Aura Tower was for Elise's annual end-of-summer party—or when she was breaking into someone's apartment. And the latter *definitely* didn't make her feel like she belonged there.

"Weird, isn't it?" Dad said, as if reading her thoughts. "Being back here."

"Yes," Ridley murmured. "Very weird."

Meera, who'd decided to come to the party after discovering no one was allowed to visit Shen in jail, cleared her throat. "So, uh … you said you're meeting someone at the restaurant on the hundred-and-fiftieth, Mr. Kayne?"

"Yes, De-Luxe," Dad answered. He placed his hands behind his back and nodded. "Someone interested in old clocks."

"Okay." Meera nodded. "How interesting." Ridley cut a sideways glance at her friend and raised an eyebrow. She knew there was not a single thing about antiques that interested Meera. "What?" Meera whispered. "It is interesting."

Though the elevator wasn't yet halfway to Elise's floor, it slowed to a halt and the doors opened. In walked Daphne Brooke and Josefina Cruz. Also on their way to Elise's party, Ridley assumed. Daphne smirked as she gave Ridley and Meera a brief once-over before turning to face the doors.

They rode the rest of the way up in awkward silence, which was nothing new for Ridley and Meera. Elise's annual party was always awkward for them. The kind of event where if the guest list wasn't automatically made up of the entire class, it certainly wouldn't have included them.

They reached Elise's floor, and Daphne and Josie hurried out, almost crashing into Lilah, who must have just exited one of the other elevators. The three of them caught hold of each other, giggling as they regained their balance. "Have fun," Dad said to Ridley as she and Meera walked forward.

"I know, right?" Daphne said Josie, in answer to something Josie must have said. She laughed again as Ridley passed her. Then, in a lower voice, she added, "He's such a weird-looking man."

Ridley stopped. She looked back over her shoulder and found Daphne watching her father through the slowly closing elevator doors. Lilah shoved her elbow against her friend's ribs. "Don't say that. Don't you know who he is?"

"Sure, he's—"

"He was a famous jewelry designer before the Cataclysm," Lilah told her. "Designers aren't supposed to be good-looking. They create amazing fashion or accessories, and that's why people love them."

"Designer? What designer?"

Meera tugged at Ridley's arm and whispered, "Just leave it." But Ridley couldn't bring herself to move away.

"Maverick Kayne," Lilah said. "Remember? The headpieces he used to create were exquisite, and his diamond work was amazing."

"But he used *magic*," Josie said in a loud whisper.

"Yes, so that's why you don't hear about him anymore,"

Lilah continued. "Anyway, my point is that most designers have kind of a weird look, don't they? So clearly Maverick Kayne isn't any different."

Daphne was nodding by now. "Maverick Kayne. Yeah, I remember that name." She looked toward the elevator, which was now closed. "My oldest sister had a Maverick Kayne tiara she wore to her prom. The diamonds had actual fire glowing in—Wait." She looked at Lilah again. "So Ridley's dad is *Maverick Kayne*?"

Lilah's eyes just about rolled into the back of her head. "Oh my goodness, where have you been for the past several years, Daphne?"

"Yes, Daphne," Ridley said loudly, unable to keep her mouth shut any longer. "Where have you been for the past several years?"

Daphne twisted around, but she didn't seem the least bit embarrassed to find Ridley still standing there. "Jeez, sorry. I don't really know you that well, Ridley, so obviously I don't know anything about your family. I only moved here after the Cataclysm, remember? And look, all I'm saying is that you're lucky you take after your mom instead of your dad. Can you imagine if you'd ended up with those huge teeth of his?"

All the better to bite you with, Ridley thought, the line from that old fairy tale flashing through her mind. She managed to hold back the words though, as well as the retort that Daphne had no idea what Ridley's mother had looked like, so how could she possibly make a statement like that? Instead, Ridley schooled her expression into a placid smile and said,

"So lucky."

"Right?" Daphne smiled. "Your mom must be beautiful, just like you."

Meera tugged at Ridley's arm once more, and this time, Ridley relented. Her eyes met Lilah's for a moment before she turned and headed around the corner with Meera. "I can't believe you were ever friends with people like them," Meera muttered as they approached the entrance to Elise's home.

"It was a long time ago."

They walked through the open door into Elise's family's glitzy apartment, already crowded with people. Neon lights illuminated the large living area, and colorful drinks lined a dining room table that had been pushed to one side of the room. "Can you tell me why we're here now?" Meera asked over the sounds of laughter and music. "Who can help Shen? And what happened yesterday afternoon? Where'd you go?"

"I, uh ... I'm not sure I should tell you who I'm here to speak to. It's kind of a sensitive business, and I don't think this person would be happy with me giving away his or her skills."

"Sensitive business?" Meera raised an eyebrow, then shrugged. "Fine. Whatever." They moved through the crowded space to the other side of the room, where floor-to-ceiling glass provided an excellent view of the city. Not as great a view as the one from the Davenports' penthouse, but still high enough that a sliver of the wastelands was visible beyond the top of the wall. Meera turned her back to the window, crossed her arms, and asked, "So where'd you go yesterday after you left my place?"

"You wouldn't like it if you knew."

"It doesn't matter whether I *like* it or not. I just want to know."

"I don't think you do."

Meera's eyes narrowed, but not before Ridley saw the hurt in her gaze. "Since when do we keep secrets from each other?"

Guilt pierced Ridley's chest at the reminder of all the secrets she kept from her best friend, and just like that, she opened her mouth and said, "I broke into Mayor Madson's house."

Meera blinked. Then she rolled her eyes. "Fine. Don't tell me what you were really up to." She lowered her arms to her sides and turned toward the window. "You're probably right that I don't want to know what it was."

"Meera." Ridley spoke slowly, unsure of what to say next. She hated that her friend thought she was lying—especially when she'd finally told the truth about something—but she knew it was better if Meera remained in the dark about Ridley's activities. She looked through the glass at the distant flicker of magic out in the wastelands. The magic that sometimes seemed to call to her, like an invisible thread attached to her chest, wanting to tug her through the city and out there into the wild. "What Archer's people did to get him off was illegal," she said. "That means we may have to stoop to the same means to prove Shen didn't do this."

"I wish that wasn't true, but ... but I think it might be." Meera sniffed, and when Ridley looked at her, she saw tears brimming in her friend's eyes. "Shen is—going to—end up dead because—because of someone else's lies." She pressed her quivering lips together.

Ridley took Meera's hand and squeezed it. "He is not. At the very worst, he'll get life in prison, but that's not going to happen. I will do everything I can to free him, even if it means using magic to break him out of prison."

"Well *that* wouldn't work," Meera said, managing a half-laugh through her tears. "The two of you would be fugitives forever if you did something like that. And where would you take him? There's nowhere to hide in the city with all the drones flying around. And out there in the wastelands—" she gestured to the pane of glass in front of them "—magic would kill you within minutes. And besides—" she sniffed again "—the prison's covered in arxium. You'd never get in, even if you were crazy enough to remove your amulets and use magic."

Ridley smiled and wrapped one arm around Meera's shoulders. "And that's why I keep you around. When I come up with crazy ideas, you're the voice of reason."

Meera nodded and sniffed again. "That's me. The practical one."

Ridley looked over her shoulder. Her eyes scanned the open space full of her fellow students, but she didn't see the person she'd come here for. She knew that person was here though. She just had to find her. "I'm going to wander around for a bit," she told Meera. "See where this person is."

"Sure. Wonderful." Meera pushed her shoulders back and wiped beneath her eyes. "I'll just stand here on my own and pretend I'm not totally—Oh. Hi, Derek."

Ridley whipped around and found herself chin to chest with the guy she'd spent many an evening working with on a group project during the last school year. She took a step back and cleared her throat. "Derek. Hi."

His warm eyes crinkled at the corners as he smiled. "Hey, Ridley. You said you wanted to talk this evening?"

"Yes, um, in a minute. I need to find someone else first."

"Someone else, huh?" Derek chuckled. He pushed one hand through his sandy locks. "I see I've got some competition this evening."

Ridley clasped her hands together—since it seemed she didn't know what else to do with them right now. "Not really," she said with a breathy laugh. "But just give me a few minutes, and then I'll talk to you." She stepped past him, but he caught her arm.

"Ridley." She looked back as he smiled his charming smile. "I'm not asking you to marry me. It's just a date. A simple yes or no will do."

"Uh …" Ridley glanced at Meera, who was staring at the floor while leaning slowly away from Derek and Ridley, as if that might somehow give them a fraction more privacy. "Then, um … it's a no. I'm sorry. You're really great. As a friend." She cringed internally as the cliched words tumbled from her tongue. Derek's hand released her arm. "I'm sorry," she said again.

His smile remained in place, though it didn't stretch quite as wide as before. "Sure. No big deal." He walked away, and Ridley's gaze fell on Meera.

Still staring at the floor, Meera whispered, "That was so awkward."

Ridley closed her eyes for a moment. "I'm sorry. He kinda caught me off guard."

Meera sighed, then waved Ridley away. "Okay, whatever. Go find this person who can help Shen. The sooner he gets out of jail, the sooner everything can go back to normal."

"Yeah, okay, I'm going." Ridley wandered through the large living area, looking around and standing on tip-toe every now and then. People lounged on plush beige couches, others mingled or danced, and a group of girls scrolled through photos of Elise's most recent summer holiday in Europe on a framed screen Ridley thought was a painting when she first walked in.

Something tightened in Ridley's chest as she observed all the activity. There was a part of her that sometimes wished this was still her life. Not only the wealth and luxury, but the entire picture that went along with it. A happy family, a father who was successful, a mother who was alive. Sometimes at night when tears wet her pillow and her chest ached at the thought of how much she missed Mom, she told herself she'd give anything in the world to have that life instead of the one she had now.

Boisterous laughter interrupted her thoughts. Her eyes landed on the source of the noise: two guys climbing onto the island separating the kitchen from the rest of the living space as their friends egged them on. Then her gaze slipped past them to where Derek was leaning close to Kat Whitely, whispering something into the girl's ear as she giggled. *Well*, Ridley thought. *He sure moved on fast.* She silently congratulated herself for dodging a bullet. She'd suspected all along that the right choice was not to get involved with any Wallace Academy boy, and here Derek was, proving her right.

She turned away from the kitchen area and scanned the room again. On the frame TV on the wall, the current photo showed Elise and her brother with their arms in the air and huge grins on their faces as they stood in the TransAt station. *Must be nice*, Ridley couldn't help thinking, *just jumping on the high-speed train when you feel like taking a quick trip to Europe.* She'd been on it once, a year or two before the Cataclysm, but she could never afford it now. Tickets were costly even before the world ended up half demolished, and those prices were nothing compared to what a TransAt ticket cost today. With magic raging across the surface of the earth and through the atmosphere, sub-oceanic trains were the only way to travel safely between continents these days.

Ridley looked away from the photos of Elise's perfect holiday and down the passageway leading to the bedrooms. She certainly didn't plan to open any of those doors, but perhaps—Yes, there she was, walking out of the guest bathroom and pressing her lips together repeatedly as if she'd just reapplied her sparkly gloss. Ridley hastened toward the passageway to stop her before she reached the crowded living room.

"Lilah," she said to the girl who was once her best friend. "I need to talk to you."

CHAPTER 11

LILAH PURSED HER LIPS into an annoyed pout before shrugging and leaning one shoulder against the passage wall. "Sure. What's up?"

Ridley looked over her shoulder to make sure no one was within earshot. She returned her gaze to Lilah and smiled. "Remember that extra-curricular activity you were getting into just before the Cataclysm? You still do that kinda thing?"

Lilah's face closed off immediately. "I don't know what you're talking about."

Ridley crossed her arms. "You know exactly what I'm talking about. You do a great job of pretending that all you care about is nail polish and celebrities and your never-ending shoe collection, but I know you speak the language of computers far better than you speak fashion."

Lilah's lips pressed into a thin line, but she did an impressive job of maintaining her composure. She flipped her sleek dark locks over her shoulder and said, "Hardly. Didn't you see that recent feature about me in Vanity Fair? My fashion taste is supposedly impeccable."

"Sure, and so are your hacking skills."

Lilah grabbed Ridley's arm and shoved her into the bathroom. She slammed the door shut behind both of them. "You have no idea what you're talking about."

"I didn't," Ridley admitted, "but now I'm almost certain you're still into hacking. Why else would you react this way?"

Lilah placed her clutch on the edge of the basin and crossed her arms. "You know I could ruin you, right? I could make your life even worse than it already is."

"Wow, thanks for that, bestie. Good to know there's absolutely nothing remaining of our former friendship."

Lilah gritted her teeth. "You come here and threaten me, and you think I'm going to just—"

"I'm not threatening you! I need your help, okay?"

Lilah paused, her perfect sparkly lips forming an O before she said, "My help?"

"Clearing the name of an innocent person." Lilah's only answer was to narrow her eyes, so Ridley hurried on. "The guy who's being accused of murdering that man behind my building is one of my best friends, and I know for a fact that he wasn't even there. The video that supposedly shows him at the scene is a fake. I don't know who put it together or how, but Shen definitely wasn't there. I was watching out of the window when it happened. I saw the stranger and two other people, but not Shen. There must have been a drone flying over, and that's what took the original video. So please, Lilah." Ridley pressed her hands together. "I just need you to find that original footage to prove Shen's innocence."

Lilah let out a humorless laugh. "If your friend didn't do it, then that means Archer did. So you're basically asking me to turn on my own brother."

"No, that's not what I'm asking. I'm asking you to find evidence of what really happened, and I think the evidence will show that Archer didn't do it. There was someone else there." She hesitated before plunging ahead. "Lawrence Madson."

"*Lawrence Madson?*" Lilah's eyes narrowed further. "You're sure it was him?"

"Yes. He was running away, which means he probably did it." Ridley hoped with everything in her that she was right. If Lilah found proof that it was actually Archer, there was no way she'd hand that proof over.

"So you didn't *see* Lawrence stab the man?" Lilah asked. "You only saw him running away?"

"That's right."

"Which means you have no idea what actually happened. You don't know what I'll find on that footage if I manage to track it down."

"Not exactly, but—"

"Nope. Sorry." Lilah shook her head. "I can't help you, Ridley."

"Lilah, please." Ridley hated begging the person who'd made sure she lost every single one of her friends after the Cataclysm. But she had better friends now, and she'd do whatever she had to in order to keep them. "Please, we're talking about an innocent guy's life here."

"We're also talking about my *brother*'s life. I'm not putting that at risk." Lilah picked up her clutch. "I'm sorry, but I have no idea why you thought I'd be able to help you. And if you tell *anyone* what you *think* I spend my spare time doing," she hissed, stepping closer, "I will make sure you pay."

Ridley shook her head. "You're all the same, you Davenports. Despicable specimens of the human race."

Lilah pasted a sweet smile onto her face as she pulled the bathroom door open. "It's been nice talking to you, Ridley. Stay out of trouble."

CHAPTER 12

THOUGH IT WAS A Saturday, Ridley woke early the following morning. Dad was heading to the other side of the city to purchase a clock on behalf of his new client from someone who needed the cash more than he needed his collection of pre-Cataclysm collectibles. So Ridley had offered to man the store for the morning, which, sadly, meant she only had about ten minutes left to lie in bed.

She rolled over and squinted at the dull morning light seeping through her curtains, anger resurfacing as the previous night's conversation with Lilah washed over her again. She and Meera had left soon after that, and Ridley had told Meera not to despair. "I'll come up with something, don't worry." Then she'd sat with her laptop and followed Ezra's instructions to locate the live feed of the listening device she'd hid in Lawrence's bedroom, but it appeared the recording had ended several hours after it began. And prior to that, the only things recorded were footsteps, the shuffling of something that might have been paper, and then some loud rustling sounds before the recording abruptly cut off. Which probably meant that stupid, paranoid Lawrence Madson had discovered the darn thing.

And that left Ridley back at square one. So she had no idea what this 'something' would be that she'd promised Meera she would come up with. Hopefully by the time she saw Meera at the Wallace dinner tonight, a brilliant idea would have presented itself.

Wallace Academy kicked off every year with a social dinner for each class—a pointless event, in Ridley's opinion—and tonight was the seniors' turn. *Yippee*, she thought dully. Pulling out her fingernails seemed more appealing at this point.

She reached for her commscreen to check the time and was about to turn over for another three minutes when a message appeared on the screen.

Unknown: I found the footage. You were right. Your friend wasn't there. LM was.

Ridley sat up quickly, her heart pounding. "Lilah?" she murmured. It had to be. She raised her commscreen closer to her mouth and watched her words transcribe across the screen as she spoke. "You changed your mind."

Unknown: I needed to know the truth. If the video had shown something else, I wouldn't have told you about it.

Of course, Ridley thought as she sighed. She wouldn't have expected anything else of Lilah. Besides, if Ridley were in the same position, could she be so sure she'd do the right thing? If she found proof that her own father had committed murder, would she be able to turn him over to the cops? She pushed the thought aside, grateful she didn't need to have that moral debate with herself.

Ridley: You're going to do the right thing, I hope? Send it to the cops?
Unknown: No.

Ridley bit down her anger before replying; her comm-screen found it hard to understand her when she spoke too quickly.

Ridley: Then why bother telling me what you discovered?
Unknown: I can't send it to the authorities. You know they're all in the mayor's pocket. He won't want anyone knowing his son was present at the scene of a murder. That video will never see the light of day if I send it to the police.

Ridley frowned at her commscreen. Lilah was probably right.

Ridley: Then what do we do?
Unknown: Look outside your window.

Ridley scrambled across her bed and pulled the curtain

aside. On the windowsill sat a small plain envelope inside a clear plastic bag. She pushed the window up and grabbed the bag. Kneeling on the bed, she removed the envelope and tore the top open. Inside was a flash drive half the size of her thumb. She sat and reached back for her commscreen.

Ridley: You're giving it to me?

Unknown: Yep. This isn't my problem, so I'm not involving myself any further. Ball's in your court now, Rid.

Within half a minute, Ridley's laptop was open on the bed in front of her, the flash drive had been plugged in, and she was biting her lip as the video file began playing. She saw the street on which Kayne's Antiques sat as if from above, confirming her theory that this video had been recorded by a passing drone. The drone moved smoothly across the street and into the alley—and there they were! Archer and the man in the maroon coat. Unfortunately, the drone had missed the moment they met, which left some of Ridley's questions unanswered. Did they know each other? Had they arranged to meet? Or had Archer seen the man doing something suspicious and walked into the alley to confront him?

She watched the two of them speaking for longer than she expected—both of them gesticulating in an agitated manner—before reminding herself how odd it was that the drone hadn't moved on. The scanner drones were normally in constant motion. The only time they ever stopped was when they detected something unusual. Ridley picked up the laptop and peered closely at the screen, trying to figure out if there were any implant scars behind the stranger's ear. But his coat collar was pulled too high for her to see his neck, and even if the collar hadn't been in the way, she doubted the recording was clear enough for her to make out such a small detail.

Then into the frame ran Lawrence Madson, his face clearly visible as he stopped beside Archer and the stranger. His hand darted forward and he grabbed a flat object from the stranger—the mysterious envelope he and Archer had spoken about?—before leaping out of reach and running away. He glanced back, which must have been the moment at which Ridley looked out her window a second time. Her eyes moved back to the stranger, and that was when he fell to the ground, a knife visible in his chest.

"Wait," Ridley murmured, reaching out to pause the video. She'd missed the moment he'd been stabbed. Had Lawrence somehow done it while grabbing the envelope? She clicked further back on the progress bar of the video window and tapped the play button again. This time, she kept her eyes fixed on the stranger. She watched as the envelope was taken from him, and then, a second or two later, a knife flashed in front of him. But where had it come from? Archer's hands hadn't moved, so it couldn't have been him.

Ridley replayed that section of the video yet again, this time tapping it forward frame by frame. The video was grainy, making small details somewhat fuzzy, but ... there! The unmistakeable flash of metal falling from somewhere above the drone's view.

"Holy crap," Ridley whispered. So it hadn't been Lawrence or Archer. The knife had come from somewhere above. From *someone else.*

She sat back against her pillows, biting her thumb nail. Why, if Archer's lawyers had access to this video, had they bothered constructing a fake version placing Shen at the center of the crime? She could see how they'd done it: they'd replaced Lawrence's head with Shen's head, erased all evidence of the envelope, and Lawrence's hand darting forward to grab the envelope had instead become a hand darting forward with a knife. She had to marvel at the effort Archer's people had gone to, all in less than a day. How much drone footage did they have to search through from the area before finding one that not only had Shen in it, but showed him from the correct angle, turning the right way? And *why*? The original video clearly showed that Archer hadn't done it.

The reason didn't matter though. All that truly mattered was that this video proved Shen's innocence. Now all Ridley had to figure out was what to do with it. If she had Lilah's skills, she'd broadcast it anonymously across every device in the city. But she didn't, and Lilah had made it clear she wasn't getting involved any further.

Movement near the window startled Ridley a second before she felt pressure on her feet. She snatched her legs up toward her chest and grabbed the laptop as she looked across the bed, her heart beating suddenly, wildly. But it was only a cat. A cat with ... four ears? A chill raced up Ridley's spine as she looked at the second pair of ears directly behind the first.

The cat turned its head toward her, and when its eyes met hers—eyes that glowed magic-blue—she knew for sure. This was a creature from the wastelands. An animal mutated by magic. She'd seen some of them before—the occasional blue-eyed rat scurrying across the street at night; birds that flew over the wall, squawking and spitting magic before the drones shot them down—but she'd never had one inside her home before.

She set the laptop aside, being careful not to bump the flash drive, and climbed off the bed. "Go on! Out!" She shooed the cat toward the window. It hissed at her, and an electric blue spark flew from its mouth. Ridley caught the magic in her hand and absorbed it before it could turn her duvet to water or light it on fire. Her eyes darted to the window to make sure no drone was hovering outside. "Out!" she repeated, motioning toward the window again. The cat leaped away, and as it landed on the outer windowsill, Ridley's hand swooped down, her magic shutting the window in an instant. She leaned across the bed and tugged the curtains closed. "Darn creepy animal," she muttered. She had nothing against cats, but a magic-mutated one would only get her into trouble. Hopefully it wandered into someone else's neighborhood.

Perching on the edge of the bed, she pulled her laptop closer, her thoughts racing once more. She needed to get this video out there for everyone to see. No doubt someone important would claim this version was fake and the doctored one was the original, but hopefully it would throw enough doubt on the whole situation that Shen wouldn't wind up convicted of murder. She could send it to some of the news networks, or upload it to all the social feeds. Or both. But it needed to come from someone else's computer and someone else's accounts. Someone with influence. Someone the public would believe.

She played the video again, ignoring the fact that she should be dressed and ready to open the store by now. As she watched Archer standing there with his hands up, staring at the man dying on the ground in front of him while Mrs. Long-bourne screamed silently from the sidelines, she realized she knew exactly who should be the one to share this footage.

CHAPTER 13

RIDLEY'S MIND REMAINED fixed on the flash drive hiding in her pocket as she paced Kayne's Antiques for most of the morning. Even while cleaning the graffiti someone had decided to decorate their front door with during the night, she couldn't turn her thoughts away from the one piece of evidence proving her friend wasn't a murderer. She scrubbed away every letter of the word 'magicist'—a slur that showed up on the exterior of their building at least once every few months—and went back inside the store to continue her pacing.

By the time Dad returned around midday, she was itching to leave. She told him she was heading out to Meera's, which was, in fact, partly true. She would go to Meera's straight *after* sharing the video that was currently burning a figurative hole in her pocket. She kissed Dad's cheek, then hurried upstairs to grab her jacket with the hood.

Half an hour later, she was inside the Davenports' apartment. Magic made it ridiculously easy. She found Mrs. Davenport sitting primly on the edge of a couch engrossed in something on her commscreen, which definitely wasn't ideal. After confirming that no one else was home, Ridley hid in the guest bathroom for a while, wondering whether to risk going into Archer's room when it was possible his mother could walk in at any moment. Fortunately, after about ten minutes, Mrs. Davenport asked the home auto system to send one of their cars out to the front of the building, and then she left.

Ridley listened to the beep of the security system arming itself, but decided not to bother with disarming it this time. She was invisible as she left the bathroom, so none of the beams protecting the artifact collection would detect her. Instead, she headed straight for the passageway and the bedrooms. As she neared the room belonging to Archer, she relaxed and let herself become visible. There were no cameras or beams in this part of the home. She remembered Lilah giving her a tour of the apartment years ago, pointing out every security device and then telling Ridley, "But bedrooms are *private* obviously. Mom didn't want robots watching her in this part of the house."

She entered Archer's bedroom, which was a lot tidier than she remembered it being years ago when she spent so much of her time in this apartment. Almost everything inside this room had changed, but it was definitely still his. She caught herself thinking, *It smells like him*, before reminding herself what a weird thing that was to notice. With an involuntary shiver, she hurried to the sleek white desk and the screen that sat on top of it. With one finger, she tapped the surface of the desk where the faint outline of a keyboard was visible.

The keyboard and screen both lit up, the screen displaying nothing but a background forest scene. *No password*, Ridley thought with relief. If it was Lilah's computer she was trying to use, she doubted she would have been as lucky.

She pulled the chair forward and sat. Then she swiped her forefinger in an upward motion across the screen. She scrolled through the various apps until she located the social feeds collection, then opened the top one. Next, she removed the flash drive from inside her jacket, reached behind the screen, and plugged the flash drive in. She located the file and began the upload. Within seconds, it was sitting there in the preview window, waiting for Ridley to write a caption to go with it.

She sucked in a breath. Then she lowered her hands to the keyboard and began typing.

This may be a mistake, but I can't keep quiet about it any longer. I can't live with the guilt of knowing an innocent guy is taking the fall for a crime he didn't commit. So here it is. Unaltered. The video showing what really happened in Demmer District three nights ago.

Ridley leaned back and read the message once more. Then she reached toward the screen, her finger hovering near the share button. Lilah would hate her for this, especially after she'd gone to the trouble of tracking down this video for Ridley. Archer would be furious too, though he wouldn't know who to direct his fury at—unless Lilah told him. But the Davenport siblings had done enough to ruin Ridley's chance at a normal life after the Cataclysm that messing with theirs didn't bother her too much. And the public already knew Archer was in the alley at the time of the murder. This video didn't change that. If anything, the way Ridley had written the post made Archer come across as the good guy in all of this. The guy who wanted the truth to be made known. The guy who wanted to save an innocent person from a life in prison.

It was too bad Archer Davenport was pretty much the opposite of that kind of guy.

With that final bitter thought, Ridley tapped the share button. She watched as the video popped up at the top of the feed. Then she opened Archer's email, typed in the various news channel contact details she'd looked up while pacing the antique store that morning, and forwarded the video to them with the same message.

Then she stood and pushed the chair back in. She pulled her sleeve down over her right hand and wiped the fabric across the computer screen and over the smooth surface of the keyboard to remove any trace of her fingerprints. Finally, she stepped out of the room and pulled the door back to the exact position it had been in when she arrived.

She turned, magic pulsing through her veins, her skin glowing blue for a moment before she vanished entirely. Then she moved down the passage, her invisible heart thumping a little too fast at the thought of what she'd just done, and made her way out of the penthouse.

CHAPTER 14

"DID SHE CHANGE HER mind?" Meera asked the moment she opened her door about half an hour later and saw Ridley standing there.

"Who?" Ridley asked.

"You know, the person who was supposed to help us last night. The person you said turned out to be a gigantic coward."

"Um ... I'm not sure." Ridley walked past Meera. "I sent her a message this morning pleading with her. I figured I'd wait until the end of the day to see if it made any difference." She walked into the kitchen and stopped at the sight of the commpad, laptop, notepaper and pens on the kitchen table. "What's going on here? Wait, are you doing schoolwork already?"

"Yes!" Meera hurried to the table with a panicked look on her face. "Didn't you see the net-mail from Wallace?"

"Uh ... no?"

"Apparently we were supposed to read *every* book on the prescribed list during summer break. I thought we only had to read these two." Meera held up her commpad and showed Ridley two book covers. "So obviously I read those, but I've barely started on the others."

"Well, you're not alone." Ridley picked up the notebook and examined the list of book titles Meera had written down. Only the top two titles had a tick next to them. "I'm pretty sure everyone else thought we only had to read these first two on the list."

"Anyway, so I've started reading this one—" Meera pointed to the third title on the list "—but I can barely concentrate thinking about what Shen must be going through right now."

Ridley's eyes moved to the fourth title. "Okay, I can start reading one of the others while you carry on with the one you've started. Then we can summarize for each other." She knew she wouldn't be able to concentrate well either wondering what was going on with the video she'd posted, but she'd already decided to ignore it until the story made it onto the news.

"Ugh, I know this is super weird for me to say," Meera said, staring dismally at her commpad, "but I don't want to be reading right now. We were supposed to meet Shen at the indoor wall this afternoon. I was even kinda looking forward to it. I can't believe things can change so drastically in just a few days."

Ridley put the notepad down. "We can still go if you want."

Meera rolled her eyes. "I wasn't looking forward to it *that* much. You know it's more your thing than mine. I only started 'cause you guys were making me feel left out."

Ridley couldn't help laughing. "Yes, I know." The indoor sports center had begun as a community project to keep kids from the city's poorer districts off the street and out of trouble. Shen loved climbing from the start and continued going, even after many of his friends lost interest. When Ridley started at Wallace and was so unhappy to discover all her old friends still ignoring her, Shen convinced her to give indoor climbing a go. She was surprised to find that she enjoyed it. She liked relying on her own body's strength and not her magic, and it gave her something to work toward. At first it was all about climbing a little higher every time. Then, once she'd mastered climbing all the way to the top, it became about climbing faster. Beating her own best time. Beating Shen—something she hadn't managed to achieve yet, though she assured herself it would happen.

These days, Shen was a volunteer instructor at the sports center. All the younger kids loved him. They must be so confused, Ridley thought, seeing Shen's face on social feeds and on the news updates that streamed across the city's public screens. Seeing him accused of murder. *I'll get you out of that jail*, she promised him. She had to do it as much for those kids as for herself, Meera, and Shen's family.

"So yeah, let's try the reading thing," Meera said with a sigh. "It has to be done. I'll try harder to focus and not think about Shen *too* much."

They sat on the couch, Meera reading her commpad and Ridley reading the one title that Meera had an actual paper copy of, mainly so she could put her commscreen aside and resist the urge to scroll through the social feeds. The minutes ticked slowly by, and no one messaged Ridley or Meera to ask if they'd seen the video. Meera's siblings didn't say anything about it. Ridley's dad didn't call her.

A paranoid corner of her mind was afraid someone might have made the video disappear. Or that every news channel had been secretly threatened and decided not to broadcast it. But she pushed her worries away and tried to focus on the book. She lasted another fifteen minutes before Anika ran out of her bedroom. "Did you see this?" she said to Meera, her eyes shining as she held a commscreen toward her sister.

"Is that mine?" Meera asked with a frown.

"Yeah, it kept buzzing on your bed. You've got all these messages from one of Shen's brothers."

"And you *looked* at them?" Meera demanded, snatching the commscreen. "Didn't we *just* have a discussion about privacy?"

"Just look!" Anika insisted.

Ridley's heart sped up as Meera tapped her commscreen. Those messages had better be about the video she posted, otherwise—

"Oh wow," Meera said. "Wow, wow, wow. Rid, look at this!"

"What?" Ridley let the book fall shut and leaned over to look at the screen of Meera's device. Sure enough, there was the video with Archer's caption above it. Below, more than three hundred comments had already been added. "Holy crap," Ridley murmured, trying her best to look more surprised than relieved. "So that's what really happened."

"Awesome, right?" Anika said. "I'm gonna tell Triven." She turned and ran from the room.

"This is proof," Meera said, her eyes bright and her smile wide. "This shows he wasn't there. He's going to be free!" She threw her arms around Ridley and hugged her tightly before pulling back and staring at the commscreen again. "Wow, so they seriously doctored this original video to pretend Shen was there. I mean, this is the mayor's son, right? No one knew until now that he had anything to do with this whole thing. Wait, but what if the cops say *this* video is the fake?" Her face fell as she looked up. "What if they think Archer's lying?"

"Um, I guess that's possible," Ridley said, pretending it was the first time the thought had occurred to her. "But this is Archer Davenport we're talking about. He has the money and connections to make sure the police believe him. And even if they don't, hopefully this video will throw enough doubt on the whole situation that they won't have enough reason to keep Shen in custody any longer." Ridley finally allowed herself to pick up her own commscreen. "I wonder if it's in the news yet." She located the live streaming feed of one of the news channels she'd contacted. "It is. Look." She leaned over and held the commscreen so both she and Meera could watch as Archer Davenport walked out of Aura Tower with his father on one side and someone Ridley didn't recognize— one of his lawyers, most likely—on the other. They stopped at the top of the steps and looked down at a crowd of reporters.

"Wow, people don't waste time in this city, do they," Meera said. "He posted that video, what, two hours ago? And already he's talking to reporters about it."

Anxiety twisted Ridley's insides as she watched Archer. *Don't you dare deny it*, she thought. She managed an uneasy laugh and said, "He probably didn't have a choice. His father probably told him to get out there and make a statement about it instead of hiding behind the social feeds."

"Yeah, maybe."

Behind her back, Ridley crossed her fingers as Archer smiled—a poor imitation that in no way resembled the real thing—and shouted above the reporters' questions. "Yes, I did post that video. It was sent to me by someone at the Lumina City Drone Surveillance Department. Someone who wanted me to know that the other video—the video with Shen Lin— wasn't real. It had been cleverly manipulated. This person at the Drone Surveillance Department was afraid to go public with it, but I wasn't. I realized Shen Lin might be innocent, and I couldn't live with the guilt. I had to make the truth known. A digital forensics team has begun examining both videos, and so far, it seems the representative of the Drone Surveillance Department was correct. The video I released to-day is the unaltered version." The reporters raised their voices once more, but Archer shouted, "That's all I have to say. If you have further questions, you can direct them to my lawyer."

Ridley exhaled slowly. *Great story, Archer*, she thought. *I wonder who came up with it.*

"I'm so happy," Meera said, falling back against the couch

and hugging a cushion. "Shen's going to be okay. I hope they release him today. I can't wait to see him again. Even if the Wallace dinner finishes late. I don't care. I just want to see him and make sure he's okay." Ridley tilted her head, watching Meera closely as something occurred to her. "What?" Meera asked. A flush rose to her cheeks. "Why are you staring at me?"

"You like him, don't you? I mean you *really* like him. I don't know why I didn't see it before."

"What?" Meera rolled her eyes. "Don't be so silly. This is *Shen* we're talking about. Our *friend*. He's not … like …" She waved her hand in the air as whatever words she was looking for escaped her.

"Not like what?" Ridley asked with a grin.

"You know. Not like boyfriend material."

"Really? He's kind and smart, and have you seen those arm and shoulder muscles from all the rock climbing? I mean, talk about swoon-worthy, right?" Ridley's grin stretched wider as Meera's blush deepened.

"Yeah, but he's *Shen*." She sucked in a deep breath, and slowly, tears welled in her eyes. "And … and I really thought he was going to be trapped in prison forever, or maybe even end up dead. I thought we might never see him again, and I could hardly bear it."

Ridley launched across the couch and wrapped her arms around Meera. "You're so totally in love," she said with a laugh.

"I am not," Meera protested weakly. And then: "Do you think I am?"

"Well, look, I'm no expert," Ridley said as she pulled back. "But it seems like it."

"Ugh, I'm never going to be able to concentrate on this stupid book now," Meera said, covering her face with both hands.

"Yeah, I wouldn't even bother trying. You know we can catch up quickly with reading once school starts." Ridley picked up her commscreen again and searched for Mrs. Lin's details. "Let's find out what's happening with Shen."

They called Mrs. Lin twice, and she answered the second time. After getting her emotions under control, she told them, "The lawyer says she's pushing for him to be released by the end of the day. And she's really good, this woman. She says they have zero legitimate evidence that points to Shen being involved."

Ridley high-fived Meera over the top of the commscreen before ending the call. They then spent the remainder of the afternoon texting back and forth with one of Shen's brothers while watching the social feeds blow up about the video Archer had shared, the corruption within law enforcement and government, and the general injustice surrounding the whole situation. Eventually, half an hour before they needed to be at Wallace Academy, Shen's brother sent one last message: HE'S OUT!

Meera squealed, then jumped up and pulled Ridley off the couch. "Okay, you gotta go. You still need to get home and get dressed. We'll meet at the bus stop?"

"Yep, I'm going, I'm going. We can visit Shen at home later."

"Yes! Yay!"

Ridley ran home, which was fortunately only two and a half blocks away, and quickly changed out of her jeans and jacket and into black pants and a blue shirt. It was one of three smart button-up shirts she kept aside for Wallace Academy events. That and the two dresses she wasn't particularly fond of wearing. She dabbed on lip gloss, dragged a mascara wand over her eyelashes, ran her fingers through her hair a few times, and decided that was good enough.

A little more than twenty minutes later, she and Meera walked up the Wallace Academy steps together. "Our last one," Meera said as they reached the tall glass doors. "One more start-of-the-year dinner. One more year of school uniforms. One more year until all the hard work is worth it. Well, then there's university, I suppose," she added. "After *that* all the hard work will be worth it. But at least we'll be done with pleated skirts and knee-high socks by the end of this year."

"Those ridiculous socks," Ridley said. "I'm so over them."

"You definitely won't need them at The Rosman Foundation," Meera said with a laugh.

If I get in, Ridley added silently. If she wasn't accepted into one of The Rosman Foundation intern programs straight out of school, then hopefully one of her college applications would work out. Many of the world's best tertiary institutions had been demolished in the Cataclysm, of course, but those in cities with arxium protection had survived. There were still some good places left around the world—if she could get financial assistance. Then she could try again in a few years for The Rosman Foundation, or something like it somewhere else in the world.

As she and Meera passed reception and headed toward the academy's grand dining room, Ridley's commscreen buzzed. She pulled the slim device from her pocket, which showed a picture of Dad's face alongside the incoming voice call symbol. "I'll catch up in a minute," she said to Meera as she turned and raised the commscreen to her ear. "Hi, Dad."

"Riddles! Did you see the news about Shen?"

"Yes! Isn't it great?" Ridley's smile stretched wide as she wandered back past the reception desk. "I heard he's out now."

"Yes, sounds like their lawyer was amazing. Ferocious woman. And with the public going nuts about rich people framing poor people for crimes they didn't commit, I think the cops felt pressured to speed up the process of releasing him."

"So is he home yet?"

"Yes. Saw him myself. He had a police escort straight to his front door."

"Awesome." Ridley stopped near the library door. "Meera and I will come over later after the dinner. I mean, if the Lins don't mind."

"Sounds great. I'll check with them and let you know. And Ridley?"

"Yeah?"

"Try to enjoy tonight."

"Yeah, yeah." She traced one finger over the gold lettering on the library door. "I'll try."

"I know you hate these stuffy traditional events, but it's your last one. At least, the last of this exact type of event. So pretend you're happy to be there. You know what'll happen."

Ridley smiled again as she lowered her hand. A smaller smile, but one no less real. In the early days of living above Kayne's Antiques, when life sucked more than it had ever sucked, Dad would say, "Let's just pretend, okay? Let's pretend it's fun to live here." So they pretended, and most of the time it actually made Ridley feel a little better. "I will," she said, turning away from the library door. "I promise. See you later." She ended the call, slid the commscreen back into her pocket, and looked up.

And took a startled step back at the sight of someone standing there, watching her. With hands curled at his sides and his expression thunderous, Archer Davenport said, "What have you done?"

CHAPTER 15

"WHAT HAVE *I* DONE?" Ridley repeated as Archer stepped past her and shoved the library door open. He grabbed her arm and pulled her in after him.

"You stole a priceless artifact from my home," he said, releasing her before she could tug her arm free. "And you posted a video that should never have been made public."

She hesitated, utterly baffled as to how he knew she was the one who'd done these things. "Even if it were true that I posted the video," she said eventually, ignoring Archer's first statement, "what are you so concerned about? It's not like it showed you doing anything wrong. You're still off the hook."

"How did you even get hold of it?" he demanded. "My father said that all trace of the original footage was gone."

"How did *I* get hold of it? You're joking, right?"

He brought one fist down on the librarian's desk. "Do I look like I'm joking?"

"You seriously don't know the things that happen under your own roof?" Ridley asked. But even as she said the words, she remembered Lilah hiding one laptop in her bottom dresser drawer and the other behind a pile of books at the top of a bookshelf. *If you tell* anyone *what you* think *I spend my spare time doing,* Lilah had said to her, *I will make sure you pay.*

Archer's eyes narrowed. "I know you were in my bedroom this evening using my computer to post that video. And since you were stupid enough to wear the exact same jacket as the mysterious thief who stole that figurine a few nights ago, I now know that mysterious thief was you."

"You don't know—"

"I *do know*, Ridley. It was you who walked past the camera in my bedroom."

Her mouth dropped open. "You have a camera in your *bedroom*?" she blurted out. "Okay, that's just creepy."

Archer's gaze grew darker. "Think whatever you want to think."

"I'm trying not to, actually. I'd rather not imagine the things you like to record in your own—"

"Ridley!" he shouted. "You have no idea what a mess you've created. Apart from the video, which I had to get creative about when explaining things to my father—"

"Oh, poor Archer," she sneered. "Did I make a *mess* for you? I guess that's what you get for going along with framing an innocent person instead of telling the truth from the start."

He leaned dangerously close to her and lowered his voice. "I had nothing to do with that. And did you ever stop to think that maybe your friend isn't so innocent?"

"No, I did not stop to think that. I don't know about the kind of people you hang out with, but my friends aren't the type who *kill people!*"

Archer swung away from her, his hands clenching into fists. Several silent moments passed before he turned back to her, his jaw set. "Just forget about the stupid video. I need the figurine, okay? That's all that matters right now."

"Why? What's so important about one stupid artifact from the old world? Your family owns so many of those kinds of things I'm surprised you even noticed it was—" She stopped then, her mouth half open and her body suddenly drenched in goosebumps as she remembered something: She'd used magic when going in and out of Archer's bedroom this afternoon. And Archer had cameras she didn't know about, which meant he now knew her biggest secret.

"What's so important," Archer said, "is that you don't get to take things that don't belong to you. Which means you need to give it back."

No, she told herself. He couldn't have seen her magic. She'd only used it while in the passageway and not inside his bedroom. He would have said something by now if he knew about it.

"Ridley!" Archer threw his hands into the air as he swore beneath his breath. "Are you even listening to me?"

"Yes," she answered, almost smiling with relief. "You were trying to get me to believe that it's somehow a big deal that I stole one of your many, many, *many* toys, and now you're demanding that I—"

"It isn't a *toy!*" he shouted. "This is serious. You have no idea what—"

Shattering glass and a loud crack interrupted Archer.

Ridley spun around. "What—" Another splintering crack reached her ears before she found herself on the floor with Archer's arm across her back. "What the hell?" she gasped. Another window shattered, and she flinched and squeezed her eyes shut automatically.

"Get up!" Archer tugged her upward and half dragged her toward the bookshelves as she struggled to find her feet. "Move!"

"Trying," she gasped as she made it onto her feet and launched herself forward. Another shot, and the screen of a nearby computer shattered just as she raced into the shadows between two bookshelves.

"Storeroom," Archer said as he dashed ahead of her toward the other end of the library. Ridley wasn't sure she agreed about the storeroom being the best place to hide, but she certainly wasn't turning back. At least, not until she'd become invisible. She needed to turn at the end of these shelves and duck away before Archer saw. She could disappear among the other shelves and let her magic—

"Hurry up!" Archer called, looking over his shoulder. Then: "Get down!"

She swerved and ducked, knocking into the shelves on the left as another crack sounded behind her. "Dammit," she hissed as books fell all around her, hitting her head and shoulders. The shooter was in the library now. She needed to disappear as soon as possible—*without* anyone seeing her magic. She pushed away from the shelves and raced forward again, then took a sharp left at the end of the row instead of continuing straight.

She dashed between the maze of bookshelves as a memory of sitting here late one evening with Derek rose abruptly to the surface of her scattered thoughts. "Dusty old things no one ever uses," Derek had said, looking around at all the books. Surrounded by their laptops and commpads, she'd had to agree with him.

She blinked the memory away and made an abrupt right into another aisle—and there was Archer, straight ahead with the storeroom door just ahead of him. "Come ON," he called to her as he looked back.

"No, we'll be trapped!" she answered, coming to a halt and looking back over her own shoulder. *And I'm trying to escape you as well*, she added silently. But Archer's hand was suddenly on her arm, pulling her back around and shoving her toward the storeroom.

"Wait, stop—"

"Trust me," he hissed into her ear before pushing her forward the final distance. Ridley's magic screamed to be let loose, to hide her, protect her, but she shoved it down and grabbed hold of the storeroom door handle. She twisted, pushed, and then she and Archer were tumbling into the room. He slammed the door shut immediately and glanced wildly about before his eyes came to rest on an old filing cabinet. He leaned his full body weight against it and heaved it toward the door. Ridley rushed to fit into the space beside him and pressed her shoulder against the cabinet. She flattened one palm against it as well—close to her chest, shielded from

Archer's view by her body—and pushed her magic as hard as she could. The cabinet screeched against the floor as it slid in front of the door. Ridley lowered her hand and stepped back.

"And now?" she asked, her chest rising and falling as she caught her breath. "We're stuck."

"We're not stuck." Archer moved toward the back of the room, and Ridley followed him. They passed rolls of plastic, reams of paper, boxes of stickers, and other supplies that probably hadn't been used in years. On the other side of a cupboard with old textbooks stacked on top of it, he turned left, and where Ridley had assumed the room came to an end, it actually extended into an L-shape with boxes piled up against the far wall. "Help me," Archer said as he began pulling the boxes away from the wall. The boxes, labeled 'Teacher Stationery,' were easy to shove aside, and in no time at all, she and Archer had cleared the space in front of the wall.

Except it wasn't a wall. It was a door. With a key sitting in the lock.

Ridley stared. "What—How did you know that was there?"

Archer reached for the key. "You didn't know about it?"

"Why would I know about it? I've never even been inside this room."

He pulled the door open and looked back at her. "Clearly you've never needed to escape the library when you weren't supposed to be there."

At the sound of a thump from somewhere behind her, Ridley flinched. "Okay, move. *Movemovemove!*" She pushed him forward and hurried after him, then reached around to pull the key free from the lock. She shut the door, locked it from the other side, then took off after Archer along a corridor she'd never seen before. He shoved his way through two swinging doors, and Ridley followed a second later. "The kitchen?" she muttered as she ran after him. Yet another part of Wallace Academy she'd never been in. They raced past counters of food, a pantry, a small office, then up a ramp and finally, through a door that led outside to the street. Ridley slowed and looked around. "Where exactly—"

"Keep moving." Archer grabbed her arm—she was seriously getting tired of him doing that—and pulled her across the street. They rounded a corner, and he ducked down beside a low window at street level. It appeared to be closed, but perhaps the latch was broken because it opened easily when he pushed it. "Come on." He held the window open as Ridley crouched down. She dropped inside, her feet striking the floor a little further down than she'd expected. A moment later, Archer landed beside her.

"Why do I feel like you've done this before?" she asked as she looked around the basement at the old furniture and boxes.

"What? Escaped Wallace Academy at night when I wasn't supposed to be there and hid in the principal's residence? I have no idea what you're talking about." He crossed the room to the stairs. "Don't stop yet. No one wants to be trapped in a basement."

True, she admitted silently. After a glance at the window they'd come through, she hurried up the stairs after him. He led her across the dining room of an old-fashioned home with wooden floors and painted portraits in gilded frames. Then across a hallway and up a spiral staircase that creaked beneath their feet. At the top, they pushed open an old wooden door, and Ridley found herself in a round room furnished as a study. A study with a view of the city in almost every direction. The small tower, Ridley realized, that she'd spent many hours staring at from Mrs. Hardman's English classroom.

She jumped as something banged behind her, but it was only Archer shoving his weight against the old door to get it to close. He finally pushed it into place, turned the key, then moved to the nearest window. He looked out, then checked every other window before saying, "I don't think we were followed."

"No one wants to be trapped in a basement," Ridley muttered, still catching her breath. "No one wants to be trapped in a tower either."

"We're not trapped. We can get out of that window—" he gestured behind him "—across the top of the house, and onto the next building over. I'd rather be up here where I can see someone coming than down on the street where I don't know if someone's still following us."

"Okay stop. Just stop." She leaned against the desk as her pounding heart finally began to slow. "Why the hell is someone trying to *kill* you?"

He turned away from the window and met her gaze. "Maybe someone's trying to kill you."

"Seriously?" If she hadn't just escaped a life-and-death

situation, she might have rolled her eyes. "Just answer the damn question, Archer."

"I am being serious." He crossed the room toward her. "Ridley, if I was certain that shooter was aiming at me, I wouldn't have dragged you with me when I ran."

She blinked. "But ... why would someone want to kill *me*?"

He stared at her a moment too long, his mouth open as if to say something. Then he pressed his lips together and looked away. "I don't know."

"You *don't know*? Surely you have a reason for saying something so crazy."

"Okay look." He faced her again. "We escaped the gun—or guns. What we need to focus on now is that figurine. I need it back tonight, so wherever you hid it, that's where we're going next."

She pulled her head back. "That's it? You believe that someone has a reason to shoot one of us, but you're happy to move on without explaining any further?"

"There's nothing to explain."

"Are you kidding?" She gripped his shoulders and gave him a small shake. "Why do you think someone might want to *kill me*?"

Archer sighed, his eyes sliding shut for a moment as Ridley lowered her hands. "Okay. It was me they were shooting at. Not you. Now it has nothing to do with you, so you shouldn't have any more questions."

Though the situation was far from funny, Ridley started laughing. "Oh, you have *no* idea how many questions I have.

You return to the city with *zero* fanfare—which is interesting enough on its own—end up at the scene of a murder right outside my home, have a cryptic conversation with the mayor's son after trying to steal an envelope from him, almost wind up getting shot, and you think I shouldn't have any questions?"

"Fine. You have questions. Doesn't mean you're getting any answers. Especially not after you *stole* from me."

Ridley folded her arms across her chest. "Did you know him? The man in the alley. The one who was killed."

"No."

"But you were talking to him. What did he say? Why was he following me?"

Archer hesitated, his eyes narrowing. "You saw him following you?"

"Yes. Earlier that afternoon. I thought I got away from him, but I must have been wrong, seeing as how he showed up outside my place." She gestured to him. "Now your turn. You answer one of my questions."

"No. Now you tell me where the figurine is."

She cocked her head to the side. "Where were you for the past year and a bit?"

"France," he answered, a little too quickly.

"What were you doing there? And why'd you come back now?"

"Where is the figurine?"

"How is Lawrence Madson involved? Why did he take the envelope that man was carrying?"

"The figurine, Ridley," Archer growled.

"Tell me what's going on!" she shouted.

He walked away from her and stood by one of the windows. After looking down, he turned back to face her. "I didn't want to have to do things this way, Ridley."

She narrowed her eyes at him. "What way?"

"If you refuse to return what you stole, I'm going to have to go to the police and show them the proof of exactly who it was that broke into our home and stole from Alastair Davenport's private art collection."

Ridley pressed her lips together and sucked in a long breath. "Blackmail. I see."

"You've given me no choice."

"Uh huh. Well, getting the figurine back is going to be a little difficult."

"And why is that?"

"Because I sold it. And I have no idea who the buyer was."

CHAPTER 16

"YOU *SOLD IT*?" ARCHER'S hands balled into fists. "What the hell is wrong with you?"

Ridley pushed herself away from the desk and stood a little straighter. "The money went to a little girl who needed cancer treatment and to an elderly couple about to end up on the street because they can barely afford their rent. You should be happy."

"I'm not happy!" Archer yelled. "I mean, I'm glad a little girl will get treatment and an elderly couple won't be homeless, but you could have stolen something else to fund your illegal donations, Ridley. *Anything* else."

Ridley stared at him, finally seeing past his anger to the desperation in his eyes. She began to realize that perhaps this really was about more than the fact that she'd stolen something from the all-powerful Davenport family. "It's that important?"

"You have no idea."

"And you won't tell me why?"

"No. I ... I can't. All I can say is that it will affect many people—many *innocent* people—if I don't get it back before it ends up in the wrong hands."

"And you really expect me to believe that you, partying playboy Archer Davenport, care about these innocent people?"

"Yes, of course. I—" He pushed his shoulders back and pressed his lips into a tight line before saying, "I'm not the same person who left the city over a year ago. I've changed."

Ridley started laughing, partly at Archer and partly at herself for almost being taken in by his act. "Oh, come *on*. Are you kidding me? I might have believed you if you hadn't pulled out that tired old cliché. You haven't changed a bit, Archer. You came back to the city and let someone else take the fall for murder without batting an eyelid. You're exactly the same as you were before."

"That was—" He cut himself off, exhaling sharply. "Out of my control," he finished quietly.

"Sure it was."

"You're a criminal," he countered. "Does that mean *you* don't care about other people?'

"Of course I care about—"

"Exactly. So think whatever you want about me, but I'm not so terrible a person that I'll let loads of people die if I can stop it."

"Die?" Ridley eyed him doubtfully. "And this is all because an ancient gold artifact might end up in the wrong hands?"

"Yes."

Ridley sighed. "Well, crap."

"What?"

"It might be too late then."

Archer stepped closer, fixing his intense gaze on her. "Why?"

"Because ..." She swallowed but refused to look away. "It wasn't by chance that I stole that particular artifact. Someone asked for it."

"Someone *asked* for it?"

"Someone was offering a lot," she rushed on, "so I wasn't about to turn down the job. I didn't realize that thing was so important. I thought it was just an ancient piece of art from hundreds of years ago that some other collector really wanted. But maybe ... maybe the buyer knew about whatever makes this figurine so important."

"Yes, Ridley, if someone specifically *asked* for it, then of course they know why it's important." He moved closer—far too close for comfort—and said, "You're going to get it back. You might not know who bought it, but there must be some kind of trail. Information you can follow."

Refusing to be intimidated, she raised her hands to Archer's chest and pushed him away. "Yes, I can probably find out from my dealer. But if the figurine is already in the wrong hands, then—"

"It's not too late. No one knows how to open it, so we might still have time."

"Open it? There's something inside?" When Archer showed no sign of answering, she sighed. "Fine. But if someone knows why this thing is so important, then they probably also know how to get inside it."

Archer shook his head. "No one knows."

"Well ... what if they just break it?"

"That won't work. At least ... I hope it won't." He unlocked the door leading to the stairway, then crossed the room to the window behind the desk. Sliding it open, he said, "Send a message to your dealer and ask to meet."

"Now?"

"Yes, now. Have I somehow failed to communicate the urgency of this situation to you?"

"Someone just tried to *shoot* one of us," Ridley reminded him. "And now you want to go back out there?"

"I'm not planning to hide in Principal Colson's house forever, if that's what you're suggesting."

"No, it's just ..." Ridley threw her hands up. "I've never been shot at before, okay? I don't know what to do in this situation."

"You do what I tell you to do."

"Wow, that makes me feel *so* much better," she deadpanned.

"Or we go to the police. Together. We can tell them all about how someone tried to shoot us, and I can also update them on the details of the robbery that took place in my home a few nights ago."

Ridley placed her hands on her hips. "Obviously I'm not interested in that option."

"I thought so." Archer nodded to the window. "Let's get moving."

"But we have to do *something* about it, right?" Ridley asked as she moved toward the window. "Because if someone wants one of us dead, they'll probably try again."

"Then we can deal with that problem after we find the figurine."

"Hopefully we're still alive at that point," she muttered. She stopped in front of the window and added, "Can I at least text Meera? She's going to worry about the fact that I disappeared straight after a shooting."

"Stop stalling!" Archer exclaimed.

"I'm not!" Ridley sat on the windowsill, swung both legs over, and balanced herself on the sloped, tiled surface. She hung onto the window frame with one hand and pulled her commscreen from her pocket with the other. "My friend cares about me, so I need to tell her *something*."

"Then make it quick."

Ridley looked at the device's screen and found three missed voice calls, one missed video call, and multiple text messages—all from Meera. Without reading any of them, she touched a button, raised the commscreen to her lips, and said, "I'm so, so sorry. I had to leave. I'll explain later. And if my dad asks, please tell him I'm fine." The words appeared on the screen almost instantly, and she tapped to send the message. "I should text my dad as well—"

"Just do it so we can get moving," Archer said as he climbed out of the window.

"Dad, I'm fine," Ridley quickly dictated into her comm screen. "I'll be home later."

"Great." Archer balanced beside her. "Now contact your dealer to arrange a meeting as soon as possible."

She shook her head. "No can do. Not with this comm-screen. I have an old one at home that I use to contact him. And even if I did message him from that device now, he'd ignore me. We never arrange meetings on such short notice."

Archer raised an eyebrow. "You'd better have a backup plan then."

"I know where he lives," Ridley said, hating that she was about to betray Ezra in this way. "That's my backup plan."

"Good. If we have to, we'll wait at his place until he returns home." Archer began pulling himself up the sloped roof. For a moment, Ridley considered vanishing, running away, hiding from Archer and whatever problems she'd caused him. But she banished the thought immediately and followed him. Archer knew where she lived, which meant she couldn't hide forever. And there was the possibility that he was serious about going to the police with the videos of her stealing that figurine and sneaking into his bedroom.

"I assume we're taking the roof in case someone's looking for us down on the streets?" she asked.

"Yes. And I assume you don't have a problem climbing across a roof. Being a thief and all that."

Ridley decided not to reply and instead focused on not slipping. Her flat-soled pumps weren't the best for climbing, but at least she hadn't chosen to put heels on. She and Archer scrambled their way to the top of the roof, walked tightrope-style part of the way across the narrow ridge, slid down the other side, and jumped easily onto the flat roof of the neighboring building. Archer was correct that Ridley had little problem with this particular terrain, but it appeared she wasn't the only one who found it easy. He seemed as comfortable up here as she was, and she wondered yet again what he'd spent his time doing since he left the city.

"He lives quite far from here," she told Archer once they'd climbed onto yet another roof. "It's going to take a long time if you're hoping to get there without setting foot on the ground."

"Don't be silly. Two more buildings and then we'll climb down. My driver will pick us up there."

"Your driver? Seriously?" Ridley paused beside a chimney. "You're hoping to get into the grimiest part of the city unnoticed in the type of car that probably hasn't been seen there in ... well, ever?"

"No. We'll drive until you decide we've reached a good point to get out, then we'll continue on foot. No public transport. I'm too recognizable."

As much as she wanted to, Ridley couldn't argue with that. Pretty much everyone knew who the Davenports were.

They traversed two more rooftops, climbed down a fire escape, and found Archer's driver already waiting in a shiny black electro-limo with tinted windows. The driver jumped out, opened the back door, and Ridley climbed in ahead of Archer. She slid across to the other side of the seat, putting as much distance as she could between herself and Archer.

As the car pulled smoothly away from the curb, Ridley turned to the window. The disorienting feeling of being thrown back in time was so overwhelming that she shut her eyes and let the memories wash over her. In her head, for just a few moments, she was a little girl again, sitting in the back of a fancy car with one parent on each side. They were driving to a movie premiere Dad had been invited to because every crown in the royal ball scene had been designed by him. She remembered the city lights flashing by, the feel of the leather seat beneath her hands, the cold air conditioning raising goosebumps on her arms and legs. Mom had tried to get her to put on a coat before they left home, but Ridley had refused. She didn't want to hide the butterflies on her dress. The butterflies with wings made of water droplets.

"Look here," Archer said, pulling Ridley from her memories. Her eyelids snapped open as she faced him, and he held his commscreen out for her to see. A news alert on the screen said something about Lawrence Madson being taken in for questioning regarding the murder outside Ridley's home. "He won't tell the truth," Archer said quietly. "At least, not all of it. And they won't be able to question him for long. Terrible publicity for the mayor though."

"I assume it was terrible publicity for your family too," Ridley said.

Archer shrugged as he put his commscreen away. "Not really. My family's not trying to convince anyone to let them continue governing Lumina City. Besides, it fits the Archer Davenport image. I think everyone was more surprised to see that I'd returned than they were to find out I'd been arrested as a possible suspect in a murder."

Ridley frowned. "You must have known there was some-one else in that alley. You knew it wasn't you or Lawrence, that someone else must have thrown that knife. So why didn't you say anything when you were arrested?"

"The best thing to do when arrested is say nothing at all. Later, when I spoke to my father and the lawyers, they told me what I should say."

"Why did you go along with it though? What was the point in creating that other video to pretend Shen was there? It seems a whole lot of effort for nothing."

"For nothing? You think hiding the fact that the mayor's son was there is nothing?"

"So ... it wasn't your father or your lawyers who decided that video should be doctored? It was the mayor?"

Archer turned his face to the window. "It doesn't matter now. What's done is done. All that matters now is finding the figurine."

They drove another few minutes in silence before the car came to a stop. The window that separated the back section of the car from the front rolled down. "Excuse me, sir," the driver said. "We've arrived at the street your companion suggested we stop at."

"Good," Archer said, reaching for the door handle. "We'll get out here."

They climbed out of the car and crossed the street, and Ridley looked back to orient herself. The limo drove away, revealing the veggie hot dog stand on the other side of the road and the family clustered in front of it.

Shen. His parents. His two younger siblings.

Ridley had to blink more than once to make sure she was seeing correctly. She let out a surprised laugh, a wide smile stretching her lips. She stepped down off the sidewalk. Archer must have known she was about to race across the road, because he gripped her arm, leaned closer, and said, "Let him enjoy this time with his family. You can talk to him when I've got that figurine back."

Ridley's smile was gone in an instant. She wanted to argue with him. She longed to run across the road and fling her arms around her friend. But Archer was right that she should let Shen enjoy being with his family now. "Fine." She wrenched her arm free of Archer's grip. "And stop manhandling me."

"My apologies." Archer held his hands up, though he hardly looked sorry. "Where to next?"

"This way," she muttered, turning away from the Lin family and marching forward. As she and Archer rounded the corner at the end of the block, she couldn't help throwing a glance back over her shoulder. They all looked so happy, as if everything was right in the world. And then they were out of sight, and Ridley had to turn her mind back to remembering the way to Ezra's apartment block. She'd been there several times, but rarely using the same route. She was fairly certain she knew where to go though.

A man sitting on the sidewalk strumming a guitar called out to the two of them as they drew near. He continued singing, and though it sounded terribly out of tune, Ridley patted her pockets, hoping to find a few coins. But it seemed she had nothing. "Sorry," she said, giving the man an apologetic smile as they passed.

"I don't have anything on me," Archer said quietly.

Ridley's only response was to raise her eyebrows. She doubted Archer would even have noticed the man if Ridley hadn't been there.

After turning several times and walking at a quick pace for another few minutes, they reached the building Ezra lived in. As they faced the neglected apartment block with the dilapidated sign that read Jasmine Heights, Ridley wondered for the first time why Ezra lived in such a run-down part of the city. Surely he made enough from all the stolen items he sold to afford something nicer?

"*This* is where he lives?" Archer asked.

Ridley looked at him. "Yes."

He sighed and shook his head.

"What?" she asked. "You know this place?"

"Let's just get inside."

Ridley was getting tired of Archer not answering questions, but she managed to keep her irritation to herself as they entered the building through a security door with a broken lock. She led Archer up the stairs to the first floor, where she turned left. She couldn't remember the apartment number, but she knew it was the seventh door on the right, so she counted until she reached the correct one.

She'd known for years that Ezra lived here. Of course, he wasn't aware that she knew. He no doubt thought he'd been clever about the secret roundabout ways he took to get home after making any exchange with Ridley, but she'd easily followed him multiple times. Once every few months, in fact, just to make sure he still lived in the same place. She highly doubted he'd be happy with her showing up out of the blue now. She figured this was probably the end of their professional relationship.

She raised her hand and rapped her knuckles against the door. Then she waited, but no sound came from within the apartment. She tried again. Eventually, with Archer sighing impatiently beside her, she bent and peered through the keyhole. She could see the side of a couch bathed in moonlight, but that was about it. "Look, he's clearly not home," she said, straightening.

"Right, so we wait. Inside the apartment where he can't possibly miss us when he gets home."

Ridley crossed her arms. "That's creepy. I'm not doing that."

"Oh, so *now* you have a problem breaking into someone else's home? What is this, some kind of thief's code of honor?"

She shrugged. "Call it whatever you want."

"Look, if we're really lucky, the figurine is inside this apartment and we can take what we came for without having to wait. So just unlock the door. It shouldn't be hard for you. Apparently you do it all the time."

"I can't," she said, her mind racing to come up with a believable excuse. She certainly wasn't about to use magic in front of Archer.

"You *can't?*"

"It's ... a different kind of lock."

His eyes narrowed. "How exactly did you break into our apartment?"

She leaned against the door, hoping to stall for another few moments. "You mean your secret surveillance cameras didn't show you how I did it?"

"*My* secret cameras are in my room only. The rest of the cameras installed throughout the living area didn't show you breaking in. All I know is that you didn't come through the front door."

Ridley smiled. "That's correct." The Davenports' double front doors each had a thin layer of arxium sandwiched between two pieces of wood. Lilah had mentioned that particular security feature years ago, and Ridley had never forgotten it.

"I'm breaking in," Archer said, not waiting for her reply before ramming his shoulder against the door.

"Hey!" she hissed, looking around to see if anyone had heard the commotion. From somewhere around the next corner, she heard a door swing open. She grabbed Archer's arm and tried to pull him away from Ezra's door. "Go tell that person nothing's wrong."

"What?"

"Just go! Tell them anything. I'll get this door open. *Quietly.*"

"Have you forgotten the part about my face being recognizable?"

"If anyone says anything, just say you always get asked

that. No one's going to believe the *actual* Archer Davenport is inside Jasmine Heights. Now *go* before someone comes this way asking questions."

She waited until his back was turned before letting magic rise to the surface of her hand. The motions required to unlock a lock with magic were a little complicated, and she hadn't tried them in years, so she simply held her hand against the lock and transformed it to air. With one hand still against the lock, she twisted the handle with the other, and the door opened easily. A second later, she heard the door around the corner bang shut.

"I guess no one's that interested in what goes on outside their own apartments," Archer said from the end of the corridor. As he turned back, Ridley pulled her hand hastily away from the lock and shoved it into her jacket pocket. The lock was visible again, and her hand was hopefully returning to its normal non-glowy state while inside her pocket.

Archer reached her side and frowned at the door that was now ajar. "You managed that pretty quickly."

"Turns out the lock wasn't that different after all," she answered. She pushed the door open, walked in, and looked around. Aside from the couch she'd seen through the keyhole, a small table, a single chair, and one moth-eaten rug, the rest of the apartment was empty. She turned slowly on the spot, taking in the empty half of the room and the kitchenette with no appliances. Crossing to the only other door, she found an empty bathroom. A fine layer of dust covered the toilet lid and bath. She walked back out as Archer opened a kitchen cupboard to reveal empty shelves inside.

"So ... he's moved?" Ridley said. "Or is in the process of moving? 'Cause this is definitely where he used to live. I've followed him here multiple times. I saw him come in here just last month."

Archer stopped beside the window—too dirty to see out of—and said, "Interesting."

"So." Ridley leaned against the wall beside the open front door and crossed her arms. "Do you still want to wait here for him? If he's already living somewhere else, it could be days before he comes back for this stuff. We could ask some of the neighbors if they know where he went. Or *I* could ask them, seeing as how you don't want to show your face. Or ..." She trailed off as she noticed the strange way Archer was looking at her. "What?" she asked. No, not *at* her; his gaze was fixed on the wall just beside her head.

She looked right, and sucked in a breath. Some sort of insect, almost as large as her hand, clung to the wall. Translucent wings covered in glowing blue spots quivered. It detached itself from the wall, and Ridley held her breath as it zoomed through the open door and disappeared into the corridor, leaving a trail of light imprinted on her vision. "It must have come over the wall," she whispered.

"So pretty," Archer said. "Don't you think?"

Her gaze snapped back to him. "I guess," she said carefully.

He paused a moment, watching her, then said, "Turn your commscreen off."

"Why?"

"Just do it."

Heaving a dramatic sigh, she pulled the device from her pocket and switched it off. "Okay, done." She put it away. "What about yours?"

"Mine's off already."

"Terrific."

She was about to tell him he was just as paranoid as Meera when he said, "You know what this building is, don't you?"

She hesitated, wondering if this was a joke. "Uh, an apartment block?"

"No."

"Okay, why don't you tell me then."

"It's an entrance."

Her eyebrows climbed a little higher. "To ... ?"

Archer cocked his head to the side. "You really don't know? Or is this you doing a great job of pretending?"

Ridley's jaw tensed. "An entrance to *what*, Archer?"

His lips curved into a small smile. "Lumina City's illicit underworld of magic users."

CHAPTER 17

GOOSEBUMPS CRAWLED UP Ridley's arms, and the hairs on the back of her neck stood on end. "Illicit underworld ... of magic?" she whispered. "Why—why would I know about that?"

He frowned. "Because you're a thief?"

"Oh." Her racing pulse slowed slightly. "Right."

He leaned forward against the back of the couch, his eyes never leaving her. "You really expect me to believe that you, a criminal, know nothing about the people who live illegally beneath the city's surface where the drones can't detect them?"

"I'm not that kind of criminal," Ridley answered. "I keep to myself. I steal things and pass them on to Ezra. That's pretty much it for my criminal life."

"Oh. That's a bit of a letdown." Archer pushed away from the couch. "Here I was thinking I've been in the company of a genuine crook."

"Sorry to disappoint you. I'm really more of a straight A scholarship student than anything else."

"That's unfortunate."

Ridley glared at him. "I assume you mentioned this alleged magical underworld for a reason?"

"Right." He sat on the arm of the couch as he looked around the room once more. "This building conceals one of the entrances. Plenty of people who claim to live here merely use this place as a route underground."

Ridley waited for him to start laughing, to crack a smile, but his eyes continued to examine the room. "You expect me to believe this nonsense? Magic is dangerous, unreliable. Totally unstable since the Cataclysm. People who use it get killed. If this underworld you're talking about really did exist, there's no way it would remain secret. There'd be underground explosions all over the place, the ground would crack apart, and buildings would cave in."

Archer shrugged. "Perhaps it isn't as dangerous as everyone believes."

"It is," Ridley said. "I've seen what happens to people who use it. So have you." She thought of the woman who'd died just days ago. She thought of Serena Adams. Ridley's own magic was different, of course. The power that existed inside her had never changed, never fought back or become uncontrollable. But the magic out there—the magic everyone had pulled for centuries—was different. She only had to look out at the wastelands or up at the stormy sky to know this was true.

"Maybe what you've seen is a lie," Archer said.

She shook her head. "Nope. I'm pretty sure I saw a woman completely lose control of magic a few days ago."

"Look, I don't know what to tell you, Ridley," he said as he stood. "This underground community exists. They use magic in the same way we used to use it before the Cataclysm." He crossed the room and peered into the bathroom, as if Ridley might somehow have missed a secret doorway inside that part of the apartment.

"Okay," she said. "Let's say I believe you. I assume the government doesn't know about this magical underworld?"

Archer turned away from the bathroom. "Of course not. It wouldn't exist if they knew about it."

"How do *you* know about it?"

"I didn't," he admitted, "until I left Lumina City. Anyway, my point is that your friend Ezra could very well be down there. If you've seen him coming in and out of this apartment, it could be because he wants to hide where he's really going."

"Or," Ridley countered, "he moved, and this is the last of his furniture that hasn't gone yet."

"A couch, a chair, and a table, neatly arranged on a little rug, all within perfect view of someone standing at the door." Archer strode to the doorway. "It's only when the door is fully open and someone steps inside that they can see the rest of the apartment is empty."

"You're saying this stuff is here to fool people?" Ridley gestured to the furniture. "So if Ezra happens to be here and someone stops by, he can answer the door and it appears as though he lives here?"

"Yes." Archer walked back to the chair.

"That's a little bit of a stretch."

"It would be," he said, dragging the chair back and crouching down, "in any ordinary building." He flipped the edge of the rug back, revealing a square trapdoor. "But we know this isn't an ordinary building."

Ridley moved to his side and frowned at the square in the floor. "Is that supposed to be a doorway to this supposed criminal-ridden underworld?"

Archer lifted the trapdoor and Ridley crouched down to get a better look. What she saw was an empty corridor dimly lit by dusty old-fashioned lamps fixed to the walls. "No," Archer said. "But I think this is the route Ezra takes to get underground once he's entered this apartment."

"Okay, I'll admit that a trapdoor in the floor is kinda weird." Ridley leaned to the side, squinting as she tried to see more of the corridor. "Maybe you're right about this underground community."

"Of course I'm right. I didn't just make it up." He sat at the edge of the trapdoor and dropped down to the floor below. "Come on," he added, gesturing for her to jump. "We've wasted enough time already."

"Yeah, yeah," she muttered, scooting on her backside toward the edge of the trapdoor. She dropped down, hitting the floor with a jolt and stumbling forward a step or two. She didn't normally do this type of thing without the assistance of magic.

"Oh, the trapdoor," Archer added, looking up. "I wonder how he closes it once he's down here."

"Well, if he really is a member of this magical underworld, then he probably does it with—"

"Magic. Right. I guess we'll be leaving it open then." He looked at Ridley. "Unless you have a way of closing it?"

She narrowed her eyes, trying to figure out if he might possibly know more about her than he was supposed to. "And what way would that be?"

"You could get up on my shoulders and pull the trapdoor down."

Ridley's eyes widened a fraction. "That's not happening."

"Okay, then it's staying open."

"Fine with me." She looked over her shoulder, but the corridor came to a dead end behind her. "I guess we go that way, then," she said, pointing her gaze forward.

They followed the passageway, making several turns both left and right, as if they were being led around and between apartments. Ridley looked up every now and then, noticing more trapdoors in the ceiling. "We'll probably be breaking the law by entering this underground area of magic users," she said after they turned a corner for the fifth time. "We're breaking the law just by knowing about it and not reporting it."

"Yes. But we've already established that breaking the law is something you have no problem with."

"True." Ridley looked at him. "I find it interesting that *you're* okay with it though." She hesitated for barely a second before adding, "Given your family's opinion of magicists."

Archer's eyes flashed toward hers, and she held his gaze as he said, "I'm not hurting anyone by going down there. In fact, I'm hopefully saving a whole lot of people. So I can live with the fact that I'm breaking the law."

No mention of his family, she noted. *Drop the subject*, she told herself. *Don't provoke him.* But somehow, she couldn't let it go. "I doubt your family could live with that fact. Your father would probably disown you for voluntarily entering a community of illegal magic users."

Instead of responding in anger, Archer's mouth quirked up on one side. "Perhaps." He looked ahead once more, and Ridley was so busy examining his response that she almost walked into the door he stopped in front of.

She brought herself to an abrupt halt with her nose inches from the plain metal door. Taking a step back, she cleared her throat. "Do you think this is it? The entrance?"

"Yes." Archer reached out and knocked twice. "This is it."

She looked at him again. "But you've never been down there before, right? You said you only found out about this underground community after you left."

"Once." Archer stared at the door as if he could see beyond it. "I've been down there once. The first time I came back."

"The first time?" Ridley squinted at him. "I thought *this* was the first time."

"Yeah. You and most other people in the city."

She was about to ask for more details, but at that moment, the door swung open. On the other side, less than a foot beyond the door, was a rose bush so large and overgrown that she couldn't see over or through it. Leaves and twigs and thorns twisted around each other, with red roses creating splashes of color here and there. Archer moved closer and reached up for the highest rose. The moment he touched it, the twigs began to retract. The entire bush instantly became magic blue, revealing that it was all a clever conjuration. The twigs swiftly untangled themselves with a rustle of leaves and moved outward to flatten against the walls and ceiling—revealing a path forward.

A path that was blocked, Ridley realized a moment later, by two thickset men standing side by side. The one on the left was pale and bald with numerous piercings in both ears, while the other's copper-colored arms were covered almost entirely in dark, swirly tattoos. Ridley couldn't help looking for the scars beneath their left ears to see if they might only have one each. She was almost disappointed to see two, but she reminded herself that two scars meant nothing. After all, her own second scar hid no AI2. And the dazzling rose bush conjuration suggested Archer might be right about people safely using magic down here.

"The moon is hidden tonight," Archer said.

Ridley frowned, then realized this odd phrase might be some kind of code. Sure enough, the bald guy nodded and asked, "Yeah?"

"Oh, uh, we're looking for someone," Ridley said. "A young man named Ezra."

"Actually," Archer said, "we're here to see Christa."

The bald guy's gaze shifted away from Ridley. "Is Christa expecting you?"

"No, but she knows me."

"I see." The bald one looked at the tattooed one, a question in his eyes.

"Why don't you just call her?" Archer asked. "She'll confirm she knows me."

"No need, pretty boy," the bald one said with a twisted smile. "We know exactly who you are. Come on in."

Ridley hesitated, her instincts warning her not to walk through that door. Clearly Archer felt just as unsettled by the man's strange welcome because he made no move to walk forward either. "What, now you don't want to see Christa anymore?" Bald Guy asked. "Make a decision, folks, or I'm shutting this door."

Something told Ridley that might be the sensible way to go, but Archer put his arm around her, pulled her against his side—which was probably the strangest of all the things that had happened since they entered this building—and said, "Thanks. We know the way."

"Great," Tatooed Guy said as Archer and Ridley walked forward.

"Still, one of us should go with you to make sure you don't get lost," Bald Guy added, shutting the metal door.

"That won't be necessary." Archer ushered Ridley ahead of him before turning to face the two men. "I told you we know the way."

"Rules are rules," Bald Guy told him. "Christa likes us to stick to them."

Archer hesitated, and Ridley had a suspicion he wasn't used to people not listening to him. With someone like

Alastair Davenport as his father, he'd probably learned to or-der people around at a young age. "Fine," he said eventually. He stepped to the side of the passageway, reaching out to pull Ridley toward the wall as well. "Why don't you walk ahead of us then?"

"No thanks." The man's twisted smile made another ap-pearance. "I think I'll stick behind you."

Archer looked at Ridley, and they had less than a second in which to exchange a wary glance before the man lunged forward, wrapping both beefy arms around Archer's neck.

CHAPTER 18

RIDLEY STOOD FROZEN, trying to figure out what to do as Archer shoved his elbow backward, then wriggled free when the huge man's grip loosened. "Run!" Archer yelled at her as he dove forward. Her feet unstuck themselves from the floor, and she turned and raced ahead of Archer along the corridor. It was bare, no rose bush against the walls, and no doors. Jumbled thoughts flashed through her mind: She could become invisible. She could fight back with magic. But Archer would see, and once they got out of here, he would hold the knowledge of her secret over her forever. Or turn her in to the police.

The corridor ended at a set of concrete stairs, and since there was nowhere else to go, Ridley ran down them. Behind her, the men yelled to one another, and Archer shouted at her to move faster. The stairs went on and on, and she began jumping down two or three at a time until finally she saw the bottom. She cleared the last few steps with one leap, stumbled forward a few paces, then carried on running. This corridor was short and soon it opened onto a wide tunnel with a canal running along it and a ceiling so high it was probably the same level as the ground way above them. But what stopped Ridley in her tracks was how unexpectedly *alive* this tunnel was. Lilies at the edge of the water, moss creeping up the sides of the canal, trees and bushes rising up from the concrete, luminous pink jellyfish propelling themselves through the water. Here and there at the edges of leaves and petals, the blue glow of magic was visible, hinting at the conjurations underlying this scene. It was all crafted from magic.

"Don't stop!" Archer yelled behind her.

With a jolt of adrenaline, Ridley raced toward the bridge that crossed the canal. She was halfway over it when a zigzag of brilliant blue light sizzled past her. The air gusted unexpectedly around her, almost shoving her over the edge of the bridge. She ducked down, lowering her center of gravity, and hurried across to the other side amid the relentless wind. *Wonderful*, she thought grimly. *They definitely do use magic.* Archer had said people used it safely here, but Ridley was more inclined to believe it would destroy this entire underground base. "You okay?" she called without pausing to look back.

"Keep going!" Archer shouted, which was answer enough. "Alongside the canal. Toward the left."

Ridley raced off the end of the bridge and immediately turned left. Archer reached her side as they began darting between the trees. She heard a sizzle of magic and risked a glance over her shoulder. Their pursuers crashed through the bushes behind them, but their larger size slowed them down, and their magic couldn't easily reach Archer and Ridley through the trees. "We can get out this way," Archer panted. "Follow me." His long legs easily moved him ahead of her.

The trees came abruptly to an end, as did the cavernous size of the space around them. The ceiling was suddenly much lower, only just above Archer's head, and the walkway on either side of the canal was wide enough for only one person abreast. Jellyfish illuminated the water, but other than that, all Ridley could see now was a circle of light up ahead. With Archer just in front of her, she ran toward it. Her arms pumped and her lungs burned, and eventually she raced out of the darkness. But she'd barely run another few steps before she skidded to a halt, realizing in complete horror exactly where they were.

Outside. On the wrong side of the city wall.

Spotlights somewhere above them cast a bright glow over the surrounding area, revealing rusted cars and crumbling buildings covered in overgrown plants. And there was that irresistible pull, so much stronger now than it had ever been while Ridley was behind the wall. The wild, dangerous power out here called to her, as if it were reaching out to touch the magic inside her. There was a part of her that longed to answer the call, but she knew it would kill her.

"Archer, stop!" she shouted to him.

"What?" he yelled as he slowed and looked back.

"We can't stay out here!"

"It's okay, we can. We'll hide—"

With a deafening crack, magic zigzagged like lightning toward them. It flashed past Archer and struck Ridley. Her eyes squeezed shut against the blinding glow, and she knew she was about to die.

Except ...

She wasn't dead. She wasn't even in pain. She opened her eyes as air spun faster and faster around her, blurring everything. A vortex lifted her from the ground. She threw her magic outward, hoping to fight back, but the glow rising from her body was whipped away into the air spinning around her. Then the tornado funnel whipped back and forth, like the tail of an angry cat, until it finally lowered her—almost gently—in a dizzy, gasping heap on the ground.

The violent winds died down as the landscape seemed to whirl around her and someone took hold of her arm. "Hey, you okay?" Archer asked.

"Everything's ... spinning," she managed to say as Archer helped her sit. She blinked and looked past him, convinced their pursuers would be on them within seconds. As the world slowly righted itself, she spotted them at the mouth of the tunnel. The wind that had dropped her on the ground now raged along the edge of the wall, blowing branches and sand against the arxium and into the tunnel. Though the men tried to step out once or twice, their hands up as they performed quick, complex conjurations, they didn't seem to be able to battle their way past the magic-enforced wind.

"We're trapped out here," Ridley said faintly.

"We're not." Archer pulled her to her feet. "See the ladder?" He pointed to a slim metal structure attached to the wall. It stretched about a quarter of the way up and ended below a small door. "We can get back inside the bunker that way. Quickly, before the wind stops holding those guys back."

Still dizzy, Ridley managed to half-stumble, half-run beside Archer while holding onto his arm. Wind tore through her hair as they reached the wall though it was nothing compared to the power that had lifted her off the ground. She squinted to keep dust and other debris from flying into her eyes. Archer went up the ladder first, and she followed close behind. At the top, he pushed the door open, climbed inside, then reached back to help pull Ridley up. Though she wouldn't normally have needed the assistance—this was easy compared to the indoor climbing she'd done—the howling wind threatening to push her off the ladder meant she was happy to reach for Archer's hand.

He pulled her swiftly inside and shut the door. In the stillness and quiet that followed, Ridley breathed in deeply and looked around at the narrow metal passageway lit by bare bulbs lining the center of the ceiling. "Are we back inside the same place?"

"Not yet." Archer hurried forward, and Ridley followed him. "You know the guys who patrol the top of the wall? This is part of their setup. Sometimes they go down the outside of the wall and patrol along the edge."

"They would see the canal tunnel then, wouldn't they?"

Archer shook his head. "There's a panel that slides down to cover the tunnel. Someone always makes sure it's down during patrol times."

"Great, so now we're about to get caught by government

employees instead of criminal magic users. And why the hell were you suggesting we hide out in the *wastelands* of all places? What is wrong with you?"

"We could have hidden if we'd got out of sight of those men in time."

Ridely shook her head. "You're insane."

"Hopefully not." Archer stopped beside a doorway and peered around the edge into the next room. "Empty," he said, stepping inside. Ridley followed him into what looked like a locker room. He moved to the set of lockers on the right, took hold of the end locker with both hands, and tugged forward. The entire row swung away from the wall, revealing a small opening into a dark space. "There," Archer said. "The way back inside."

"You sure seem to know this illegal underworld pretty well considering you've only been there once."

Archer didn't answer as the two of them slipped around the lockers and into the darkened space. He pulled the lockers back against the wall. After blinking a few times and letting her eyes adjust, Ridley found that it wasn't entirely dark. Tiny lights at floor level lit the way forward along another metal corridor. They hurried along it, reached a square hole in the floor, and climbed down, down, down. Ridley couldn't see the bottom through the dim light, which, she decided as she clung tightly to each rung of the ladder, was probably a good thing.

When her feet eventually touched a solid surface, it was concrete, and she suspected they were below ground again. "Another corridor," she muttered as Archer jumped down beside her. She looked both ways, seeing nothing particularly exciting in the light of the same old-fashioned lamps that lit the corridors of Ezra's apartment block.

"That way," Archer said, pointing to her right. "Quickly. I doubt we'll be able to get back out through the door in your dealer's building, so our best option now is to find Christa. I know where she—"

"There!" someone shouted, and Ridley and Archer both whipped around.

"See?" one of two solidly built figures said. "Told you they'd come back this way."

The men began running, and Ridley and Archer took off once more. "This stupid … figurine … had better be worth it," Ridley panted. The corridor ended at a door, which Archer yanked open moments before Ridley reached it. They ran through, and she found herself alongside the canal again, running between trees. Nearing the edge of the forested area, she saw the bridge, but Archer swerved away from it, heading deeper into this underground world instead of back the way they'd first come in.

They left the yawning space behind them and raced into a smaller room, where they found another stairway, this one winding in a spiral. They raced upward, Ridley trying her best to keep up with Archer and ignore the shouts from behind her and the occasional sizzle of magic. Around and around and up and up they went, passing numerous landings. By the time they stopped and turned onto one of them, Ridley's legs ached and her breath burned her throat.

They both hurried forward along the passageway, which turned out to be more of a gangway. While doors lined the wall to her right, there was nothing but a railing on her left, and beyond that, open space. She veered closer to the railing and saw the steep drop to the canal far below. Just ahead of her, Archer came to a halt. "Dammit, I've gone too high."

"What?"

"I think Christa's place is further down."

Ridley looked around at the sound of footsteps on the stairs. "They're almost here." She ran to the nearest door and tried the handle, but the door was locked. Making sure her back was turned fully toward Archer, she bent over the handle and let her magic flood free of her body. She was about to shove it hard against the door when wind whipped her hair past her face and sent her stumbling a few paces backwards. She tripped and landed on her backside just as Archer lunged toward her. She looked up, saw the bald man at the end of the gallery with his hands raised, and felt Archer's grip on her arm as he pulled her up.

The air crackled around them. "Get down—" Archer began, but the powerful blast of wind sucked his words away, knocked him toward the railing and clear over the edge.

"No!" Ridley gasped, throwing herself against the railing and looking over the edge as Archer plummeted toward the magic-made forest and the concrete it grew from. She didn't stop to think. She threw both hands forward and hurled everything she had at the water below. The light that escaped her body almost blinded her, but the water responded instantly. A tidal wave arced up toward Archer, catching him before he hit the concrete. Ridley scooped her hands through the air, and with the power of a geyser just released from the ground, the column of water shot upward, carrying Archer straight toward the balcony.

Ridley was vaguely aware of her pursuer shouting something at her, but a moment later, the canal water crashed over the balcony like a wave over the edge of a pier, dumping Archer on the gallery floor along with several pink jellyfish that shimmered, became blue, and dissolved into water. Utterly exhausted, Ridley slid down onto her hands and knees and crawled toward Archer. He rolled onto his side, drenched and spluttering. "Are you … okay?" Ridley managed to ask.

But before Archer could answer, a dripping wet figure loomed over them. "I've never seen anyone pull such a huge amount of magic so quickly." Ridley barely had a moment to look up before Bald Guy tugged at the air, pulling magic from it and spinning his hands once. He shoved the magic at her, and the next thing Ridley knew, she and Archer were swept backward across the wet floor and through one of the now-open doors. "Christa will be most interested to meet you," Bald Guy sneered. Then he slammed the door shut.

CHAPTER 19

ARCHER HAULED HIMSELF to his feet and banged on the door, which was covered in arxium on this side. "Tell Christa to come quickly!" He coughed several more times before sucking in a deep breath. "It's urgent!" When no one responded, he thumped his fist against the door one last time before moving away from it. Ridley pulled herself up and leaned against the wall, waiting for her pounding heart to slow. Archer, his breathing still heavy, slid down the wall opposite her and sat. She didn't say a word, and neither did he, but she knew they couldn't ignore what she'd done. At some point, she'd have to confront the fact that her secret was no longer secret.

She mustered enough energy to pull her commscreen from her soaking wet pocket. As she suspected, the screen remained blank instead of lighting up when she tried to switch it on. She pushed it back into her pocket. Her eyelids slid shut, blocking out the dull light of the single bulb hanging from the center of the ceiling. *He doesn't know the biggest secret of all*, she reminded herself as a dull pain began to throb behind her eyes. *He doesn't know the magic came from* inside *you*. She swallowed, opened her eyes, and dared a glance at Archer. It seemed he'd just about caught his breath by now. Slowly, his eyes rose to meet hers. "You sure waited long enough to use your magic," he said.

A beat of confused silence passed before Ridley said, "What?"

"Your magic. You could have used it the moment they attacked us. Or at any other point while we were being pursued. I assume the reason you didn't was because you didn't want anyone to see?"

She breathed once, twice, a third time, but Archer's words—and the fact that he wasn't the least bit surprised at what she'd done—still didn't make sense. "W-what?"

He wiped one hand over his face, pushing his wet hair off his forehead. When he repeated the words "Your magic," it seemed there was a slight emphasis on the word 'your,' as if he knew she hadn't pulled it from the environment.

Her heart thudded several painful times before she could speak. "You were expecting me to—but how did you—" He couldn't have seen anything when she snuck into his bedroom to share the video. She'd definitely been on the other side of the door when using magic. Her mind flashed further back to the night she stole the figurine. But he couldn't have seen any magic then either. She'd turned her body away from the cameras as she transformed one side of the glass box into air so she could stick her hand inside and remove the figurine. "You shouldn't know," she said. "I didn't let any camera in your home see my magic."

He shook his head. "No. Long ago, before the Cataclysm. You were at the apartment visiting Lilah. You used magic. Magic that come from ... *inside* you. You were alone in a room, but I saw you. I saw the magic glowing under your skin."

Again, Ridley had to wait several moments for her brain to make sense of the words before she could answer. "You've known all these years that I'm some kind of unnatural freak?"

Archer leaned his head back against the wall and draped one arm over his knees. "I'm not sure about the freak part, but yes, I've known about your magic for years."

"And did ... did you ..." Ridley was too scared to ask.

"No," he answered. "I didn't tell anyone."

"And you won't tell anyone *now*? I know we're in this secret part of the city where people use magic freely, but it's still nothing like my magic. No one else has this stuff *inside* them. I don't need other people knowing about this."

"Look, I've kept your secret long enough, haven't I? There's no reason for me to give it away now."

"Okay. But ... *he* might know," she said quietly, the realization chilling her. "The bald guy. He might suspect I'm different. He said he'd never seen anyone pull so much magic that quickly. He might guess that it came from inside me."

"Why would he guess that?"

Ridley rested her head against the door. "I don't know. I just ... I hope he didn't see what you saw all those years ago."

Silence followed, and she let her eyes close again. The headache wouldn't be gone for another few hours, but she could at least ease the discomfort by blocking out the light.

"Hey," Archer said, then waited until she cracked her eyes open to look at him. "Thank you. For saving me. I know you don't even like me, so I appreciate you giving up the kind of secret that could get you in serious trouble."

It was too much effort to roll her eyes, so she simply let her gaze slide away from him. "Right, like I was going to let you *die* just because I don't like you. I may operate on the dodgy side of the law, but I'm not *that* bad."

"I know, I just ... thought I should say thank you."

She shook her head. "I could have done better. I should have caught you and lowered you to the ground beside the canal. You could have gotten away. But it was difficult to tell how high you were when I caught you, and I didn't want to drop you if it was *too* high, and to be honest, there wasn't really much time to think things through—"

"Ridley," he interrupted. "I'm happy to be alive. Seriously. *Very* happy. That's why I'm thanking you."

She met his eyes again. "Okay. You're ... welcome. I guess."

"You obviously have no AI2," he said. "How do you fool the scanner drones?"

Ridley remained silent. Archer might know her biggest secret, but that didn't mean he needed to know any of her other secrets. And it wasn't like he'd been particularly forthcoming about all the things he seemed to be keeping from her.

"You obviously carry your AI2—and AI1 as well, I'm guessing—somewhere on you at all times. Since you can't have them embedded beneath your skin, but you need them in order to pass safely beneath any scanner. Or ... do you even need the AI1? The protection amulet? Or does having your own magic mean your body is protected from magical interference?"

Ridley's heart pounded, sending fresh waves of pain throbbing through her head. How the hell did Archer know these things?

"I mean, I'm just guessing," he added. "Magic is inside you, and magic and arxium don't play well together, so I assume you can't have it underneath your skin. Therefore no AI1 and no AI2." He paused. "Or am I wrong?"

"You're wrong," she answered, far too quickly, and she could tell from Archer's smug smile that he knew she was lying.

"Is it the chain you always wear around your neck?"

Dammit. Here she was thinking he hadn't paid her any attention since her friendship with Lilah ended, but if he'd noticed she always wore the same chain, then he clearly hadn't been as oblivious as she assumed during his time at Wallace Academy.

"So your amulets are on the necklace," he continued when she didn't answer. "That's dangerous. What if the chain breaks and falls off without you realizing? You won't last a day in this city without a scanner drone flying over and finding out you have no implants."

"Good thing I have backups then," Ridley muttered.

"Backups?" Archer frowned. "But you can't get backup amulets. They're each registered to a specific person. One AI1 and one AI2."

She smirked. Finally, something he didn't know. "Well," she said with a shrug. "I guess I'm screwed then." Archer was right, of course. She couldn't *legally* have copies made of her arxium amulets. But that hadn't stopped her from getting duplicates made illegally two years ago. Ezra had found someone to do it, no questions asked. Then Ridley had used Dad's tools to bend each one into a small cylinder shape, exactly as he'd done for her original AI1 and AI2. She wore them now on a short chain around her right ankle.

Archer shook his head. "You're not screwed. Clearly you've made sure of that."

Ridley inhaled slowly, folded her arms across her chest, and closed her eyes yet again. "In case you haven't gathered, I'd prefer not to talk about anything to do with the freakish fact that magic exists inside me."

Archer, however, continued undeterred. "So that's how you got to the top of Aura Tower and into our apartment undetected. You used magic. That's why there was no sign of forced entry. That's why the beams didn't detect you. Your magic disabled them somehow. And here I was thinking you were an expert burglar."

"I am an expert burglar," Ridley said without bothering to open her eyes. "One can't disarm a complicated alarm system using magic without knowing exactly what to *do* with one's magic."

"How'd you get into the apartment though? You obviously knew about the arxium inside the front door, which is why you didn't attempt coming in that way."

"Yes."

"So how then?"

She knew she shouldn't answer him, but she couldn't help herself. She cracked one eye open. "Your front door might be made of arxium, but your floor isn't."

"You—" Archer blinked. "You got in through the floor?"

She smiled. "Perhaps I'll show you some time."

"The floor," he repeated. "You seriously came in through the floor?"

"The people who live below you don't have an arxium front door. They're obviously not as concerned about someone breaking in with magic as your family is. It was easy to get into their apartment."

Archer cocked his head to the side. "How long, exactly, have you been doing this?"

Ridley's eyelids remained half open, but she decided not to answer.

"You seem quite experienced," he continued. "Is stealing something you excel at, the way you've always excelled at school?"

She bit her lip, still holding her words back. Archer didn't need to know anything more about her than he'd already guessed.

"It must have been hard, after the Cataclysm," he said quietly, "with your father losing everything. I guess I can understand why it might have felt like the easy option to steal in order to get by."

Ridley bit down harder on her lip. *Don't respond*, she reminded herself. *Let him think whatever he wants to think.*

"I guess I'm just surprised," Archer continued. "It's not as though I knew you that well when you were friends with Lilah, but you always seemed to have a strong sense of right and wrong. It seemed like you had morals—"

"I have morals," Ridley hissed between her teeth, her eyes flashing open.

"You take things that don't belong to you and sell them. That doesn't sound like—"

"You want to talk about right and wrong?" She pushed herself away from the wall and stood, ignoring the throb at her temples. "I'm not stealing for *me*. I'm trying to correct the wrongs of the past. I'm trying to balance the scales." She placed her hands on her hips. "Do you know what really happened after the Cataclysm?"

"Of course I know what happened," he retorted as he rose to his feet.

"You don't have a *clue*, Archer! You wouldn't because your family has always had plenty, and after the Cataclysm, your wealth only grew bigger. Being the owner of more arxium mines than anyone else in the world paid off big time for Alastair Davenport."

"Ridley—"

"Anyone whose livelihood had anything to do with magic ended up with nothing. And what did everyone else do? People like you and your family? Did you help the rest of us? No! You looked down your noses at us. You claimed you'd always believed magic couldn't be trusted and would be the downfall of anyone foolish enough to use it. That we were essentially all getting what we deserved. Then you climbed over the rest of us and used the new laws to further build your wealth while—"

"Oh, please, it was *not* like that. Systems were put in place to help with housing and job placement and—"

"And you think those systems actually worked? Do you think there was *ever* enough funding for those kinds of things? Seriously, Archer, how naive are you? Those systems could only afford to help a fraction of the people affected by the Cataclysm, and it didn't help when influential people publicly argued that our limited government funds shouldn't be going to pay for the lifestyles of those who should have known better than to get mixed up with magic. Instead, all resources should go toward restoring our broken world. *That's* what people like your father said."

"Well we needed protection!" Archer argued. "The wall needed to be built, and we needed to get more panels into the air above the city, otherwise none of us would have survived those early years after the Cataclysm."

"Yeah, and in the meantime, people ended up selling their homes and possessions so they could afford to eat. So they could afford medical care. And when that money dried up, they got kicked out of their crappy roach-infested rental apartments and ended up on the streets."

"There have always been people on the streets, Ridley. It didn't bother you when you were living in Aura Tower, did it?"

"I was eight, Archer. I didn't know about those people until I was living in a community surrounded by them. So yeah, I started stealing. And I know it isn't right, but I sleep just fine knowing that my crimes have helped hundreds of people. They've kept children away from starvation, or given people just enough to get by on rent for another few months, or provided decent clothing for someone lucky enough to get that one important job interview that could change everything. And do my actions affect the people I steal from? Hardly. Their annoyance doesn't come anywhere near being a life-or-death situation."

Archer shook his head. "There are ways to help people without stealing."

"Not for someone like me. At least, not yet. Sure, I can tutor underprivileged kids who don't go to fancy schools, but how much does that really help if some of them don't get dinner when they go home?"

A long moment of silence passed before Archer asked, "So you had zero moral debate when it came to stealing from *us*? My family. The girl who used to be your best friend. The apartment you used to spend hours hanging out in."

Ridley squared her shoulders and didn't blink as she stared through the dim light directly into Archer's eyes. "No moral problem whatsoever. Have you forgotten about the stigma that arose after the Cataclysm? The stigma of having once been a magicist? *Your father* was one of the primary forces behind creating that stigma. He made it impossible for people like my dad to land any kind of respectable job. So no, I didn't hesitate when someone asked me to steal from your family."

Archer was quiet again. Then he said, "From what I'm hearing, this is more about bitterness and revenge than about justice."

"You can choose to hear whatever you want, Archer. Doesn't change my motives."

"And this has nothing to do with Lilah either?"

"Lilah? Why would this have anything to do with her?"

"Your best friend stopped talking to you after the Cataclysm. She didn't want to be around you anymore. The rest of your circle of friends did whatever she told them to. So you worked your ass off to get into Wallace Academy where you knew all your old friends were going so you could be with them again. But they continued to shun you once you got there. And now you want to tell me that robbing the very people who turned their backs on you is about social justice and has nothing to do with getting back at them for hurting you?"

Ridley stepped closer, hardly able to believe that Archer would dare venture into this specific area of their past. Her hands shook, and her voice was dangerously low when she said, "And do you really want to tell me that Lilah came up with those ideas all on her own? Do you think I don't know that *you* were the one who put them in her head to start with?"

Archer's confident expression faltered. "I didn't—"

"Don't lie. This week wasn't the first time I broke into your home. The first time I did it was years ago, when Aura Tower management wouldn't let me up to visit Lilah because when they called your apartment to check whether you were expecting me, *someone* answered and said they had no idea who I was. So I snuck into one of the elevators and went all the way up to the top. I didn't need magic to get into your home; the front door wasn't even locked when you guys were there. So I let myself in, and I overheard you and Lilah talking." She let out a snort of disgust. "You're exactly like your father, not wanting to taint yourself by associating with anyone who fell from grace after the Cataclysm. Lilah didn't care who had once used magic, but you *made* her care."

"Ridley ..." Archer trailed off, his gaze moving back and forth across her face. He bit his lip, then said, "I'm sorry I hurt you."

She was normally so composed. On any other day, she might have smiled her sweet smile and told him she had no idea what he was talking about. But she was tired and headachy and she'd just saved Archer's stupid, selfish life, and now he was bringing all this up? Questioning her motives and suggesting that this was all about *revenge*? How dare he!

Her hands flew up and she shoved him. So hard he stumbled backward. "Don't you dare tell me you're sorry. That means nothing to me. It changes nothing."

"I know, but ... Ridley, if the Cataclysm happened now, I would never say those things to Lilah. I wish I could take back—"

"Shut up." She spun and strode away from him. She banged one fist on the door and peered through the small glass pane. "Hey! Let us out of here!"

"I know the past should stay in the past," Archer contin-

ued. "I wasn't trying to hurt you all over again. I was just—"
He cut himself off, letting out a groan of frustration. "I don't
know, I was just trying to get you to see the real reason you're
so happy to steal from the type of people who used to be your
friends. I just wanted you to see that it's *wrong*. You said you
want to right the scales, but this isn't the way to do it. You
don't want to be this person. You're better than this."

Slowly, she turned to face him. "You know what? You're
right. You, Archer Davenport, really have changed." She
heaved a sigh and pasted on her most fake smile. "You've
turned into a gigantic hypocritical slime-weasel."

"Ridley—"

"No, seriously." Her smile vanished. "Where the hell do
you get off telling me that what *I* do is wrong? What about all
the things *you've* ever done wrong? Vandalizing school property, setting that fire at one of the Wallace dinners and getting
people injured, squandering your parents' money on parties.
Not to mention the appalling way you treated the string of
girls always clamoring for your attention. Oh yes, and let's not
forget about you turning Lilah against me. Then you leave the
city for a while and when you come back, you're all high and
mighty, wanting to tell *other* people about right and wrong?"

He lowered his head into his hands. After several beats
of silence, he looked up. "Trust me, I am all too aware of the
many, *many* times I've screwed up. I have to live with myself
knowing all the things I've done, which is why I'm telling you
to stop before you end up like me. Before you end up doing
something worse than just stealing."

"I'm not going to do anything worse than—"

"*I* ruined your life after the Cataclysm," he shouted, "and now I'm trying to keep you from ruining it further!"

She stared at him. With his hands shaking at his sides, his breathing shallow, and his dark eyes pleading with her, she wondered if she was finally seeing the real Archer, or if this was all part of his act. "What were you really doing this past year?" she asked quietly. "Tell me the truth, and maybe I'll believe that you actually care enough about my future to want to keep me from ruining it."

He let out a long sigh, but his eyes never left hers. "I can't. I'm sorry, but I can't."

She shook her head and turned back to stare out of the tiny window again. "You know why else I don't believe anything you say, Archer? Because you haven't said a word about the stolen figurine that you were apparently so desperate to find that you were willing to hand me over to the police—thereby ruining my life *forever*—if I didn't help you. If it's so important, then why aren't you trying to beat down the door to get someone to let us out?"

"I would," he answered quietly, "if I thought it would make any difference. But Christa will come as soon as she finds out I'm here, and no amount of yelling will make that happen any faster. And just so you know, I was never going to tell the cops about you. That was just—"

"Hey." Ridley stepped away from the door as a figure came into her line of sight on the other side. "Someone's here."

She heard a key slide into a lock. The lock turned. The

door swung open, and on the other side was a woman whose waist-length brown hair was streaked with gray. "Archer," she said. "You should have told me you were coming."

CHAPTER 20

"CHRISTA," ARCHER SAID, moving to stand beside Ridley. "How was I supposed to tell you? You said it wasn't safe to call."

She placed her hands on her hips and pursed her lips. "True. I did tell you that."

"I thought it was fine to just show up and ask for you. Instead your guys attacked us and tossed me off a balcony. I came this close—" he held his thumb and forefinger a fraction apart "—to cracking my skull open beside the canal."

"They don't know you're on our side. You've only been here once, and someone else was on duty then."

"I knew the pass code."

"You're also a Davenport." Christa gave him a pointed look. "Son of one of the most vocal members of the anti-magic movement straight after the Cataclysm."

Archer gritted his teeth. "I'm not my father."

"*I* know that. But they don't." She turned her gaze to Ridley then, examining her with one brief, bright green glance before focusing on Archer again. "I heard it was quite an impressive display of magic that saved you."

"It was. Quite a surprise, actually. I had no idea she had it in her."

Ridley glared at him. *Nice pun, idiot*, she thought.

Christa inclined her head toward Ridley, but her eyes remained on Archer. "Is she ..."

"No. She isn't."

"I'm not what?" Ridley asked.

"Not trained," he said, speaking over whatever Christa was about to say. "But clearly she's taught herself a lot. Look, Christa, we're trying to find someone. A guy named Ezra. He's ..." Archer turned to Ridley. "What does he look like?"

"Short, tanned, dark hair?" Christa asked before Ridley could say anything. "He's the only Ezra I know."

"Yeah, that's him," Ridley said. "Does he live down here?"

"Yes. He's been with us for years."

"Great," Archer said, walking past Christa out of the room. "We need to see him immediately." When Christa made no move to follow him, he looked back over his shoulder. "It's urgent."

"We like to protect our own," she said, "which I'm sure you're well aware of. Just as I would never tell anyone where to find this young lady—" she placed one hand gently on Ridley's shoulder "—I'm afraid I can't tell you exactly where to find Ezra."

"Protecting people is exactly what I'm trying to do," Archer said fiercely, taking hold of the doorframe and leaning back into the room. "Remember what I told you about last time?" His eyes darted for a moment toward Ridley before he added, "It's out there. And Ezra knows who has it."

Christa cursed beneath her breath. Then she stepped out of the room past Archer. "Okay. Walk with me. You can wait in the rec room while I find Ezra."

Ridley hurried after them, her shoes striking puddles of water on the gallery as she shoved everything Archer had said to her into a dark corner of her mind—where she would most likely ignore it. Then she made a conscious effort to push her frustration aside as well. Christa clearly knew exactly what Archer was talking about, while Ridley was still in the dark.

"I assume you didn't know until today that Ezra's part of our community?" Christa said as Ridley reached her side.

"I didn't even know he uses magic," Ridley said. "I've known him for years, and I had no idea."

"Does he have any idea *you* use magic?" Christa asked. When Ridley shook her head, Christa said, "Well there you go. When it comes to magic, we all prefer to keep our secrets."

As they reached the stairway and began the long descent, Ridley asked, "What is this underground place? How has it remained secret for so long?"

Christa stopped and frowned at Ridley. "You didn't know this community existed?"

"Uh, no. Not a clue. For all I knew, I might have been the only person in the whole city safely using magic. I certainly wasn't going to ask anyone else if they've been doing the same thing."

Christa turned her piercing green eyes on Archer. "Are

you sure we can trust this girl? I know she uses magic, which would suggest she's automatically on our side, but that doesn't stop her from being a spy."

"A *spy*?" Ridley started laughing. "Who would I be spying for? The government? The people who would lock me up and sentence me to death for violating magic laws?"

"She isn't a spy," Archer assured Christa. "She doesn't know anything. Even if she wanted to give away information about this place—which she doesn't—she wouldn't have any idea who to tell."

"Because you insist on keeping me in the dark about everything," Ridley muttered.

"Because it's none of your business," Archer retorted before continuing down the stairs ahead of them.

"So," Ridley said as they followed. "This place? I'm only asking because I'm curious. Because I'm—Well, because it seems like the kind of place I could maybe live in." As she said the words, she realized there was a part of her that actually meant them. She knew barely anything about this community, but not having to hide the use of magic was an appealing idea.

"It's essentially a bunker," Christa explained. "An enormous one, with many rooms and tunnels. Built by Aldous Layne before the Cataclysm."

"Aldous Layne? That property development guy? The one who also designed the Liberty Monument?"

"Yes."

"But then surely the government knows about this place. The plans would have been filed in some official government department, right?"

Christa shook her head. "He did it all off the record while demolishing an old apartment block and putting up several new ones. The workers who were involved knew about it, of course, but with enough money, you can buy silence."

Ridley couldn't help glancing at the back of Archer's head as he descended the stairs ahead of them. She knew all too well that money bought silence. Archer's family had proved this repeatedly. "What prompted Aldous Layne to build this place? Was he some kind of doomsday prepper?"

"Pretty much. The Global Simultaneous Magic-Energy Conversion was proposed years before it was ever agreed upon. Years before they began putting plans in place to make it happen. You probably weren't even born yet. There were plenty of people who argued against it from the beginning. Some people kept fighting it—as I'm sure you're aware—while others went ahead and made their own plans. This was Aldous Layne's plan."

"If this was his plan, then why was he outside the arxium wall at the time of the Cataclysm?" Ridley asked. "We all knew exactly when the GSMC was happening. It's not like he could have got the date wrong. If he doubted it so much, why wasn't he hiding in his secret bunker?"

"He was."

Ridley frowned. Her education had included stories of exactly where many of the world's famous people had been when the Cataclysm killed them. Aldous Layne, the architect who designed the Liberty Monument, had been at the very top of that monument where he'd supposedly told people they could get the best view of the global magical event that was about to change history. Teachers always went on about the irony of this when relating Aldous Layne's story. "It certainly changed history," they'd say. "But not in the way he—or anyone else—hoped it would."

"He was close to retirement at that time," Christa continued. "He made a public statement about planning to watch the GSMC from the top of his most famous work, then came to his bunker instead, along with all those to whom he'd promised a spot in exchange for silence or money or some favor. He planned to live out the rest of his days down here, and if anyone survived on the surface, those people would assume he'd died."

"Wow. Okay. And when it turned out that all the cities with arxium shields had survived, he didn't change his mind? He didn't want to go back up there?"

She shook her head. "Magic was outlawed. The legislation for the AI2 was proposed. Some people didn't seem to mind all that much. They figured it was worth giving up the freedom to use magic in exchange for living on the surface in the fresh air and sunlight. Well, occasional sunlight," she added grimly. "But most people down here were happy living the way they'd always lived. So they stayed. And every now and then, others join us."

They reached the bottom of the stairway. "So he's still down here? Aldous Layne?"

Christa shook her head as the three of them stepped onto

the bridge. "No. He died three years ago. Old age."

"Oh." They crossed the bridge and walked among the trees and plants on the other side of the canal. "How do you know all this about him?"

Christa gave Ridley a sad smile. "He was my father."

"Oh. I—I'm sorry."

"No need to be sorry. He had a long life. It was his time to go."

Ridley nodded, but her mind couldn't help turning to her mother. It definitely hadn't been her time to go. Her mother should have lived many more years. "So, um ..." Ridley cleared her throat. "You don't feel trapped living underground all the time?"

"Some of us still move around above the ground, carrying illegal amulets to get past the scanners. I assume that's how Ezra survives without getting caught. But we're not entirely trapped down here. We've extended our longest tunnel in recent years. It stretches right out into the wastelands."

"Not this one?" Ridley said, gesturing to the canal.

"No, our longest tunnel goes beneath the wall, and the opening is much further out."

"But ... why? People can barely survive minutes out there before the magic kills them."

Christa shook her head. "That, my dear, is a lie."

Ridley came to an abrupt halt. "A lie? But why would anyone lie about that?"

Christa shrugged. "I'm sure there are plenty of conspiracy theories we could come up with about those who govern our world today. I'm not sure exactly which one is true. But the notion that the magic out there will kill you is a lie. After all, you're fine, aren't you? The guys told me you and Archer ran to the end of the canal tunnel. Magic tossed you around a bit, but it didn't kill you. It didn't even hurt you."

"A fluke," Ridley said immediately. "One chance in a million. I got insanely lucky."

Christa raised her eyebrows. "You really think that?"

Ridley didn't answer. At this point, she didn't know what to think.

"Can we argue about this at another time?" Archer asked, looking back at them. "We have more urgent matters to attend to."

"Yes, of course." Christa gestured through the trees away from the canal and said, "This way." They emerged from the conjured greenery, and Ridley noticed several arched doorways at intervals along the wall. Christa walked beneath the nearest arch and said, "This is one of our rec rooms. You can wait here while I see if Ezra's home."

Ridley looked around as she entered the room just behind Archer. She'd expected another concrete area like the room they'd been locked in and the concrete tunnels they'd run through. But this room managed to be both large and cozy. Thick rugs covered the floor, and flames danced in a huge fireplace on the far side of the room. *Do they have a chimney all the way up to ground level?* she wondered vaguely as her eyes traveled across the walls. They were painted to depict large windows looking out onto one continuous beach scene. A palette of ocean blue, warm sand, and foam white. But it was paint infused with magic, the type that could be conjured to move in looping motion, as if she were really watching waves rolling up a shore before slipping back into the sea.

Ridley blinked and swallowed against the intense emotion that rose out of nowhere and made her eyes sting and her throat ache. She looked away from the walls to the people sitting at tables or lounging on couches. Some played games, others read commpads or paper books, and an old woman sat with her hands motionless at her sides. Her knitting needles flashed through the air in front of her, tugging continuously at the ball of wool that twitched on her lap as it unraveled. A boy—younger than Ridley had been at the time of the Cataclysm—ran up to the fireplace and made pulling motions with his hands near the flames. Tendrils of blue magic separated themselves from the fire, and the boy gathered them carefully before performing a series of simple hand movements around the magic. Then he pushed the glowing mass toward a cushion and beamed as the cushion rose into the air. A woman sitting on the floor nearby clapped and laughed.

"Magic," Ridley whispered. She hadn't realized how much she missed the way things used to be until now, standing here and feeling as though something misaligned inside her had just clicked back into place. This was what the world should be. What it *would* be if people hadn't become too greedy and tried to pull too much.

"Pretty cool, right?" Archer's voice broke through her thoughts.

She nodded. "So, everyone's using magic down here, and it's just ... normal. Not out of control."

"Yes." She waited for him to say something along the lines of *I told you so*, but the words never came.

"And Christa thinks it's like this out there in the wastelands?" Ridley asked. "That it's safe?"

"Not *safe* exactly, but certainly not deadly."

She looked at him. "And you believe her?"

"I do."

Ridley shook her head. "Okay, maybe I can believe that it's fine here. Maybe as long as people pull from the air and the water and everything that's within the city, then it's okay. But out there?" She jabbed her thumb over her shoulder. "Out there it's dangerous. I've seen what happens when people try to use magic nowadays. You know, like when kids dare each other to do stupid things, and one of them finds a way over the wall, and a surveillance drone catches them being sizzled to a crisp by a spontaneous magical fire or turned into a stone statue."

"You think that's real? The things you see streaming on the screens across the city and on every device?"

She threw her hands up. "What would be the point in staging something like that? The government *wants* us to take back the wastelands. They're always sending out research teams or ... I don't know, those people dressed in weird arxium suits. They're always checking to see if it might be getting safer out there, and they always report that it's still just as deadly."

Archer sighed and moved to the nearest couch. "The magic out there might be wild, but it won't kill you. At least, not if you're careful."

Ridley's eyes traveled across his face as the truth dawned on her. "You've been out there. Like, for more than the minute or two we were out there earlier. That's how you know this." She hurried to the couch and perched beside him. "When? And why would you travel through the wastelands when a train would be much—"

"I can't tell you, remember?" Archer said. "There are things I just can't tell you."

"Ugh, seriously? Surely you can tell me this *one thing*. It has nothing to do with the figurine."

"Ridley, please." He rubbed one hand over his face. "If I tell you *one* thing, it'll lead to another question, and another and another. At some point I could start lying to you. Make up some story so I won't get myself in trouble. But I'd prefer not to. So can you please stop asking?"

She crossed her arms and leaned back, but her eyes never left him. "I think you just enjoy being mysterious. Or perhaps it's a lie, and you haven't been out there." Her weak attempt to provoke him into talking failed, and his lips remained sealed as he stared at the floor. "You said you came back to the city once before," she continued after a few moments of silence. "It definitely wasn't public knowledge, so maybe that was when you came through the—"

"Ridley?"

She twisted in her seat and found Ezra staring at her, disbelief coloring his face. Then his eyes darted to Archer. "No," he muttered. He turned, but Ridley jumped up and grabbed his hand.

"Wait, please!"

He tugged free of her grip just as flames licked down her right arm. She gasped, clapped her hand over her arm, and water gushed down her sleeve, extinguishing the flames immediately.

"Holy—"

She whipped her arm down to her side and hid her hand behind her back, hoping Ezra assumed the blue glow had come from the air and not from beneath her skin. "Ezra, please just—"

"You—that was—*magic*?" he asked.

"Yes, I pull magic, and apparently you do too. So don't look so shocked."

"But ..." His eyes darted over her shoulder before he lowered his voice. "What the hell are you doing down here with a Davenport?"

"Because he needs help. I messed up, Ez. That figurine I stole last week? It's way more important than either of us knew. I need to get it back."

Ezra shook his head. "No, no, no. That's not the way this works. You got *paid* for that thing, Ridley. You can't just take it back now. And *you*—" Ezra took a step back as Archer stood and moved closer. "You shouldn't even be here. The doormen should have killed you the moment they opened up and found you on the other side."

"Ezra!" Ridley scolded.

"Christa knows me," Archer said. "I've been here before. Do you really think she'd bring you out here to talk to us if she didn't trust me?"

"Please just tell me who has the figurine now," Ridley said. "We'll handle it from there. You don't have to be involved."

Ezra shook his head again. "He'll come after me if it goes missing."

"He?" Archer asked.

"He won't come after you," Ridley said. "He'll have no reason to suspect you gave up his name. We'll ... I don't know. We'll steal a whole bunch of valuable things, so it'll look like a coincidence that the figurine is one of the stolen items."

Archer, standing beside her now, folded his arms. "I doubt that's the best way to go about things."

"Look, you want this thing back, don't you?" she said to him. "Well this is the only way to do it without raising suspicion. This is how we keep Ezra from landing in trouble."

"Right, to keep the guy who deals in stolen goods from getting into trouble. Remind me why that makes sense?"

"See?" Ezra cried, throwing his hands up. "Nobody should have let this guy down here. We're supposed to be *safe* in this place!"

"You *are safe*," Ridley insisted. "I don't like him any more than you do, Ez, but it seems he has bigger things to worry about than turning in a bunch of magic-users." She looked at Archer. "Right?"

"Right," Archer grumbled after a moment's pause. He held his hands up in surrender and took a step back. "I guess I can go along with one robbery, if that's what it's going to take."

Ridley turned back to Ezra. "See? All good. So can you give us a name?"

He released a long sigh. "It's gonna take a seriously good thief to steal that figurine back. If it was anyone else, I'd have my doubts, but you're probably the best I know."

"Yeah, well, in case you haven't figured it out, I have magic on my side."

Ezra's mouth dropped open. "Wait, you use magic *out there*? Are you insane?"

"A name, Ezra," Archer reminded him. "Give us a name."

"Fine. But if this gets back to me, I'll make sure he knows it was you who stole that thing back. You rich people can battle it out on your own without involving the rest of us."

"You rich people?" Archer repeated.

"Yeah." Ezra folded his arms. "It was the mayor's son. Lawrence Madson."

CHAPTER 21

"DAMN," ARCHER MURMURED, turning away from Ezra and Ridley. "He knows."

"Knows what?" Ridley took hold of Archer's arm and tried to pull him back around.

"You're welcome," Ezra said loudly. "Can I go now?"

"Um, yes." Ridley looked over her shoulder at him. "Thank you, Ezra." Then she hurried to block Archer's way forward. "Why the heck does Lawrence Madson need to steal from your family?"

Archer's eyes rose to meet hers, but it was as if a wall had come down over them. "Thanks for your help, Ridley. I can handle things from here."

She dropped her hands to her sides. "Seriously? That's it?"

"That's it. Your job's done. You can go back to your friends." He made to move past her, but she put her hand out and stopped him.

"Hang on. Just wait. I can help you with this. It's easy for me, remember?"

"I managed before," Archer said, "when I was hoping to

get the envelope back. I think I can manage again."

"Okay, but ..." Realizing her hand was still pressed against his chest, she hastily lowered it. "All I want is to understand, Archer. A man I don't know started following me. He was killed in an alley behind my house. An alley that both you and Lawrence happened to be in. Lawrence took an envelope that you, apparently, wanted just as badly as he did. And now it turns out Lawrence is stealing from you. I know you said it's none of my business and I should just walk away, but it *is* my business. That man was following *me*. It was *my* home he died outside of. So please, just give me *something*."

Archer's eyes rose to meet hers. He opened his mouth, then closed it without saying a word. Ridley threw her hands up in frustration. "If it's something sensitive or confidential and you're worried I'm going to go and tell a whole bunch of people, then you've obviously forgotten that you know my biggest secret. You know about—" she paused, looked around, then lowered her voice "—my magic. You know about my criminal life. So I have a very big incentive to keep quiet about whatever you tell me."

Archer shook his head. "Look, Ridley, you just ... you can't be involved any further, okay? You need to get back to your normal life. You've got school on Monday, and—"

"You're seriously reminding me about school right now?"

"It's your senior year, Ridley. It's important."

"So is this, apparently! Whatever 'this' is. And life is never going to be normal again. Someone *shot* at me. And there's a secret underworld of magic. Oh, and to top it all off, magic isn't actually the wild, deadly entity we've all been led to believe. Life doesn't just go back to normal after discovering these kinds of things."

"Well it has to."

She shook her head. "You might refuse to tell me what's really going on, but you can't keep me from being involved. I'm going to get that figurine back. *I* made this mess, Archer. I stole the figurine and—"

"Earlier today you weren't the least bit interested in fixing your mistakes. How about we just pretend nothing's happened since then, and you can continue being disinterested."

"Because now I know that people's lives are in danger. At least, they are if you've been telling the truth."

"Of course I've been telling the truth. I wouldn't lie about something so—"

"Okay, then let me do this. I'll get it done quickly. Quicker than you, at least."

"No."

Her eyes darted over his shoulder. She could run. She could get around the corner, become invisible, and he'd never be able to catch her. She shoved past him and ran, but he lunged after her and caught her arm. "Don't! Please, I'm serious, Ridley."

She tried to tug free, but his fingers dug into her arm. "Why?"

"Because someone doesn't want you involved!"

She stopped struggling. Her arm went limp, and Archer's grip loosened. "Someone?"

"Don't even try to ask who," he said, shaking his head. "You know I'm not going to tell you. Just know that someone has put a great deal of effort into keeping you safe from all of this, and you need to respect that. I promised not to involve you, and I've already strayed too close to breaking that promise. I can't tell you anything more."

"I ..." She blinked, shook her head. "Okay, now I have even more questions."

Archer sighed. "You need to forget all this. The world is more dangerous than you know. If you keep digging, you're probably going to get yourself killed."

"Someone already tried to shoot me, remember?"

He let go of her arm. "I think it's a lot more likely someone was trying to shoot me. Which is my problem, not yours," he added before she could say anything, "so I'll deal with it. It's not exactly a brand new experience for me. Being Alastair Davenport's son isn't without its risks."

Ridley held his gaze for several long moments as questions flooded her mind. But it was clear by now that Archer wouldn't answer any of them. "So ... you want me to go home now and pretend none of this happened?"

"Yes. Go hang out with your friends. I'm sure there's some kind of celebration happening now that one of them's no longer being charged with murder. Oh, and if you could stop stealing, that would be great too."

Heat flared in Ridley's cheeks and ears at the memory of everything Archer had said to her while they were locked up. But she had no desire to revisit their argument, so she merely turned away from him, muttering, "Don't hold your breath."

"Wait. Ridley, wait." He caught her arm again—hadn't she told him earlier to stop doing that?—and turned her back to face him. He sighed and said, "I'm sorry. It's just ... If I'm wrong about the shooter being after me, then you're in danger."

"If you're wrong," Ridley responded, "then I'll figure out how to protect myself. I'm not entirely helpless, in case you hadn't noticed."

"I know you're not helpless, but you won't be able to do much about someone with a gun aiming from a distance."

"Perhaps not. But that isn't your problem."

"It might not be, but that doesn't mean I can't help. There's a security company my dad often works with. Personal security. Bodyguards and—"

"No."

"I can arrange for one or two people to keep an eye on you. If they notice anything suspicious, they'll handle it before anything happens to you."

"No." She leaned a little closer and held his gaze, hoping he would understand how serious she was when she said, "I don't want strangers following me and knowing my every move, especially not if they're strangers who work for you and your father."

"I'm just trying to help, Ridley."

"Don't. The last person I need help from is a Davenport."

"Fine. Then I guess I'm done here. I need to get that figurine back." He strode past her and left the room without a backward glance. For some reason, Ridley found it immensely irritating that he was the one who got to storm away first. She shut her eyes and counted to five, putting just a few seconds of distance between herself and Archer. Then she opened them and walked forward.

"Leaving so soon?" a voice asked, and Ridley stopped short of walking into Christa in the doorway.

"Yes. Is that a problem?"

"No, of course not." Christa stepped to the side. "We don't keep prisoners down here. Well, unless it's someone spying on us and planning to jeopardize the existence of our entire community."

Ridley's hands twitched at her sides, wanting to reach for her magic, to pull it around herself and become air, or to shove fire or water at this woman before running to escape this place. "And have you satisfied yourself that I don't fall into that category?"

"Yes, don't worry," Christa said with an easy laugh. "I have my reasons for trusting Archer. If he says you're no threat to us, then I believe him."

"Too bad the guys at the door didn't believe him," Ridley countered.

"A misunderstanding for which I've already apologized, and I'm sure Archer understands how seriously we take security here. But as I was saying, you're free to leave and come back whenever you'd like. I just thought you might want to see more of our bunker before you go. Since you said it might be the kind of place you could live."

"I ... I don't know. Maybe next time."

She took a step forward, but then Christa asked, "Do you ever play?"

Ridley stopped. "Excuse me?"

"With magic. Do you experiment, have fun? Or do you only pull it when you need it?"

"Uh ..." Ridley faltered, trying to remember a time when she'd associated words like 'fun' or 'play' with magic. She wasn't sure if that had ever been the case. Even before the Cataclysm she'd been taught to keep her own magic hidden. "I just use it when I need it. That's risky enough without adding experimentation into the mix, don't you think?"

Christa nodded. "I understand. Up there, it's easy to get caught. But down here, you'd have the freedom to experiment. You already seem quite skilled—at least, from what the guys told me about how you saved Archer. But there's so much more you could learn. We have three trained magicists living down here. They could teach you all the movements you don't already know."

Ridley's eyes narrowed. The prospect was enticing, she had to admit, but no one was this friendly and welcoming in real life. What secret agenda did this woman have? "Yeah, maybe," she said noncommittally. She didn't add that she barely knew any movements at all. Her own magic was different. She simply willed it into something—air, mainly—and it obeyed. Sometimes, if necessary, she might pull from the environment and try some of the easier motions she remembered from school, but there was hardly ever an occasion when her own magic didn't suffice.

"'Maybe' sounds good," Christa said. "That's better than 'no.'"

"Uh huh. But right now, I really need to go. My father will be wondering where I am." At the thought of Dad, a pang of guilt shot through her. Dad would probably be beside himself with worry.

"Of course." The wrinkles at the corners of Christa's eyes crinkled further as she smiled. "Just know that you're welcome to return any time."

"Thanks. I'll think about it. So, if I just walk back to that main door, they'll let me out?"

"Absolutely."

"Great." Ridley stepped beneath the archway and strode through the trees. She told herself that living in a place like this was crazy. It came nowhere near the future she'd been working toward the past couple of years. But as she walked alongside the canal, the idea of being free to experiment with magic—and the possibility of learning the many intricate gestures that had been forbidden since the Cataclysm—refused to leave her mind. How much more would she be capable of if she had proper training? Surely she could help more people, probably in magical ways she'd never even dreamed of.

It would still be illegal though. Taking her life in that direction would make her a criminal forever. Dad would hate the idea. He would spend the rest of his life disappointed in the choices she'd made and terrified of her winding up caught. Could she really do that to him?

No.

She ascended the stairs, leaving the city's underworld of magic behind her. She would forget about this place, and she'd forget about that gold figurine. Archer had made it clear he would take care of that problem without her help. It was just as Ezra had said: *You rich people can battle it out on your own without involving the rest of us.* She didn't need to get herself or Dad involved. Life was safer when she stayed away from people like Archer and Lawrence. And with things looking like they were about to return to normal, she'd have no need to go anywhere near either of them again.

CHAPTER 22

"RIDDLES!" DAD EXCLAIMED the moment Ridley opened the back door of Kayne's Antiques and stepped inside. Something hit the floor in the main part of the store before Dad came hurtling through the back room and wrapped his arms around Ridley. "You're okay," he breathed into her ear. She brought her arms up around his back, squeezed tight, and breathed in the familiar scent of his aftershave. "Where have you been?" he asked, pulling back but not letting go of her. "Why didn't you answer my calls? Do you have any idea how worried I've been?"

"Dad, I'm so—"

"Meera said you were fine, but the two of you ended up separated in the crowd outside the school after everyone evacuated. She couldn't find you, and we both tried calling, but you weren't answering." He eased back a little further, and Ridley's arms slid away from him. "I know I give you a lot of freedom, but that's because you almost always answer my calls. If I'm worried, you let me know you're fine. But then something like this happens and afterwards you *don't answer*?

What was I supposed to think, Ridley? Anything could have—"

"I'm sorry, Dad!" She grabbed hold of his arms and squeezed them. "I'm really sorry. My commscreen died, so I couldn't call you. I was with a friend, and I didn't realize how much time had passed, and then it was really late, so I just came home as quickly as I could."

"You were with a friend?" Dad's brow creased. "Someone who wasn't Meera or Shen?"

Ridley opened her mouth, considered lying, then allowed the truth to escape her lips instead. "Archer."

The wrinkles marring Dad's forehead grew more pronounced as his eyebrows climbed higher. "Archer Davenport?"

Ridley lowered her arms and reached behind her to pull the door shut. "Yes."

"Since when is he a friend?"

She turned the key before facing Dad again. "Okay, so *friend* is stretching the truth. We were ..." Again, she considered making something up, but it was easier—and more believable—to go with some version of the truth. "We were arguing, actually. I wanted to let him know exactly what I thought of him going along with the cover-up of what happened out there the other night." She gestured over her shoulder to the alley on the other side of the door.

"Riddles," Dad said, slowly exhaling. "That probably wasn't the best idea."

"I know. I was just so angry about the whole thing."

Dad nodded, then paused before adding, "It must have been a very long argument."

"It, uh …" Ridley looked at her shoes. "It morphed into a bigger argument. About more than just the other night. You know, stuff about the past and about Lilah and everything that changed after the Cataclysm. I was furious by the end of it, so …" She lifted her shoulders, preparing herself for the small lie she was about to slip in. "So I went for a walk. A long one. To cool down. And when I remembered the gunshots at school and how worried you must be, it was really late." Her eyes rose to meet her father's. *I'm sorry for lying*, she whispered silently. But telling him where she'd really been was out of the question. She'd already added to Dad's gray hair and wrinkles this evening, and she couldn't bear the thought of making him worry more.

"Okay, well …" Dad reached out and rested a hand on her shoulder. "At least you're safely home now."

"Yes. And I'm so sorry for making you worry."

"Ah, it's okay." He swung one arm around her back as they headed for the stairs. "It's part of my job as your father to worry about you."

"Perhaps, but that doesn't mean I should make you worry any more than necessary."

"I know it's late—" he glanced at his watch— "but do you want something to eat? There was obviously no dinner at Wallace, so you must be—"

A bang on the door caused Ridley's legs to freeze and her stomach to tighten. Adrenaline kicked in, and before she knew it, she'd ducked down, pulling Dad with her as if to protect them both from the gunshot she felt sure was coming.

"Hey, Ridley?" a familiar voice called from the other side of the door.

"Sweetie, it's just Meera," Dad said with a smile that didn't do much to mask the concern in his eyes. He straightened, adding, "Are you sure you're okay?"

Ridley rose from her crouch, laughing off her reaction. "Yeah, I'm fine. Sorry, the knocking just startled me. Meera usually calls or texts instead of banging on the door." She crossed the small space and turned the key. "But I guess with my commscreen being dead, she couldn't really—" The door flew open, almost knocking Ridley backward. She barely had a second to make out the faces of her two best friends before they both wrapped her in a tight hug.

"We saw you crossing the street and came over immediately," Meera said, just as Shen added, "I'm so glad you're okay."

"Me?" Ridley laughed as she squeezed her arms tighter. "I'm so glad *you're* okay. You've been wrongfully imprisoned for three days and you're glad *I'm* okay?"

"Yes." Shen lowered his arms and took a step back. "The murder took place right outside your home. Something could have accidentally happened to you if you'd walked outside at the wrong moment. And then this evening—the shooting at your school—and no one knew where you were." Ridley looked into the eyes of her tall, broad-shouldered best friend, and for the first time, she saw genuine fear. "I really thought something might have happened to you," he finished quietly.

"Yeah," Meera added, wrapping her arms around herself.

"We really did. Where'd you go?"

Without answering Meera, Ridley pulled Shen into another hug. It felt all kinds of wrong to see him afraid of something. Even years ago when he was close to death, Shen hadn't been afraid. Probably because he'd been too sick then to know what was going on. "You really don't need to worry about me," she told him. "I'll tell you later what happened. I'll tell both of you," she added to Meera, peering at her other best friend over Shen's shoulder. "But how are *you*?" she asked Shen.

"I'm ... I'm fine." But as he pulled away, she couldn't help noticing the way his smile didn't reach his eyes. "I mean, I'll *be* fine," he corrected. "It was a lot to deal with in a short space of time, thinking I might end up spending my life in prison, or that maybe those crazy lawyers would try to prove I had something to do with the magic on the knife and I'd get the death penalty. Then suddenly I was being released instead." He made a weak attempt at a laugh. "I think my head's still spinning."

"Just give yourself some time," Dad said, reaching up to place one hand on Shen's shoulder. "Things will return to normal again eventually."

"What have you done since you got home?" Ridley asked, almost adding that she'd seen him at the hot dog stand before remembering that no one knew she'd been in that part of town.

"According to his family, he spent like an hour in the bathroom," Meera said with a laugh.

"Yeah, I've always been a shower kind of guy, but ... I don't know." Shen lifted his shoulders, and when he gave Ridley a sheepish grin, he looked almost like himself. "My body ached from spending the past few nights on a super thin mattress, and I just felt kind of grimy. Like, you know. All that *prisonness* seeped right through my skin and I needed to soak it all out. I don't think I've ever enjoyed a bath more than I did tonight. And then we went out for veggie dogs to celebrate. And then Meera came over. So, a pretty great evening."

"Shen?" They all turned at the sound of a new voice. Mrs. Lin leaned in through the doorway, the lines around her eyes crinkling as she beamed at her son. "Ah, sorry, I know I'm being paranoid," she said with a chuckle. "I feel like I can't let him out of my sight for long right now."

"Completely understandable," Dad said.

Mrs. Lin's gaze moved to Ridley, and she added, "Glad to see you're okay. You gave your father a bit of a scare."

"Um, I know. I'm sorry." Ridley's insides tightened with shame as more guilt piled itself on top of the healthy dose that had already settled there.

"At least all our children are safely home now," Dad said, moving to put his arm around Ridley's shoulders. "And since it's late, the three of you should probably catch up tomorrow."

"Oh, yeah, we just came over to say hi quickly," Meera said. "My dad's on his way to the Lins now so I don't have to walk home on my own."

After saying goodnight to everyone, Ridley closed and locked the door for a second time and headed upstairs with Dad. She got ready for bed, and the last thing she did before turning off her light was get the old commscreen out from the bottom drawer of her desk and send a message to Ezra.

Ridley: I'm so, so sorry about earlier. I know you probably think I've betrayed you, leading a Davenport right to your magical doorstep. But this is bigger than you or I know. I had to do it in case he was telling the truth. In case it really would affect many innocent people. I hope you understand, but I won't hold it against you if you don't want to work with me ever again.

CHAPTER 23

THE SOUND OF A GUNSHOT pierced through Ridley's dream, and she jerked awake, her heart racing and her body sweating. She sat upright, looking toward the window where dull morning light seeped through the curtains. She waited for several heart-pounding seconds, but no sound came from outside her window.

The gunshot must have been part of her dream.

She lay back down, staring at the ceiling. The fact that she was still alive this morning and that no one had attempted breaking in during the night was a good sign. If yesterday's shooter really was after her, he or she would know where Ridley lived, right? They would have come during the night to finish the job. Archer had said it was far more likely someone had been trying to shoot him, and he was probably right. Ridley was sure he had way more enemies than she did.

Her mind traveled back over the previous day's revelations: *Magic isn't deadly. There's a secret underground community of people who still use it.* And how was it possible that this community had remained a secret for so long? Surely there must have been people who'd heard of it and gone down there pretending to want to be part of it when their actual agenda was to expose it. And was there really some major government cover-up going on to hide the fact that the magic out there wasn't as dangerous as everyone thought? The idea seemed ridiculous. Maybe Archer and Christa had both been lying.

Something hard dug into Ridley's shoulder as she rolled onto her side. She sat up again and found the old commscreen she'd contacted Ezra with last night. She tapped the screen, but there was no reply from him. To be honest, she hadn't really expected one.

She slid the old device onto her desk and picked up the one that had been well and truly drenched in a small tsunami of canal water the day before. Life had not returned to it during the night, and Ridley suspected it would never switch on again. Good thing tomorrow was the start of a new school year. The scholarship administrator at Wallace Academy would have a brand new laptop and commscreen ready for Ridley, just to make sure she didn't fall behind the other students in the technology department. For today, her commpad would have to suffice.

Leaning over a little further, she tugged the top drawer of her desk open. Her hand fished around inside until it located her commpad. She pulled it out, unlocked the screen, and sat back against her propped-up pillows. After opening the app displaying all her social feeds, she located Meera's name in the private messages section and dictated, "Last day of holidays. What do you want to do?"

Meera's reply came less than a minute later: I don't mind. Whatever. I'll be happy as long as I'm with you and Shen.

Ridley grinned as she raised the device closer to her face. "As long as you're with *Shen*, I'm guessing."

Meera's reply was almost instant that time: Well … maybe ;-) ;-) ;-)

Ridley couldn't help laughing at that. "I would pretend I'm offended," she said to the commpad, "but I'm not. I'll have to find an excuse to leave you guys alone for a bit."

I don't know if I'm ready for that! Then another message: Talk later. Just helping Mom with breakfast now. But we must do something fun later. Reading can definitely wait!

As Ridley returned the commpad to her desk, Christa's words returned unbidden to the front of her mind: *Do you ever play? Do you ever experiment, have fun?*

"Nope," Ridley said out loud. She'd made her decision the night before. Magic helped her to steal things, but that was it. She wouldn't do anything with it other than what was necessary. At some point in the future, she wouldn't need to use it at all.

She leaned across the bed and pulled her curtain open. Her heart jolted at the sight of something stuck to the outside of the window. It was a note, facing inward so she could see the sloppy letters:

STAY AWAY FROM ARCHER DAVENPORT

A knock on the door made her jump. "Riddles?" Dad called.

She pressed her hand against her chest and took a deep breath, giving herself a moment to recover before she shut the curtain and called out, "Yes?"

The door opened and Dad looked in. "Thought you might want to go out and have a late breakfast somewhere together. Last day of vacation. We can go somewhere fancy, if you want." He stepped further into the room. "I ended up buying *two* clocks from that man yesterday—he had a vintage mantel clock he'd forgotten all about—and my new client loved them both. She's paid already and sending someone to collect them tomorrow."

"Sounds good," Ridley said, trying hard to focus on everything Dad was saying instead of the threatening note now hidden by her curtain. "Where do you want to have breakfast?"

"Remember that little place on 7th Avenue where we used to go with Mom? You loved it there. We haven't been back since—"

"Since I found out I got the Wallace scholarship and we went for tea and cake to celebrate," Ridley said, her lips stretching into a smile. "Yeah, I'd love to go back there."

Blue Cherry House was *almost* perfect: Country chic tables and chairs, charmingly mis-matched crockery in pastel tones, and a tiny but beautiful garden to look out at. But it was rain-ing, of course, and the background music was overlaid with the distant rumble of thunder. The words 'Stay away from Archer Davenport'—and, more importantly, the question of who had stuck the note to her window—plagued Ridley's thoughts the whole way to Blue Cherry House. Despite the fact that their building's fire escape was rusted and broken and too danger-ous to use, someone had climbed up to her window. Was it the person who'd shot at her and Archer the day before?

She and Dad sat, and a smiling waiter brought them two menus. None of the waiters who worked at Blue Cherry House now had been employed here at the time of the Cataclysm, meaning none of them recognized Dad. There was no need for anyone to cast suspicious glances his way while having whis-pered conversations with managers. She and Dad could pre-tend, for just an hour or two, that they were like everyone else sitting inside this cafe. And though Ridley generally preferred *not* to pretend she was in any way similar to the kind of people sitting around her, this place was different. It was still special because it had been Mom's favorite.

Ridley looked down the menu until she found the most affordable tea—one that was at least manufactured somewhere on this continent rather than the horrendously expensive im-ported stuff. She and Dad both selected a simple breakfast, and the waiter returned to take their orders. Then the two of them chatted about Shen and school and the fond memories they had of past visits to Blue Cherry House while Mom was still alive.

The waiter brought two teapots to the table and poured a

cup for each of them. As he left, Ridley looked up and saw a group of girls at a table on the other side of the cafe. A bunch of Lilah's friends. A bunch of *Ridley's* old friends, if she was going to get technical. For a moment, it felt as if nothing had changed in ten years. She and Dad were at their favorite breakfast spot, Mom was about to join them, and Ridley would run over to say hello to all her friends before rejoining her parents.

Thunder grumbled overhead, and in an instant, the thought was gone, leaving a hollow ache in Ridley's chest. Mom wouldn't be joining them ever again. She lifted her teacup and, with some difficulty, smiled across the table at Dad. At least she had him and Meera and Shen.

She sipped her tea and glanced over Dad's shoulder again, wondering why Lilah wasn't here at Blue Cherry House with her friends. Perhaps she hadn't been invited. Perhaps her friends were giving her the cold shoulder because of her brother's involvement in a murder investigation, the same way Lilah had shunned Ridley so many years ago for something out of her control. Ridley's lips turned up in a smug smile.

This is more about bitterness and revenge than about justice.

The echo of Archer's words jarred her so badly she almost lost her grip on the teacup. It slipped sideways, sloshing hot tea over the side, which burned her fingers and dripped onto her lap. She sucked in a breath and hurriedly placed the teacup down.

"You okay?" Dad asked as she grabbed the napkin to wipe her fingers, then dabbed at her skirt.

"Yes, sorry, just being clumsy. I'm gonna go to the ladies' and clean myself up." She stood, pulled her purse onto her shoulder, and headed for the restrooms, giving a wide berth to the table of girls. She cleaned up quickly in the cafe's restroom, but as she walked out, her purse began buzzing. Startled—her commscreen was sitting lifeless on her desk at home, wasn't it?—she flipped the top open and looked inside, and remembered that she'd brought her commpad instead. On the screen blinked an image of Delilah Davenport's perfectly smiling face—the most recent profile picture she'd uploaded to the social feeds.

Ridley stepped back into the restroom, pulled the commpad out, and tapped the screen. The profile picture winked out of view and was replaced by a video call displaying Lilah's far less happy face. "What the hell happened yesterday?" she hissed, her eyebrows pinching together as her face moved closer to the screen.

"Uh ... hello to you too, Lilah," Ridley answered. Her eyes darted around the edges of the screen, but she couldn't tell where Lilah was.

"I'm serious. I know Archer came to Wallace before the dinner began. I saw him go into the library with you, and I heard you guys arguing. And, as everyone now knows, that's where the shooting happened."

"You know he wasn't shot, right?" Ridley said, wondering if perhaps Archer hadn't been home yet and his family was just as worried as her father had been last night.

"Yes, I'm aware of that, but—"

"Then I don't have much else to tell you. I have no idea who was shooting at us."

"I want to know what happened *afterwards*," Lilah said, "because he didn't come home for hours, and when he called for a car to go fetch him in the early hours of this morning, someone blew up that car."

"Holy crap." Ridley's hand rose to cover her mouth. "Is he ..."

"He's alive. He was near the car, but not in it. He's covered in cuts and bruises, and there are some fractured bones, I think, but other than that he's fine. And it was one of our driverless vehicles, so no one else was hurt. But my *point*, Ridley, is that you were the last person I saw him with, and I want to know what happened in between the shooting and the time at which my brother was almost blown up."

"Why do you think I would know?"

"Because he was with you!" she shouted. "Wasn't he?"

"Look, even if I was with him, that doesn't mean I know who wants to kill him."

"Sure, okay, but maybe you saw something. Or someone. Where did you guys go last night? Just give me *something* to work with."

"I didn't see anyone. I promise. And we were—" Ridley hesitated, unsure whether Lilah knew anything about her brother's visits to the underground part of the city. Archer didn't seem to know about Lilah's hacking hobby, so perhaps all the Davenports were keeping secrets from each other. "We were just visiting someone I know. Archer needed to find something, so I took him to a friend who might be able to help. But that person wouldn't have done anything to Archer. He'd have no reason to—"

"Details, Ridley!" Lilah's voice screeched so loudly through the device's tiny speakers that Ridley flinched. "You're not giving me anything useful here."

"Look, the only person I can think of is Lawrence."

"Lawrence Madson? We're back to the mayor's son again?"

"Look, you don't have to believe me, and I don't actually know if it was him. But you asked for details, and that's the only thing I can think of."

"It can't be Lawrence," Lilah murmured, her eyes focusing somewhere beyond the device she was speaking to. "That doesn't make sense."

Ridley gripped her commpad with both hands. "Lilah, did Archer say anything about a figurine? Did he manage to get it back?"

"What?" Lilah focused on Ridley again. "A figurine? The thing that was stolen from my dad's collection last week?"

"Yes. Lawrence is the one who has it."

Lilah's eyes narrowed. "That doesn't make any sense either. There's no reason for the mayor's son to steal from us. And no, Archer didn't say anything about it. He just keeps telling anyone who'll listen that he can't stay here at the hospital, and that he has extremely important business to attend to, though he won't tell me what it is." She rolled her eyes. "Total nonsense, I'm sure."

Ridley had a feeling it wasn't nonsense. If Archer was

desperate to leave the hospital, he probably hadn't found the figurine yet. "Which hospital?" she asked.

"Lumina Private. Obviously. Anyway, I suppose I can look into Lawrence Madson's recent activities, just in case you're telling the truth."

"All I'm telling you is what I've been told. Lawrence has that figurine, and Archer was probably trying to get it back last night before his car exploded. Make what you will of that information."

"Fine, well, I can't say you've been *helpful*, exactly," Lilah said as she looked over her shoulder, then began walking, "but I'll see what I can find out." She brought her hand up to the screen and ended the call before Ridley could respond. Ridley leaned against the restroom wall and stared at the blank screen, her mind working. So Archer had insisted he didn't need her help anymore, but now he was stuck in hospital, and most likely hadn't got that darn figurine back yet.

It will affect many people—many innocent *people.*

I'm not so terrible a person that I'll let dozens of people die if I can stop it.

Which people? A bunch of Archer's rich friends? Did it even make a difference who he was talking about? Ridley knew it shouldn't, but she had trouble feeling as much empathy for the people filling the upper floors of Aura Tower as she felt for those in her neighborhood in Demmer District.

This is more about bitterness and revenge than—

She pushed away from the wall and away from the reminder of Archer's accusation. She still didn't know if he'd even been telling the truth, but if there *were* innocent people involved, then they needed to be protected. Which meant she had two options: get the figurine back herself, or make sure Archer could do it.

She stopped outside the restroom and typed a quick message to Meera.

Ridley: Turns out I have an excuse to leave you and Shen alone this afternoon after all. Enjoy ;-) See you guys this evening?

CHAPTER 24

MADE OF AIR, IT WAS EASY for Ridley to sneak into Lumina Private Hospital. Finding out which room Archer was in took a little more effort, but she drifted around for a while, listening to snippets of hospital employees' conversations, until eventually she heard the words 'Alastair Davenport's son.' She twirled around a corner on a gust of air, and followed a woman in a suit and several security guards. "No, we've been told to keep the press away," the woman said. "I don't care that people have nothing better to do with their time than follow the lives of the city's rich and famous, but if I see *anyone* with a camera on the twelfth floor, I'm holding the entire team responsible."

Twelfth floor. Ridley turned back, heading for the nearest elevator.

She didn't have to wait long before the doors slid open, someone stepped out, and another few people stepped in. As the numbers blinked their way up toward number twelve, she couldn't help remembering the words stuck to the outside of her window: STAY AWAY FROM ARCHER DAVENPORT.

Believe me, she silently answered the unknown author of the note. *I'd like nothing more than to stay away from him.* What was more important, though, was the safety of innocent people. If she had to spend a little more time with Archer in order to ensure that outcome, then so be it.

She found him in a private ward, of course. No sharing for Archer Davenport. She watched him through the glass pane of the door, but before she could figure out exactly how to get through it without raising anyone's attention, a nurse came toward her. Ridley moved out of the way, and once the door was open, it was easy to follow the nurse inside. She was a pretty young woman, and when she stopped beside Archer's bed, she gave him a dazzling smile. "You called, Mr. Davenport?"

Mr. Davenport. Ridley would have rolled her eyes if she hadn't been looking around the room to make sure no one else was here. "Have you found out yet when I can leave?" Archer asked in a tone that suggested he'd asked this same question a dozen times already.

"Uh, no, I'm sorry. Your doctor is still waiting for the results of some tests. You're probably fine, but he needs to be certain that you don't have—"

"Is my sister still out there?" Archer craned his neck to see past the nurse through the open doorway, his face twisting into a grimace. "Please can you—"

"No, I'm afraid she isn't, sir. Visiting hours are over. But, uh ..." The nurse twisted a stray strand of hair around her finger. "It's almost the end of my shift, so I can come back in a few minutes and keep you company if you'd like." At that,

Ridley did turn her invisible eyes toward the ceiling. *Unbelievable*, she thought.

Archer fell back against his pillows with a groan, shutting his eyes. His breaths became quicker, shorter. "No, thank you. But if you could up the pain meds, that would be great."

"Sir, you've already received as much as—"

"Yes, okay. Thank you. That's all then." He raised one hand—covered in a plaster cast—as if to dismiss her.

"Okay. All right." Somewhat reluctantly, the nurse turned away from the bed and left the room. She pulled the door closed behind her, and as it clicked shut, Ridley pushed a flurry of air away from her and across the room to drop the blind over the door's glass pane.

Archer opened his eyes and frowned at the closed blind, swinging gently back and forth against the door. But he must have thought it was nothing more than an accident, because instead of calling the nurse back or looking around the room with suspicion, he simply turned his head toward the window and stared out, his brow furrowing.

Ridley followed his gaze. Up here on the twelfth floor, they could *just* see over the top of the wall. Not much of the world beyond was visible, but Ridley could see the afternoon sun streaming through breaks in the clouds, lighting up the tops of the tallest ruined buildings that remained. Her encounter with the elemental magic out there came to mind, but she did her best to push the memory away. She didn't like thinking of how utterly out of control she'd been while magic tossed her around.

She turned her back to the window as she pulled her magic back toward herself. The blue glow shimmered just above her skin as she reappeared, then settled back inside her body. "Hi," she said simply.

Archer's head jerked up as he took in a sharp breath. "Ridley, what the hell?"

"Do you ever look out there," she said, nodding over her shoulder, "and think we got what we deserved?"

"Uh ... what?"

"We ruined the earth, used up most of our natural resources, then tried to take advantage of nature even further by pulling the most gargantuan amount of magic ever, and magic was like, 'Screw you guys. I'm taking over now.'"

"Ridley," Archer said on an exhale. "How did you get in here? Wait, never mind. Stupid question."

"Lilah called me earlier. Told me about the car. She suspected we were together last night after the shooting, and she wanted to know if I'd seen anything suspicious. She also mentioned you were desperate to get out of here, which I assume means you haven't got that figurine back from Lawrence yet."

Archer sighed. "I told you not to involve yourself any further."

"You did, and—surprisingly—I decided you were right. I'm happy to forget about all of this and get on with my own life. Which is exactly why I'm here." She walked closer and leaned her hip against the bed. "If you're not able to find the figurine, then I'm going to have to do it, and I'm not interested in going back to the mayor's house. So I'm here to make sure you can leave this hospital as soon as possible."

Archer glanced at the door, then lowered his voice. "So you're here to—to *heal* me?"

"I'm here to do what I can. I can't heal any of your bruises and cuts. I mean, I *can*, but I won't. It would be far too suspicious if your surface wounds suddenly disappeared. Someone would know it's magic. But I can try to get rid of the fractured bones so you can move about easily. Once that's done, it's up to you to talk your way out of here. Or pay your way out, since that probably works better for people like you."

"I would pretend to be offended, but that's exactly what I was planning to do. At least this way I'll be able to move without pain and use my hand once I get out."

"See? I know exactly what kind of person you are."

"Ridley ..." His hand that wasn't encased in plaster reached toward hers. Then he appeared to think better of it and lowered his hand to the blanket instead. "I'm sorry for the things I said last night. At least ... I meant what I said, but I'm sorry it all came out in a way that hurt you. And I'm sorry—*truly* sorry—for influencing Lilah all those years ago. For turning her against you." He shook his head. "After the Cataclysm I was ... scared. But that's no excuse. I shouldn't have interfered."

Ridley looked into Archer's pleading eyes and found herself wanting to believe him. But she'd spent so many years hating the Davenports that she wasn't entirely sure how *not* to hate one of them. She tore her gaze away from his and lifted one shoulder in a careless shrug. "Well, you know. Lilah isn't one to be manipulated. She'd probably already made up her mind by then that I was no longer good enough for her."

"Perhaps. Doesn't mean I shouldn't apologize though."

Ridley heaved a sigh and turned her attention back to the reason she was here. "Anyway, there is one more option for getting you out of here—aside from you talking or paying your way out. Once you're healed, I could sneak you out with magic. But I'm guessing that might create more trouble than you're looking for."

"Uh, yeah." Archer nodded. "I'd rather be officially discharged than be reported missing and have a bunch of people searching for me."

"Okay then. I'll heal you, and then you'll bribe your doctor into discharging you immediately. Shall we get started?"

"Sure. Just wondering when exactly you acquired all these magical healing skills."

"I, uh … I have a book."

He lifted an eyebrow. "A book?"

"You know what I mean."

He let out a quiet laugh, then clutched his side as his face screwed up in pain. When he'd recovered, he said, "Of course you still have a book. Why am I surprised? Ridley Kayne would never have handed over any of her books to be destroyed after the Cataclysm."

"For your information," Ridley said, "Dad and I handed over every magic book in our possession. I found this particular book months later, inside Kayne's Antiques. It was on a shelf with a bunch of dusty old books with thick, heavy covers. Music theory and dance history. I was going to show it to my dad, but then I just …" She shrugged. "I ended up hiding it in my bedroom instead."

"How mysterious. Did you read it under the covers at night?"

She folded her arms and met his smirk with a deadpan expression. "Yes, by the secret light of my own magic."

He started laughing again, then seemed to remember the pain it caused him the first time and stopped. "I'm guessing that's a no then?"

"It's a no. I've barely looked at the book in the past few years."

"And now you want me to trust that you can heal me?"

"It's just a few fractured bones. I practiced the movements before I came here. They're not too complex. It's not like manipulating cancer cells or something." She unfolded her arms and moved a little closer to him. "So. Are we trying this? Or are you happy to bribe your way out of here while still in pain and unable to use one hand?"

"We're trying this. Hopefully it works quickly so I can get to Lawrence's place before he leaves to hand over the figurine this evening."

Ridley walked around to the other side of the bed. "How do you know he's handing it over?" She pulled the curtain far enough to shield the bed from view of the door. Just in case someone decided to walk in unannounced.

"Eavesdropping. After I left the bunker, I found him in

one of his favorite clubs. Overheard part of a commscreen conversation. He's meeting someone at Brex Tower tonight." Archer eased himself up a little more and held his right hand out. "My wrist," he said. "Underneath this stupid cast, which I'll have to break off once you're done. And a few ribs on this side," he pointed to the right side of his chest. "It really isn't too serious. I can't see why these doctors won't just let me leave."

"I suppose they're being cautious," Ridley said. "Wouldn't want to let a precious Davenport leave the hospital if there might be some serious underlying damage." She raised her hands, then added, "Don't freak out, okay?"

"Why would I freak out?"

"Because nothing about my magic is normal. It comes from *inside* me. I get all glowy and weird looking."

One side of Archer's mouth lifted. "I think I can handle it."

She hesitated before letting her magic free. "So …" she said slowly. "Like I said, I really don't want to be involved, but if I heal you, will you consider telling me why that stupid figurine is so important?"

His gaze moved across her face, his lips pressing into a thin line. "So that's your deal. Fix my broken bones in exchange for information."

She shook her head as she looked down at her raised hands. Her magic rose slowly to the surface of her skin. "No. I'll heal you either way. Just figured I'd ask one more time." She didn't look at him as magic began to pulse visibly beneath her skin. It rose away from her body in glowing blue wisps. She started the movements, first gathering the wisps with precise scooping motions, one hand and then the other, before sweeping both hands away from each other. Her fingers traced the air in specific patterns, manipulating the magic into something that would heal broken bones. She'd been clumsy and stiff when she began practicing earlier—crossing fingers over fingers and touching fingertips to fingertips hadn't come as easily as she'd assumed. But after working through the pages of pictures detailing every movement of this conjuration multiple times, it had become easier.

"So graceful," Archer murmured. "I always enjoyed watching magicists at work. It always looked a little bit like a dance, no matter what kind of magic they were doing."

Ridley didn't respond. Though she'd practiced the movements so many times before coming here that they were now automatic, she'd rather not draw Archer's attention away from the magic and toward her. No one other than her parents had ever watched her using her own magic. She felt naked and vulnerable. *Don't*, she reminded herself. *He already knows about your magic. Who cares if he sees what you look like when using it?*

The set of movements ended with her nudging the magic toward Archer's wrist where the plaster cast began, but the book had told her to repeat the set at least three times for each area of injury, so she began again.

"You surprised me the other day," Archer said. "The day we came to the antique store."

Her hands almost faltered, but she managed to keep the movements going without pause. She finished the second set, then let her magic fade a little before saying, "*I* surprised *you*? Are you kidding? I'm pretty sure the most shocked person in that situation was me."

"You just seemed different from the person I remembered."

"The person you remembered? The eight-year-old you last had a conversation with before the Cataclysm? Yeah, I can see why I might have seemed a little different from that girl."

"I don't mean that. It's not like I haven't seen you since then. There were several years when we were both at Wallace. I mean you seemed different from when I left the city at the beginning of last summer." He leaned his head back with a sigh. "I don't know, maybe it's just me. Everything I look at seems different now. As if I wasn't seeing anything properly before. It was all distorted, and now everything is clearer."

Ridley returned her attention to her magic and began the third set of movements. "Maybe that's the pain meds talking," she said quietly.

"I hope not. I'm pretty sure these are the same thoughts that have been running through my head the past few days. I just haven't put them into words until now."

Ridley's thoughts chased after one another as her fingers danced and her arms swept through the air. She'd laughed at Archer the night before when he told her he'd changed. She'd accused him of being exactly the same person he'd always been. But running around the city and putting his life in danger in order to save other people wasn't anything like the person she used to know. Being involved with the magic community certainly wasn't like a Davenport either.

"How did you really break into our house?" he asked.

She looked up, being sure to keep her hands moving. "I told you before," she said, watching the way his eyes followed the magic swirling around and between her hands. "Through—"

"The floor. I know. I just wondered … how, exactly. And how did you get to the alarm system to disable it without crossing any of the beams?"

She looked at her hands again to make sure her thumbs met each other in precisely the right position before her fingers spread out and scooped through the magic. "I made a hole in the floor," she explained. "Well, not a hole, exactly." She finished the third set and lowered her hands to the edge of the bed before she continued explaining. "It's not as though I took away part of the floor. The magic tells part of the floor to fold back in on itself, which creates a section where the floor no longer exists. I climbed through that bit. Then reversing the movements makes the floor fold back out of itself and reform. Something like that. I'm probably not explaining it properly." He was watching her face now, his eyes moving across the magic she knew was glowing in her cheeks.

"But most of the time," she continued, speaking faster as she tried to get him to focus on what she was saying and not the way she looked, "I don't use movements at all. My own magic doesn't require it. It just sort of … responds to my will. I haven't experimented much. I generally just use it to become invisible. Like air, you know. So that's how security beams and cameras and things don't see me. As long as I *stay* invisible, of course. Which I don't always do. It's tiring. Gives me a headache after a while."

Archer tilted his head. "Invisible? Really?"

"Yes, I can ... well ..."

"What?"

"Never mind, it sounds stupid." She lifted her hands again. "Where exactly?" she asked, gesturing to his side. "We should finish this before someone comes back in. And you're in a rush to get out of here, remember?"

"What sounds stupid?" he asked, lifting one arm up and indicating a bruised area on the side of his ribcage with the other.

Ridley shook her head. "I should concentrate." She began again, saying nothing as she made sure to curve her hands in the correct way, then sweep her arms outward at the right time, and let her fingers weave through the magic in the required patterns.

"Whatever it is that you think sounds stupid," Archer said as she neared the end of the third set, "I'm sure it isn't."

"I can ... become the elements," she said quickly, as if speed might make the statement sound less weird. Her hands twisted around each other, met together, and nudged the magic toward Archer's side for the last time. "Or, at least, my magic can conceal me as any of the elements. I'm not sure of the exact technicalities. Maybe because magic comes from the elements, and that same magic is inside me. Air seems to be the easiest. I use that the most. I'm scared of earth. I don't know, it just seems so … suffocating. So solid. Like I might not be able to return to normal afterwards. And water and fire … Well, fire is quick and volatile, and water can be that way too. I feel out of control when I'm either of those two elements, so I tend to avoid them."

Archer didn't answer. She looked up and found him staring at her. "Great," she muttered. "I can see I've totally weirded you out with this."

"No, sorry." He shook his head. "I'm just … thinking."

She looked away. "It's okay. You're right to find the whole thing extremely weird. This isn't normal. *I'm* not normal. At all." She caught sight of the blue glow in the reflective surface of one of the machines beside the bed and turned her head fully to look at her face. At the vibrant electric blue that pulsed through her veins, and the patches of her skin that lit up, then faded, then lit up again. At the luminous blue glow in her eyes and lips. She returned her gaze to Archer and, fighting the urge to smother her magic, she said, "You can't tell me you see anything other than a complete freak of nature right now."

"Actually," he said, his eyes traveling slowly across her skin, "I think it's beautiful."

Beautiful. Her mother had said the same thing when Ridley first discovered magic inside her own body, but Ridley had never agreed. Her magic was unnatural. It had to be hidden. Now, though, she remained still beneath Archer's searching gaze, willing herself not to be ashamed. To show herself for who she truly was.

And at that moment, the door opened.

"Crap," Ridley hissed. Her magic flared for a second before responding to her first thought—*air*—and surrounding her in nothingness.

"Mr. Davenport?" Someone pulled the curtain aside, and Ridley slipped beneath the woman's arm in a quick rush of air. "Is—is everything okay?" she asked, smoothing her hair down and looking around with a frown. It was the same nurse from before, no longer in uniform. "I just ... was that a flash I saw when I walked in?"

"Yes," Archer said. He looked toward the window. "Another storm coming. It must be windy out there. I could feel a draft coming in beneath the door, which is why I closed the curtain."

"A draft? Really?" The nurse threw a perplexed look at the door, which presumably had never let a draft in before. "Um, well, my shift is finished," she continued, looking at Archer again. "I just came to say—in case you're no longer here when I get to work tomorrow—that I hope you recover soon."

"Thank you," Archer said to her. "And on your way out, please let my doctor know that I need to speak to him urgently."

"Oh, yes, okay."

"And please close the door on your way out," he added.

"Yes, of course." She left quickly, pulling the door shut behind her.

"Ridley?" Archer whispered, his eyes searching the room. "Are you still here?"

"Yes." She crouched down on the other side of the bed beneath the window before letting herself become visible again, just in case Archer's doctor entered as abruptly as the nurse had. "Do you feel any better? Did the magic work?"

Archer twisted his torso from side to side. "Yes. Not perfect, but way better than before." He sat straighter and breathed deeply. "Almost no pain. That's amazing. Thank you."

"Good. I'd better get out of here then."

"It's a flash drive," he said before she could rise to her feet. "Inside the figurine. That's what Lawrence is after. The information on the flash drive."

Ridley slid down against the wall until her backside met the floor. "I see," she murmured, afraid to voice any of her questions in case Archer decided to close up again.

"The first time I came back to the city—about ten months after I left—it was to give that flash drive to someone. But ... things went wrong. I had to leave quickly. So I hid it, and someone was supposed to collect it. Without anyone in my family knowing, of course." His gaze darted over his shoulder before returning to Ridley. "But she never made it there. She was killed."

"Killed?"

"Yes. Serena Adams. Someone discovered her using magic. She was killed for it."

"Serena Adams? But ... wasn't her death an accident? She

was using magic and it got out of control, and she ended up killing herself."

Archer's expression darkened. There was no doubt in his voice when he said, "It wasn't an accident. She was murdered. So the flash drive remained hidden until recently, when Lawrence must have found out where it was and hired someone to steal it."

"But what's on this flash drive that's so important it means life or death for—"

"I can't say. I'm sorry, but you're not supposed to know anything more."

"Then why tell me anything at all?" Ridley pushed herself to her feet. "Don't you know it only makes me want to know more?"

"I just ... I felt like I owed you something. For helping me. And because I need you to understand that there are people in this city more dangerous than you think. If they know what you can do, they'll chase you onto the top of a building—or out into the wastelands—and blow you up, just like they did to Serena."

"Was Serena ..." The question hovered on the tip of Ridley's tongue. A question so absurd she almost couldn't voice it. If it were true, people would know about it. It would be a normal part of the world, just like regular elemental magic. But still ... she had to ask. "Was she like me?"

Archer hesitated, his brow drawing low over his eyes as he searched her face. "There's no one else like you."

Disappointment flooded Ridley's chest as she looked up

at the sound of footsteps outside the door. "Time to go," she muttered, magic already lifting away from her skin to conceal her. "Good luck," she added.

"Thanks. Stay away from trouble."

CHAPTER 25

RIDLEY ARRIVED HOME AT the same time as her father, reaching the corner of their block just as Dad came out of the Lins' restaurant across the road. "Is Shen home?" she asked as Dad walked toward her.

"No. I was just paying his parents a visit." Dad paused, a frown creeping across his face. "Weren't you just with Shen and Meera?"

Ridley realized her mistake a moment too late. "Um, I actually decided to give the two of them some time alone together."

"Ah. Shen and Meera. How interesting." They continued down the alley toward the store's back door. "I would never have guessed they felt that way about each other."

Ridley shrugged. "They can both be quite shy sometimes. Maybe that's why?"

"Mmm. Yes." Dad pushed his key into the lock of the back door, then leaned a little closer when it wouldn't turn. "Odd," he murmured. "I'm sure I ..." He pushed down on the handle, and the door opened easily.

"Didn't you lock it when you left to see the Lins?" Ridley asked.

"I'm sure I must have." Dad pushed a hand through his scruffy hair and squinted at the partially open door. "Why wouldn't I?" He pushed it open fully, and Ridley peered through the back room and into the store. She couldn't see much from this angle. They wouldn't know whether anyone had broken in and stolen anything until they moved further inside.

Ridley exchanged a look with Dad, but neither of them said a word. This was the point at which a normal person might have said, "Should we call the cops?" But Ridley wasn't normal, and Dad had spent a long time keeping her away from the attention of anyone in law enforcement. Having the cops right outside their door last week was close enough; they weren't about to willingly invite them inside their home now.

"I can check it out," Ridley whispered, "without anyone seeing me. It'll be easy."

"Absolutely not," Dad answered. "One of our nosy neighbors might notice the glow before you vanish. You'd have to wait until you're inside, and by then, whoever's in the store might see you. *If* there's someone in the store, that is." He stepped inside, adding, "I'll take a look."

"Dad!" Ridley hissed, reaching forward to tug him back and missing his arm by inches. She followed him inside, but he turned his furious gaze back over his shoulder at her, mouthing something about her waiting outside. She shook her head, just as insistent as her father. No way was she leaving him to confront whoever was inside their store.

"Go back outside," Dad whispered.

Ridley leaned back, tugged the door shut, then shoved her magic outward as she lunged forward and pressed herself against Dad's side. They both vanished as her magic turned to air around them. The air moved them forward at Ridley's mental command, and at the back of her mind, she couldn't help noticing the irony of the situation: She was a thief about to get a taste of her own medicine. About to find her family's store robbed of everything valuable.

Except ... it wasn't. Not a single item appeared out of place. She swirled the two of them through the air as she examined the shop, but it was exactly as she and Dad had left it that morning before heading out for breakfast. The magic dissipated around them, revealing them bit by bit until they were fully visible, Ridley still pressed against Dad's side.

He stepped away and swung Ridley to face him. "What the hell was that?"

She hesitated, startled for a moment by his anger. "I was trying to keep us both safe, okay? Anyone could have been inside this store, and you just walked in, unarmed."

He leaned closer to her, lowering his voice. "You're not supposed to have used magic in years, and yet you turned us into air almost faster than I could see. That suggests to me that you've been practicing."

Ridley swallowed, then pulled herself a little straighter. "Maybe."

"I don't want you doing that ever again."

"If it means protecting you, I will."

"I'm supposed to protect *you*," Dad reminded her. "Which is what I'm doing when I tell you not to use magic."

"I know, Dad, but you won't be around to tell me anything if you end up getting yourself killed by walking into a potentially dangerous situation unprepared."

Dad stepped past her, shaking his head as he walked back through both rooms to the door she'd banged shut. She followed him, saying nothing. He retrieved his keys from where they were still dangling in the keyhole outside and locked the door, then turned to face her. "Fine. I'll be more careful if you promise not to do anything with magic again."

"I won't promise that." She moved to the staircase leading up to their apartment. "If I need to hide myself, I'll hide myself. If I need to protect someone, I'll protect someone."

Dad turned the handle to check the door was indeed locked, then joined Ridley on the stairs. "I know I can't control what you do," he said as they walked up. "Just ... please, *please* be careful. Can you at least promise that?"

She smiled as he looped one arm around her and pulled her against his side. "I'm always careful."

"Good. Though I doubt that'll help me sleep any easier at—" Dad's voice cut off as they reached their living room at the top of the stairs. His hand tightened around her arm, his wedding ring pressing into her skin.

"Dad, what's—" Then she saw him: The pale, blond young man sitting in one of their ratty old armchairs with one leg crossed over the other and a gun held loosely in his hand.

Lawrence Madson.

Ridley's heart stuttered as Lawrence raised the gun a few inches, pointing it directly at her father. "Make a single move, Miss Kayne, and your father is dead." Ridley forced her hands to remain still at her sides. Her eyes darted to the two figures standing in the shadows at the edge of the room before returning to Lawrence. "I know what you are, Ridley. I know about the magic inside you."

"That's crazy," Dad said immediately, pulling Ridley tighter against his side. "She has her amulets, just like everyone else. She must have been scanned thousands of times since the Cataclysm, and nothing's ever—"

"Quiet," Lawrence snapped at Dad. "I know what I'm talking about. I know her amulets are not beneath her skin. I know what makes her different from you and I."

"H-how do you know that?" Ridley asked.

"Your name is on one of the letters. The letters inside the envelope that man was carrying when he was killed outside your building." Lawrence shrugged. "Presumably that's why he was here: to give you your letter. What's interesting, though, is that the letters didn't appear to be addressed to anyone when I first looked at them. It was only later on that I noticed a name had appeared on the outside of each one. Almost as if ... by magic." He snapped his fingers. "Not entirely sure where that magic came from, but that doesn't matter. The names have since vanished again, but I made a note of them all before that happened. Including yours."

He rose from the armchair, keeping the gun trained on

Ridley's father. "Anyway, I'm here because I need a favor. A magical favor."

"She won't be doing any—"

"I guess I could have tracked down any of the names inside that envelope," Lawrence continued, speaking over Dad as if he wasn't even there, "but the name 'Ridley Kayne' was the easiest. A little more unusual than the others, and I recognized it from my time at Wallace. I figured you wouldn't mind helping out an old school friend."

"I'm not helping you with anything," Ridley told him.

"Really? Even if I threaten to put a bullet through your father's head?" Ridley swallowed, and Lawrence smiled. "I don't generally do my own dirty work," he added, "but I'll make an exception if I have to." Ridley pressed her lips together, choosing to say nothing more. "I need you to open this," Lawrence said, holding his empty hand out to the side. One of his burly bodyguards stepped from the shadows and passed something to Lawerence: the gold figurine Archer was so desperate to get back. The figurine that would probably still be safe if Ridley hadn't stolen it in the first place.

Lawrence held it out toward her. "I assume you know the movements to open something that's been sealed by magic? If not, I'd be happy to show you."

"Why do you want it open?" Dad asked, his fingers digging into Ridley's arm as he held her tightly. "What's inside it?"

Lawerence turned a bored expression toward Dad. "I'm not sure why you think I'd tell you."

Ridley stared at the roughly human-shaped figurine with its string of green stones embedded around its neck. People would die. That's what Archer had said. But she knew without a doubt that Lawrence wasn't playing around. If he said he'd shoot her father, he meant it.

"Whatever crazy plan you're cooking up inside that fair head of yours," Lawrence said, "I'd advise against it. You're not a save-the-day kind of person, Ridley. Especially if saving the day means losing your father and the future you've worked so hard for since the Cataclysm cost you everything."

"I ..." She looked up at him. "How do I know you won't kill both of us anyway as soon as I've opened this for you?"

"You don't. But if you refuse to open it, your father will *definitely* die. So it's up to you, I guess."

She didn't want it to be up to her. She didn't want to have to choose between her father and whoever it was that Archer was so determined to save. Maybe there was still a way she could get out of this. If she used different movements—if she opened a hole in the floor and let her and Dad fall through it—then maybe they'd have a decent chance of—

"OPEN THE DAMN THING!" Lawrence yelled, striding across the room and shoving the barrel of the gun against Dad's forehead.

"Okayokayokay!" Ridley gasped, taking the figurine from him. She turned it quickly in her hands, looking for a seal or seam while her mind raced over the movements that would cause magic to create a hole beneath her feet. As far as she could tell, the figurine was a solid piece of gold. She shook it, but nothing seemed to move around inside. She remembered Archer saying that no one would know how to open it, and that breaking it apart wouldn't work either. "So it's—it's sealed with magic?" she asked.

"Yes. The movements are different from those that would open something locked with a key or sealed with glue or something else non-magical."

"I don't know—"

"Good thing I made sure to find out exactly what those movements are then," Lawrence said. He nodded to the man who'd handed him the figurine, and he walked over to take Lawrence's place in front of Dad. Ridley watched in terror as the gun moved to the bodyguard's hand while remaining firmly pressed to Dad's head. One wrong move—one finger squeezing in the wrong place—and her father would be dead.

"Pay attention," Lawrence snapped as he raised his hands. "If you don't get this right first time around, you can kiss your daddy goodbye. *After* Charlie's blown his brains out. Oh, and in case you're thinking of trying something else with your magic ..." The second man stepped out of the shadows and strode past Ridley. He stopped behind her, and a moment later, she heard a click and felt something cold and hard against the back of her head. "One wrong move—and by 'move' I mean magical movement—and you're both dead."

A shiver raced from Ridley's scalp down to her toes, and she squeezed her hands around the figurine to keep them from shaking. Any hope she might have had of escaping this situation fizzled away.

"Ridley, just ... just do what he says," Dad told her. "Everything will be okay." He had no way of knowing that, of course, but Ridley couldn't blame him for trying to comfort her.

"Are you watching?" Lawrence asked.

"Yes," Ridley breathed, though she was hyperaware of the weapon pressing into the back of her head.

Lawrence moved to stand beside her and began the series of movements required for this particular conjuration. It wasn't a long one, but there were a few complex finger patterns near the end. When he began a second time, Ridley's fingers twitched against the figurine as she mentally copied the motions. "Right. Got it?" he asked when he was done.

"Can—can I practice? Just the movements, no magic. To make sure I've got them right." When Lawrence narrowed his eyes, she added, "I'm not trying to trick you. I just don't want to wind up with a bullet in my brain because I accidentally turned my hand the wrong way."

"Fair enough." He took the figurine from her hands and watched closely as she ran through the movements. "No, not that way," he said when she was almost done, reaching forward to correct the way her two forefingers traced a circular pattern in the air. She almost jerked away as his hand touched hers, but she managed to remain still. "Yes, correct. Now do it again." Finally, when she'd practiced successfully several times, he said, "Okay, now with magic. And only do *exactly* what I showed you. Anything else, and you're dead."

He held the figurine out on his palm, and Ridley took a steadying breath before raising her hands and letting her magic drift away from her. She scooped up the wisps, touched her fingers gently together in the starting position, and attempted to block everything else out. She began the conjuration, focusing intently on the exact way her hands and fingers moved. Her heart rate slowed, and by the time she reached the end and nudged the magic toward the figure, she felt almost calm.

Something sizzled. A line formed around the figurine's neck, just above the ring of green stones. Lawrence gripped the head part and twisted it. It came away easily from the rest of the artifact. He turned the body upside down, and something small and dark landed on his palm: a flash drive, just as Archer had told Ridley. For the briefest moment, surprise flashed through her, and she realized that up until this point, she hadn't entirely believed him.

"Finally," Lawrence whispered. Then he laughed. A genuine grin spread across his features as he stared at the flash drive. "Thank you, Ridley. You have no idea what this means for me and my position." He looked up. "And the fact that I get to hand you over along with this information makes it even better."

"Hand *me* over?" Ridley repeated at the same time Dad said, "Don't you dare touch her!"

But before either of them could do anything, pain sliced through her head, and all she knew was darkness.

CHAPTER 26

SHE DREAMED OF THE DAY the world almost ended. She was in Aura Tower's penthouse hanging out with Lilah and Josefina Cruz. The three of them had taken advantage of the fact that Lilah's annoying older brother wasn't home and had claimed the entire living area for themselves. Blankets were draped across nearly every item of furniture, creating a maze of fluffy tunnels. But they'd grown tired of the tunnels some-time earlier that morning, and the treasure at the center of their blanket maze—Lilah's brand new robotic unicorn—lay forgotten next to a pile of wrappers from the sweets Josie had snuck past Lilah's mom.

It was a good thing Mrs. Davenport wasn't home now. They all knew she'd freak out at the sight of her lounge. But they'd promised Grace, the nanny, that they'd clean every-thing up before Lilah's parents got home. So Grace, whose patience seemed to have no end, had moved all the priceless relics and art pieces to the edge of the room where the girls wouldn't accidentally knock them over.

Josie was currently sitting on the cushioned stool in front

of the grand piano, playing a near-perfect rendition of the theme music that accompanied their favorite VR game, Dragon Slayer Princess—which was yet another thing Mrs. Davenport didn't approve of. But Lilah had somehow got hold of a copy, and the three of them played whenever they were at Josie's place. Right now, though, with Grace watching them from the kitchen while she made lunch, they had to make do with pretend dragon slaying. So Lilah and Ridley leaped about the living room with invisible swords, ducking to avoid invisible flames, and jumping over invisible obstacles.

"Hey, we could make *actual* flames," Lilah panted, coming to a halt and breathing heavily. She grinned at Ridley. "You can do it. You're super good at that stuff."

"No magic inside the house," Grace called to them. "You know your father's rules, Lilah."

Lilah rolled her eyes. Grace had impeccable hearing. Even when the girls whispered, she always seemed to hear them. Ridley sometimes wondered if she used a conjuration.

"You're no fun, Grace!" Josie shouted as her fingers hammered the piano keys.

"No magic inside the house," Grace repeated.

"Fiiiiiine," Lilah groaned. "Oh, hey, your mom's calling, Ridley." Lilah ran to a wall near the kitchen area and touched the screen above the home auto system's control pad. Ridley's mom's face appeared on the screen, along with the interior of her car. "Hi, Mrs. Kayne," Lilah said, jumping up and down and waving.

Ridley reached Lilah's side. "Hi, Mom."

"Hey, Riddles. Hey, Lilah." Mom grinned in the direction of her commscreen camera before looking back at the road. "You guys having fun?"

"We made a blanket maze," Lilah said.

"And we're sword fighting."

"Hi, Mrs. Kayne!" Josie squealed, crashing into Lilah and Ridley.

"Hi, Josie," Mom said, smiling at the camera again. "So, blanket mazes and sword fighting huh?" she said as her eyes returned to the road. "I hope you're not making too much of a mess for Grace."

"No, no, we said we'd clean up," Ridley told Mom as Lilah and Josie nodded beside her.

"Okay, well I just wanted to say hi and tell you I'll only see you tomorrow. I left a little late, so you'll probably be asleep when I get home tonight."

"Okay. See you tomorrow," Ridley said.

"Alrighty. Have fun and be good. Love you lots."

"Love you, Mom."

Lilah tapped the screen to end the call. Then she leaped around, brandishing a make-believe sword. In her deepest voice, she said, "Beware, princess. Dragons guard this land."

"Dragons cannot stop me!" Ridley and Josie shouted in unison. "I will complete my quest!"

"Girls, go wash your hands," Grace interrupted before they could launch themselves into a full-blown imaginary dragon battle. "Lunch is ready."

Lilah lowered her sword hand, her shoulders slumping.

"Fine. We can carry on after lunch."

Five minutes later, the three of them were seated on stools at the kitchen island eating ravioli lasagne. Grace sat on the other side, watching the news on the screen that popped up out of one end of the island. "Grace, can we watch *Milo & Mara*?" Josie asked.

"Yeah, this is boring," Lilah said. "Oh, wait, is that the big magic thing?" she asked, pointing her fork at the screen where a drone camera was zooming out over something round and copper-colored and probably as wide across as a city block. "They keep talking about it at school."

"Yes, the GSMC," Grace said. "This is historic, girls. We should be watching it. In years to come, everyone's going to be talking about the day we ended the global energy crisis, and you'll remember sitting here eating your lunch as you watched it."

"Doubt it," Josie grumbled.

"If it's so important, why aren't my mom and dad watching it?" Lilah asked.

"They are, they're just watching it somewhere else on a big fancy screen. That's how important it is."

"Oh." Lilah peered a little closer at the screen, so Ridley and Josie did the same. Dozens of people stood in a ring around the circular thing, each of them with one hand placed against it. As the camera zoomed further out, they saw a line of people connecting one ring of people to another enormous ring of people. Then another and another, and multiple lines of people extending toward a large body of water.

"Those are all magicists, right?" Ridley said.

"Yes," Grace answered. "This is happening all around the world at this very moment."

"Duh, that's what the G stands for," Lilah said. "Global."

On the screen, the magicists began their conjuration, everyone pulling from the air or the water with one hand while touching either the circular device or the person next to them. Magic materialized, and the screen glowed bright blue. It was like a large-scale dance, every free hand near the device moving in the same way, pushing outward, swinging back in, twisting back and forth, cupping the air, and then trailing fingers in patterns too small to see.

"Don't they need both their hands for a conjuration?" Josie asked.

"Not for magic-energy conversion," Grace said, her eyes glued to the screen. "That kind of conjuration only requires one hand for movements and one hand touching the ... uh, battery? I'm not sure exactly what they call the other part, but it's basically like a battery."

"Oh. We haven't done that conjuration at school yet," Josie said.

"I think you'll only learn it if you become a magicist," Grace told her. "Anyway, I heard they're doing something new here where all the people who're *not* touching a battery are just pulling magic and sending it toward the magicists who are touching it. So they can do the conversion conjuration faster, I think."

"Okay," Ridley said. They watched for another minute or

two, but by then it was just more of the same thing and it was starting to get boring. She picked up her fork again, but a thunder-like rumble startled her. She looked up, and a second later, the rumble sounded through the screen's speakers. The blue glow hanging above the gathering of magicists flashed too bright to look at, before the feed suddenly went blank.

"What happened?" Josie asked.

"I don't know," Grace said, frowning at the screen.

A second rumble came from outside, louder this time. Then the sizzle and crack of lightning, followed by a crashing boom that sent a shudder rippling through the floor.

"What's happening?" Josie whimpered, clutching the counter top.

Grace muttered something beneath her breath, her brow furrowing as she stared past the girls toward the windows on the far side of the living area. Ridley and Lilah spun around on their stools and jumped down. Together, they ran to the windows and looked out. In the distance, in one of the outlying suburban areas, raged the largest fire Ridley had ever seen. "That's where one of those battery things was," Grace said, reaching the window with Josie hanging onto her hand. "By Menlow Lake."

As they watched, buildings near the fire began heaving and crumbling as the earth cracked around them. *Earthquake*, Ridley thought, but then lighting zigzagged out of a cloudless sky and struck something too far away to see. No, not lightning, because it was definitely blue. "Is that magic?" Ridley asked.

"I think so," Grace said.

"We're all going to die," Josie whispered.

"But there are panels over the city that reflect magic," Lilah reminded them. "My dad told me those would keep us safe if anything magical ever went wrong."

"They can keep us safe from above, but what about everything out there?" Ridley said pointing a shaking finger at the fires in the distance. "And the magic in the ground underneath us."

"Don't some foundations have arxium built into them?" Grace said. "We'll be fine, don't worry." But Ridley couldn't help hearing the shudder in her voice.

"Look up there!" Lilah said. "Those are the panels, right? The arxium ones. They're moving." They watched as the panels spread out, while above them, dark clouds gathered unnaturally fast. "They're, like ... making sort of a dome? See, so we'll be protected from the side as well," Lilah said, nudging Ridley's arm.

"But then the spaces between the panels are way too big," Ridley said. "They were big already and now they're just *massive*. That magic lightning is gonna get through and—" Her eyes shut automatically as magic flashed down into Lumina City. "See?" she said, her eyes opening and her voice now a high-pitched whisper.

"But ... maybe only a little bit of magic will get through," Lilah said, though she sounded far less certain now. "And we'll still get protection from the side. So ... so we'll be okay."

"I don't want to be up here," Josie said, close to tears as

she backed away from the window. "We're gonna fall down like those other buildings."

Ridley's feet remained frozen to the spot as she stared beyond the distant fires. *Please be okay, Mom. Please, please, please be okay.*

Then Dad was suddenly there, tugging at Ridley's hand, pulling her away from the window, and she became abruptly aware that she was dreaming. She remembered that this was the day Mom died. This was the day her entire life came crashing down around her. Nothing would ever be the same again.

She pulled free of Dad's grip and spun away from him, desperately clawing her way through the swirling confusion of the dream world and toward consciousness.

CHAPTER 27

RIDLEY WOKE SLOWLY, becoming aware bit by bit of the dull pain in her head, the aching throughout her left side, the hard surface beneath her body. She peeled her eyelids apart as she probed at her memory, trying to dredge up her last waking thoughts before—

Crap. Her heart leaped into action, sending renewed pain shooting through her head as the scene in her apartment rocketed to the surface of her mind. She pushed herself up and took stock of her surroundings: An empty, unfamiliar room. A closed door. A single window. And no Dad.

"Dad," she whispered as her hand rose to the back of her head. Her fingers moved through her hair until she found the source of her headache: a large lump. One of Lawrence's men must have hit her. "Where are you?" she muttered, climbing to her feet. Her thoughts tumbled over one another, arriving all too quickly at the worst possible scenario. She was alive and trapped somewhere, which meant she was valuable to Lawrence. But Dad wasn't like her, which meant he wasn't valuable. Would Lawrence really have left him alive? Left him in a position where he could go to the police and tell them exactly who had broken into his home and abducted his daughter?

No, came the silent answer. *Of course not.*

But he can't be dead, she thought immediately. *He CAN'T be.* But the fact that Dad wasn't locked up here only served to confirm her worst fears. She hurried to the door and twisted the handle, though she knew already that it would be locked. When the door wouldn't budge, she jiggled the handle more desperately. A sob clawed its way up her throat, tightening her chest and stealing her breath.

"Stop it, stop it," she whispered fiercely to herself, stepping away from the door and forcing her hands to her sides. "Don't. Panic." She took several deep breaths, then let her magic rise away from her body. Before attempting any specific movements, she nudged the magic toward the door. It curled lazily through the air, brushed against the door, then rebounded instantly in a jagged flash, zigzagging back and forth almost too fast to follow. She stepped backward and out of the way just as the magic erupted into an explosion of sparks and vanished.

In the darkness that followed, Ridley let out a grim sigh. It was just as she'd expected: an arxium door. Or at least, it had arxium hiding somewhere inside it, since the door appeared to be made of wood. She turned and moved toward the window, where the heavy clouds blotting out most of the light made it hard to determine whether it was late afternoon or early evening. She nudged her magic toward the bars crisscrossing the window. The blue glow drifted slowly, then burst away from the window in a rush of angry sparks. Ridley ducked down, only rising again once the magic had vanished. "More arxium," she muttered. Another brief magical experiment informed her the floor, ceiling and walls also contained arxium.

Wonderful. Magic certainly wasn't going to get her out of here.

She gripped the bars and peered out of the window. Her eyes took in a perfectly landscaped garden with manicured hedges and white modern art sculptures, and in the distance, a familiar house. "Holy crud," she whispered. Even if she hadn't recognized the house, the oddly shaped sculptures would have given it away.

She was a prisoner on the mayor's property.

In his pool house, to be more precise, if she correctly remembered what she'd seen of his garden. It made sense, of course, given who had abducted her. But still, it seemed crazy that Lumina City's mayor had a room like this on his property. It couldn't have come about by accident. This room would have been made specifically to confine a person who might want to escape using magic. She doubted she was the first prisoner to inhabit this cell, which meant the mayor of Lumina City—and his son, it would seem—were in the habit of locking up magicists.

Ridley folded her arms and stared at the door she couldn't get through. Lawrence said he knew about her magic, but did he know exactly what she could do with it? Hopefully not. Because when he opened that door, she was going to get the hell out of here. How long would it take before he showed up though? Archer said Lawrence was meeting someone at Brex Tower tonight. The shorter, less extravagant version of Aura Tower. Had he left already, or would he come by to check on her before going?

Wait, hadn't he said something about *handing her over*? She frowned in concentration, trying to remember exactly what Lawrence had said before she was knocked unconscious. He was excited to have the flash drive. And even more excited that he'd be able to hand *her* over along with it. A chill raced across her skin, but with it came a sense of optimism. If she was supposed to be going with Lawrence to Brex Tower, then it wouldn't be long before he came to fetch her. And she would make sure he never got his hands on her.

She waited near the window, her eyes glued to the sliding door leading onto the deck outside the main house. Lawrence might approach the pool house from somewhere else, of course, but there was no other door for her to watch, so she kept her eyes trained on it. Eyes she knew must be glowing with magic. She let it ripple across her skin and hover in the air around her, ready to use the moment anyone showed up outside the pool house.

Fortunately, she didn't have to wait long.

They came from the side somewhere, not the back of the house, so she was startled by the figures that moved without warning past the window. She shrank back into the darkness, knowing they must have at least seen a blue glow, if nothing else. There were three of them, and she guessed it was probably Lawrence and the two bodyguards who'd been at her apartment. The thought of what they might have done to Dad caused her chest to tighten again. But she fought against the panic. She couldn't do anything for Dad if Lawrence's men knocked her out now.

She let her magic turn her to air and drifted closer to the door as she heard the shuffle of footsteps beyond it. They would be prepared for magic, of course. Maybe they had arxium clothing or bullets or something. But would they be prepared for a mini tornado? She spun the air around herself in an imitation of the magic that had scooped her up outside the wall the night before. It whirled faster and faster, lifting her up and howling past her ears. She couldn't hear a thing beyond the wind's roar, but Lawrence must surely be about to open the—

The door flew open, and Ridley spun toward it. Something hissed, like the sound of a deodorant spray can, but she was already flying out the door and up. She spun higher and higher as nausea hit her stomach. *No!* she screamed internally as she sensed her body becoming heavier. *I am air, I am weightless, I am AIR!* She breathed through the nausea, which already seemed to be lessening, and relinquished all control of her magic. She'd always been afraid of going too high. Afraid the air currents might be stronger the higher she got, or that her magic would fail her and she'd fall a great distance. But her desperation to escape overrode her fear.

Within seconds, she was tossed beyond the wall around the mayor's property. She tried to direct herself downward, but a strong gust scooped her up and flung her higher. She rose and fell and tumbled about as she tried to keep breathing and not let panic take over. She was vaguely aware that she was moving away from the edge of the city and toward the center, but other than that, she had no concept of exactly where or how fast the wind was carrying her.

Just don't panic, she kept telling herself. She pictured her street as if from above. The old shop, the apartment upstairs, and Dad. Because Dad had to be there. He *had* to. If Lawrence's men had done something to him. If they'd *killed* him—

She sucked in a sob as an ache swelled in her chest. Then her heart leaped into her throat. She was falling. Swiftly. Looking down, she realized she was almost completely visible again. *Nonono!* She squeezed her eyes shut so she wouldn't see the city streets rising rapidly toward her. She shoved her magic outward, reminding herself she was made of air, and a breeze caught her and carried her forward instead of down.

Breathing out a shaky breath, she opened her eyes. She was close enough to the ground now that her feet—if they weren't made of air once more—could almost have touched the rooftops of the low buildings she was flying above. She moved down past the three- or four-story buildings and directed herself toward a quiet side street. Letting her magic sink back inside her body, she landed, breathless and dizzy, and threw her hand out to steady herself against the wall. She blinked and looked around, hoping no one had seen her appear out of nowhere. Luckily, the buildings she stood between didn't have windows facing onto this narrow street.

Once her dizziness had passed, she hurried into the next

road and examined the buildings and signs. She didn't recognize anything. If she had her commscreen on her—and if
it worked—she could easily have found her location. But she
would have to resort to more traditional means. She ran down
another two streets before finding a bus stop and a map. Her
heart skipped a surprised beat as she figured out where she
was. Much closer to home—and, hopefully, to Dad—than
she'd thought, which was fortunate, because without her
commscreen, she had no way to pay for a bus.

She looked around, checking for somewhere to hide as
she considered handing herself over to the mercy of the wind
once more. But without being able to control exactly which
direction it moved in, she might end up taking even longer to
get home. So instead, she took off at a run.

She was slower than she wanted to be, with her left side
still aching from where she must have landed on the floor
earlier. But she managed to keep running, and eventually she
turned, sweating and breathless and with a cramp in her side,
into the alley behind Kayne's Antiques. She rushed up to the
door, hoping it would be locked because that would mean Dad
was inside and he was okay. But the door stood ajar.

"Crap, crap, crap," she muttered as she pushed it open and
ran upstairs. She ground to a halt at the top of the staircase,
her heart beating in her throat and a sick feeling twisting her
stomach as she took in the scene. The lamp in the corner had
been knocked over, the small coffee table was split in half, and
something large had smashed through the window behind

the couch. But the most alarming part was the pool of blood smeared across the floor.

Ridley gripped the top of the banister as her legs became oddly weak. Her breath shook and her eyes remained trained on the blood as she slowly lowered herself to her knees. For a moment, she considered the possibility that she was entirely alone in the world. Tears blurred her vision. She squeezed her eyes shut, letting the tears fall.

"He's not dead," she whispered shakily. "He's *not dead*."

She refused to believe it. If Lawrence's men had killed him, wouldn't they have left him here? They could easily have made it look like a break-in and an accidental shooting. They must have taken him for some reason. *Alive*, she told herself firmly, opening her eyes. *They took him alive.* She reached for the banister again and pulled herself up, then wiped beneath her eyes. If Lawrence had taken her father, where would he—

Something rustled behind the couch. The curtain moved. Ridley held her breath and prepared to transform into air, but before she could push her magic outward, something leaped onto the back of the couch. "Holy crap," she breathed. It was that darn cat with the four ears and the glowing eyes. She shook her head and exhaled slowly.

Then, without bothering to shoo the cat out the window, Ridley turned and headed back down the stairs. Dad was missing, and she didn't have time for magic-mutated animals that couldn't find their way back out to the wastelands. What she needed to do was get to Brex Tower. That's where Lawrence would be tonight. He might not have *her* any longer, but he still had that flash drive. She knew it was stupid to go after him, but there was no other option. Lawrence knew what had happened to Dad, and Ridley wouldn't rest until she got her father back.

CHAPTER 28

BEFORE RIDLEY COULD find her father, she had to go to Aura Tower. She knew which building Lawrence would be in tonight, but she didn't know exactly where *inside* Brex Tower he would be. For that, she needed Archer. She managed to get into the Davenports' private elevator while invisible, then took the longest damn elevator ride of her life all the way to the top. By the time she reached the penthouse, she was almost in tears from sheer frustration.

I'm running out of time! her internal voice screamed inside her head. She knocked repeatedly on the double front doors, then almost cried with relief when it was Archer who opened up. She'd had no explanation ready if it turned out to be someone else.

"Ridley, what are you—"

"He took my father," she said, the words escaping her in a rush as she stepped through the doorway.

"What? Who? Wait, are you okay?" His eyes darted across her face, no doubt taking in her ruffled hair and red eyes. "What happened?"

"Lawrence. He was waiting at my place, and he made me open the figurine with magic, and then one of his guys knocked me out and I woke up in an arxium room inside his freaking *pool house*, of all places. But then I managed to get away, and I went straight home to see if Dad was okay, but he was *gone*. And the table was broken, and the window, and there was blood on the floor, and it was a *lot*, Archer. I mean, I don't know how much is too much, but it looked like a lot. But Dad wasn't there so—"

"Okay, just calm down." Archer gripped her shoulders.

"But he must be *alive*, right?" she insisted, staring pleadingly into his eyes and hoping he would agree with her. "I mean, that's what you'd assume, isn't it? He's alive. It wouldn't make sense to take him if he's dead. So he has to be *alive*—"

Archer pulled her against his chest and wrapped both arms around her. "Seriously, you need to *calm down*. Lawrence would be an idiot to kill Maverick Kayne. We'll find your father, okay?"

It was both extremely strange and oddly comforting to be hugged by someone she'd known since she was four years old but had barely spoken to in almost a decade. She shut her eyes and replayed Archer's words in her head. They sounded so reasonable when he said them. She didn't know why Lawrence would be an idiot to kill her father, but she was happy to go along with that reasoning.

"So Lawrence has the flash drive now?" Archer asked quietly.

Ridley sniffed. "Yes. So you need to get it back before he

gives it to someone else, and I need to get my father back." She removed herself from Archer's embrace and stepped backwards. "Do you know where he'll be at Brex Tower tonight?"

"Yes. Sapphire 84. That restaurant on the eighty-fourth floor with all the private balconies, so I'm assuming he'll be on one of those."

"Okay. Let's go." She turned toward the open door.

"Wait, hang on." She looked back at him. "I'll do it. I'm going anyway." He picked up the object she hadn't noticed sitting on the table below the hallway mirror—a gun—and slipped it into the back of his jeans. "I promise I'll get your father back."

Ridley blinked at the spot where the gun had been, shivering as she imagined a cold, hard object pressed to the back of her head. She forced herself to forget it and look at Archer instead. "No way in hell am I staying out of this now. We're going in together. You'll get the flash drive, I'll get Dad—or find out where he is, at least—and then we'll get far away from Lawrence."

"And then?"

Ridley frowned. "Then what?"

"Lawrence knows what you can do. You won't be safe, even if you do manage to get us out of Brex Tower alive."

"Then I'll ... I don't know." Ridley shook her head, turning away as her breath caught in her throat. The strands of her life were rapidly beginning to unravel. Her secret was out. Once she got Dad back, they couldn't stay in their current home. Perhaps they couldn't even stay in this city. She'd never get into The Rosman Foundation. She wouldn't get into any college either. Hell, she couldn't even go back to school tomorrow, she realized with an icy jolt.

She shoved her whirling thoughts away and turned back to Archer. "Right now, my priority is my father. I'll figure everything else out afterwards."

"You realize this is probably a trap, don't you?" Archer said. "Lawrence probably took your father so that if you escaped, you'd have no choice but to go back to him."

"Yes, I've thought of that. But it doesn't change anything. And just because Lawrence planned for me to return to him doesn't mean I have to walk up and hand myself over. I'll be invisible, remember?"

"And if you're not? What if something goes wrong? Can you guarantee you won't be carted off by security if someone sees you sneaking around Sapphire 84?"

"I trust my magic. Even if it reaches the point of driving a blinding ache through my head, I won't stop using it."

"Really? What happened at the Madsons' house? Something certainly went wrong then."

"That was—" She cut herself off when she realized she had no answer for why her magic had made her so dizzy and nauseous that she'd actually passed out while sneaking through the mayor's lounge. To be honest, she'd forgotten about the strange experience in the wake of everything that had happened since. "Look, I don't know what that was, but that was the only time it ever happened, so I don't expect it to happen again. Now can we please go? We're wasting time, and my father's *life* is on the line!"

"I know, but so is yours! That's why *I* need to do this, not you."

"This isn't negotiable, Archer."

"And when things go wrong inside there? Or wherever it is that your father's being held? When you find yourself trapped, surrounded by all those bodyguards Lawrence likes to keep nearby? I know you've got magic on your side, but you're a thief, Ridley, not a fighter."

"I'm not going there to fight." She turned and strode into the still-open elevator without hesitation. "I'm going there to steal."

Stealing her father back was likely to be the most challenging heist of her life, but Ridley didn't allow herself a moment's doubt. There was no room for failure. "Security isn't quite as tight as Aura Tower," Archer said as they stood in the shelter of a doorway across the street from Brex Tower. "But there's still a sign-in process. I can probably talk my way in without a reservation at Sapphire 84, and you can do your invisible thing."

"No," Ridley said. "I can get us both in. It'll be faster." The front door of the fashion boutique they stood in front of was set into a recess, allowing Ridley to move further back and out of sight of most of the road. "Don't freak out," she said to Archer as vibrant, pulsing patches of blue appeared across her skin.

He looked back at her. "You said that before. I didn't freak out, remember?"

"Yeah. But this is different." It was also potentially awkward, she reminded herself, and so she did it as quickly as possible. She rushed forward and wrapped her arms around him as her magic lifted away from her body. It swirled around them both, turning them to air within seconds. Ridley's momentum spun them away from the door, and the next thing Ridley heard was a startled curse in her ear. "Told you," she said. "It's freaky stuff."

A breeze caught them and twirled them above the cars and across the street. Ridley then directed them both up the wide stairs and into Brex Tower. It was an unexplainable thing, being somehow weightless while also having the sensation of Archer's arms tight around her. Like the memory of a touch instead of something tangible. She tried not to think about it too much and instead whisked between people, leaving fluttering hair, billowing skirts, and a few shocked gasps in her wake. She headed over a turnstile, past the elevators—where too many people were stepping in and out—and toward the stairwell. Then straight up through the center of the spiral staircase, her eyes keeping track of the numbers flashing by on each landing until eventually she saw the number eighty-four beside an open doorway. She stopped but didn't let go of either Archer or her magic.

"Whoa," Archer breathed. "That was *weird*. Like a rollercoaster without any actual machinery."

"Yeah. Sorry. I'm in a rush." Ridley moved them both beyond the stairwell and onto the eighty-fourth floor. A sign with the words Sapphire 84 directed her toward the right. She followed the arrows around the corner toward the floor-to-ceiling glass panes that separated the restaurant from the rest of this level. Music, chatter, and the clink of glasses reached her ears. Heading swiftly through the open doors, she looked past the tables to the numerous balconies jutting out from the side of the building, each of which was strategically concealed from the view of the indoor patrons by trellises covered in lush greenery.

"We'll need to go to each one and take a look," Archer said. They began at one end, looking through the doorway onto each balcony as quickly as they could. Ridley hoped desperately that she was about to look out and see Dad on one of them. Even if he was tied up or unconscious, at least she'd know for sure he was alive.

But when they found Lawrence, he was alone at the far end of the balcony table, speaking to a commscreen. A cold fist tightened around Ridley's heart, but she tried to look on the positive side. "At least his bodyguards aren't here," she murmured as they hovered in the doorway.

"They're inside," Archer whispered. "I saw two of them eating together. There might have been more of them sitting at other tables."

"Well at least they're not out here. Ready to move closer?" she asked.

"Yes. Wait until we're behind him and I've got the gun out. Then you can make us visible. Or just me. I'll force him to hand over the flash drive and tell me where your father is."

"And if he refuses? Are you actually planning to shoot him?"

"Would you try to stop me if I did?"

Ridley hesitated. "I don't know. He's a despicable human being, but I'm not okay with murder."

"Do you think people deserve to die for using magic?" Archer asked. "Because that's what will happen if I don't stop Lawrence. Many, many people's lives are tied to the information on that flash drive. Once the wrong people know exactly who they are, they will all be killed."

Ridley let his words sink into her brain. "It's about the bunker, isn't it," she guessed. "All those innocent people just getting on with their lives, using magic in secret underneath the city. That's the information on the flash drive."

Archer was quiet for several heartbeats. "Do you think they're worth saving?" he asked.

Ridley already knew her answer. She moved Archer and herself out onto the balcony. A pane of glass on the outer edge of the balcony railing provided protection from the wind—and prevented anyone from falling over the rail—while still allowing for a spectacular view of the city.

"... pity I lost her," Lawrence was saying to his comm-screen, "but she might be back if she can't find her father."

Ridley turned her attention back to him. Clearly he was talking about her.

"Yes, it would be a bonus if you had her," said the woman on the device. Ridley had a feeling she'd heard her voice before. Lawrence's mother, perhaps? "But the flash drive and the letters will be more than enough to secure you a position at the table. Plus the evidence against Archer Davenport."

As they moved closer, Ridley sensed Archer's phantom arms tighten around her. "I know," Lawrence said. "It's shocking the amount of information he's been hiding. I won't tell you now—you never know who's listening in—but I'll show you everything at home."

"You made a copy?"

"Of course."

Archer made a sound like a suppressed groan. Lawrence looked up, but of course, there was nothing for him to see. He focused on the commscreen again. "Dad's going to hate me for going behind his back like this."

"He won't *hate* you, honey. He just ... he's been underestimating you, that's all. He didn't realize you had what it takes. Now you can show him—and the others—that you do."

"Yes. Finally." Then, almost in one movement, Lawrence dropped the commscreen and grabbed a small spray can from below the table. His hand shot out, and he sprayed the contents of the can in a wide arc in front of him. Back and forth, and then all around as well as behind him.

Nausea hit Ridley's stomach about two seconds later. She sucked in a breath, but she was already losing control of her magic. Dizziness overwhelmed her, and she felt herself falling sideways. Through the spinning of her surroundings, she became aware that she was no longer invisible. Then Lawrence's voice reached her ears: "Ridley. I was hoping you might find your way back to me."

CHAPTER 29

DARKNESS CLOUDED RIDLEY'S vision and pulled her downward, and she was pretty sure she lost consciousness for a few moments. Then her stomach heaved, and she *almost* threw up. Gasping and swallowing, she peeled her eyelids apart to find that the only thing keeping her upright was Archer's arm pinning her to his side. His other hand pointed the gun at Lawrence. "Give me the flash drive," he growled.

Lawrence sighed. "I thought I might see her—" he nodded at Ridley "—but you're an unpleasant surprise. I thought you were in hospital."

"You can *give* me the flash drive," Archer said, "or I can put a bullet through you and then *take* it."

"Fine, fine," Lawrence drawled. He removed the flash drive from an interior pocket of his jacket and slid it across the table. Archer let go of Ridley just long enough to grab it, then caught her as she swayed.

"Next," he said, "we'd like to know where Ridley's dad is."

Lawrence raised his hands, palms facing up. "I wish I knew. He attacked my guys and fled. Almost killed them both."

"That's … a lie," Ridley managed to say. Her father was one of the gentlest people she knew. He wasn't capable of *almost killing* anyone. Especially not two muscled men with guns.

"The truth, Lawrence," Archer said, raising the gun a little higher.

But the mayor's son only smiled. "Threatening to shoot me isn't going to help," he said. "If I'm dead, I can't exactly tell you anything, can I."

Fury burned inside Ridley's core. Though it made her want to hurl and caused bright spots to dance in front of her eyes, she managed to force a tiny bit of magic out. She slumped forward, grabbed the edge of the table, and sent fire rushing down the center of it and up Lawrence's arm. He cried out, his chair skidding back slightly. Then he grabbed a napkin and managed to smother the flames. "Bitch," he gasped. He slapped the napkin down and glared at her. "I hope you're suffering for that. Not nice, is it. Breathing in arxium particles." He pushed his chair further back and stood. "Good thing I had my trusty anti-elemental air freshener handy. Oh, and look. It's the guys I pay to keep me safe, finally come to check if everything's okay."

Archer swung around, but someone in a suit stepped onto the balcony and knocked his arm aside. The gun clattered to the floor. Someone else shoved Ridley onto her knees, while the first guy wrestled with Archer until he managed to get both of Archer's arms behind his back.

"Move a little bit this way, please," Lawrence said, his tone impatient. "We don't need anyone inside getting worried about what's happening here." The one bodyguard pushed Archer closer to the table, while the other dragged Ridley against the trellis so she was out of the way. Looking up through her haze of dizziness, she realized she didn't recognize either of them. Were the other two guarding her father somewhere?

"Well, isn't this lovely?" Lawrence said, rubbing his hands together. He walked around the table and picked up the flash drive Archer had dropped on the floor. "You're both here, and I have the flash drive—" he placed it on the table "—and this special envelope." He moved his side plate, picked up a large yellow envelope Ridley hadn't noticed before, and placed it beside the flash drive.

"You're going to kill ... all those people ... who use magic?" Ridley asked, leaning her head back against the vines trailing down the trellis. Archer shoved backward against his captor, and the bodyguard twisted Archer's arms further behind him until he groaned out loud in pain.

"Me?" Lawrence said. "No, I won't be killing anyone. I don't like to travel that far. And other people generally do my dirty work, remember? Nope, I'm just passing on the information in order to better my position in the society."

Ridley figured he had a pretty good position in society already. It didn't get much better than being the mayor's son. Well, unless you were a Davenport.

"Just let me explain things to you," Archer said, struggling against his captor. "Let me tell you about them. They're good people. Magic isn't this huge *threat* that has to be—" The guy restraining him grabbed the back of Archer's head and smacked his face down against the table. Archer slumped to the floor, groaning as he clutched his nose.

"Archer," Ridley mumbled, trying to crawl toward him. "Are you—"

The other guy grabbed her and dragged her back. The world swirled around her again, but it wasn't as bad as when she'd first breathed in the spray. She seemed to be recovering faster this time than at the mayor's house. Maybe because her heart was racing along at such a high speed this time, getting rid of the arxium faster. Was that possible? She had no idea. She'd never heard of this stuff before.

It didn't matter how it worked though. All that mattered was that she reach a point where she could use magic without her stomach wanting to turn itself inside out. She'd have to be quick when she did it. She didn't want to give Lawrence a chance to use that spray again.

"You know who I'm meeting here tonight, don't you?" Lawrence said to Archer. He walked closer, planted one shoe against Archer's chest, and kicked him down onto his side. Archer coughed, still clutching his nose, and Ridley saw blood drip down his hand. "Oh, it's going to be delicious indeed to hand you over along with—"

Before Lawrence could finish, a dark shape flashed downward, landing in a crouch on the table: A man, hooded and carrying a knife in each hand. The bodyguard beside Ridley launched away from her, but the man on the table was already whirling around, his knives glinting in the light. One struck Ridley's guard in the chest, while the other embedded itself in

Archer's guard's neck. Both guards slowed, stood still for two or three seconds, then fell. Horrified, Ridley watched magic curl lazily away from each knife and vanish.

Holycrapcrapcrap. This was the person who'd murdered the stranger in her alley. It must be. With the oversized hood pulled completely over his head, she still had no idea what he looked like. No way to identify him if he managed to kill anyone else here tonight and get away without being caught.

The man turned toward Lawrence as he drew another knife from a sheath at his hip. "This time, you're dead," he said in a gruff tone. The knife flashed through the air, but Lawrence had already dodged, and the knife struck the glass pane behind him before hitting the floor. The man let out a low laugh at the sight of Lawrence's wide eyes and pale face. "Oh, you got lucky. So did you," he added, looking down at Archer. "But not this time." He reached behind him, and Ridley watched as he swiftly pulled a gun free from beneath the hem of his hoodie.

"No!" she shouted. She launched forward on hands and knees, fire racing away from her glowing blue hands and up the leg of the table. The man leaped free and landed just past Archer. The gun swung Ridley's way as he turned fully toward her, and she finally saw his face.

She stopped breathing.

"Shen?"

CHAPTER 30

"RIDLEY?" SHEN SAID. "What—how are you—why are you here?"

"Why are *you* here?" Ridley demanded, managing to climb to her feet despite the world still swaying around her. The flames she'd sent running up the table leg fizzled away, and an entirely new kind of nausea filled the pit of her stomach. "Oh, watch out!" she shouted as Lawrence lunged for the gun. Shen swung his arm around and elbowed Lawrence in the face. He fell back against the railing, his head smacking on the glass as he let out a yelp.

"I don't ... I don't understand," Ridley said. It was as if the world had tipped upside down and she was looking at everything from entirely the wrong angle. Her best friend wanted to kill people, and the guy who represented everything she hated was the one helping her to right her wrongs and find her father. "Did you ... were you the one ... Did you kill that man in the alley?"

Shen's grip tightened on the gun. His eyes moved to Ridley's hands, where the blue beneath her skin was fading away now that she was too shocked to focus on her magic. His eyes rose to meet hers, and there was no sign of surprise in them. "Yes."

"But you weren't there. You were somewhere else. Doing a delivery or—"

"He was there," Lawrence said, rubbing the back of his head. "I looked up and saw him on your roof. That's why I had no problem telling Archer's lawyers to comb through the drone footage from the area and stick his face onto the original video."

"That was *your* idea?" Ridley asked.

"I should have killed you then too," Shen hissed, pointing his gun at Lawrence again. Archer moved as if to get to his feet, and Shen swung the gun toward him.

"No, wait, please," Ridley said. "You don't need to kill anyone here."

"I know you've tried to kill me before," Lawrence said to Shen, his voice oddly calm given the situation. "You probably don't know that I saw your face that time, but I did. Never knew who you were, of course, so I couldn't go after you. But I recognized you immediately when I saw you in the alley on top of that roof."

Ridley's eyes bounced back and forth between the two of them. The effect of the arxium particles she'd breathed in had just about worn off. She could probably turn herself to air now. She could try to take Archer with her and get out of here before Shen hurt either of them. But she was so confused, and her feet seemed rooted to the spot, and she just needed to *know*. This was her best friend standing here with a gun, and she needed to understand what had led him to this point. "Shen, what's he talking about?" she asked. "Why would you have tried to kill him before?"

"Because he killed Serena," Shen said, squeezing both hands around the gun and pointing it at Lawrence again.

Lawrence's expression didn't change. "I will neither confirm nor deny that accusation, but either way, what's it to you if I had anything to do with Serena Adams' death?"

Shen ground his next words out between his teeth: "I loved her. And you killed her because of magic."

"That doesn't explain why you killed that man outside Ridley's place," Archer said. He'd risen to his feet now, and his hands were raised at his sides. His nose was swollen, and blood covered part of his upper lip and chin.

"I was trying to kill *you*!" Shen shouted. "But you moved!"

"What a terrible tragedy," Lawrence deadpanned.

"But why?" Ridley cried. "Just ... *why*? I know we've never liked the Davenports, but why would you want to *kill* one of them?"

Shen gave her a pleading look. "You have to trust me on this, Rid. You don't know who these guys are. You don't know what they've done and what they're capable of. As soon as I saw Davenport was back in the city—that he was *in your shop*—I had to do something. I had to get rid of him, to make sure he'd never go near you ever again."

"Hang on," Ridley said quietly. "Did you put that note in my window? The note telling me to stay away from Archer?"

"Yes. I didn't want to risk you being anywhere near him like you were before at the library."

"The library? That was *you*? Frickin' hell, Shen, you almost shot *me*!"

"No! Ridley, I would never. I was aiming past you. Aiming for—"

"And how was that even possible?" she continued. "You'd only just been released. You wouldn't have had time to get there."

"I did have time." He looked at Archer again. "It was the first thing I did after I got home."

"Goodness, you have messed up priorities," Lawrence said. "The cops free you, and the first thing you do is get hold of a gun and try to kill someone? Did you like jail so much you wanted to go straight back?"

"I did it then because my family thought I was at home. No one would ever suspect my involvement."

"But they must have noticed you were missing for ..." Ridley trailed off as she remembered what Meera had said. "They thought you were in the bathroom the whole time," she murmured.

"Never noticed I was gone," Shen said. "Neither did they notice when I snuck out in the middle of the night to blow up that car. Too bad he wasn't in it."

"I was just about to ask if that was you," Archer muttered.

Instead of answering, Shen twisted one arm and glanced at his watch. "This needs to be done." He swung the gun back to Archer, and then again to Lawrence, as if he couldn't decide who to take out first. "I've wasted enough time already."

"I'm happy for you to take your time," Lawrence said.

"Shen," Archer said carefully, "you're about to make a mistake." He kept his hands raised as he took a step toward Shen. "You already made a mistake when you killed the man outside Ridley's place, but you don't need to make things any worse. Whatever you think you know about me, it isn't true."

"Sure," Shen said bitterly. "Anyone would say that with a gun pointed at them."

Ridley moved a tiny bit closer, almost close enough to put her arm on her friend's shoulder. "Shen, just … just think of your family. Your parents and your brothers. And Meera. Everything's going to change if you do this. Your life will never—"

"My family understands. They know what's at stake, and they know I'm only doing what has to be done. They've looked out for you too, just as I have."

Ridley shook her head, confusion mounting upon confusion. "What are you—" But a gunshot cracked through the night, and she jumped, squeezing her eyes shut instinctively. With her heart banging against her ribcage, she forced her eyes open. Across the balcony, Lawrence slid down to the floor with one hand pressed against his chest. He tried to gasp out a few words, but then his hand rolled to the side and he became still. From his wound rose a wisp of magic.

The next second, the gun was trained on Archer. Before she had time to think, Ridley rushed in front of Archer and raised her hands. "No, please don't!"

"Ridley, get the hell out of the way!" Archer hissed.

"He's been *helping*," Ridley told Shen. "He's been trying to *save* all those people who use magic."

Shen's eyes narrowed, but not before she saw the confusion—and the hurt—in his eyes. Then he threw a glance over his shoulder. Was someone coming out here? Surely people must have heard the gunshot. Shen looked at his watch and muttered something. Then he swung the gun away from Ridley and shot the glass pane instead. Once, twice, three times, until finally it shattered. "Get out of here, Rid," he said as he lowered the gun. "Air, water, whatever. Just get away quickly." She barely had time to register what he was saying—that he *knew what her magic could do*—before he was running toward the shattered hole in the glass.

"No!" Ridley shrieked, lunging after him. But her fingers clutched at empty air. He jumped, sailed right through the opening, and fell into the night. Ridley threw herself against the railing, one hand stretched out, magic lifting instantly from her body. But looking down, she saw Shen clinging to one of the larger scanner drones, zooming away from Brex Tower.

"What the hell?" Archer said as he reached her side and looked over.

"Hey!" someone shouted behind them, and Ridley made sure to pull her magic back within her before turning.

"Down!" Archer shouted, and the next thing she knew, he'd pushed her to the floor as another gunshot sounded. She scrambled toward the table before looking up. The newcomers were a man and woman, smartly dressed and each holding a gun. More of Lawrence's bodyguards?

And then ... was that a man in a blue masquerade mask? And a beanie? He raced onto the balcony, pulling magic from the air as he went. He moved his hands—a conjuration too quick for Ridley to see—then tossed magic at the trellis. It immediately duplicated itself, the second one sliding to the side to cover the doorway. The woman bodyguard aimed at the masked man, but Archer, who now had a chair in his hands, yelled and swung the chair at her. She cried out and fell against one of the trellises.

As the masked man spun his hands in a new conjuration and aimed magic at the other bodyguard, Ridley's eyes landed on the forgotten flash drive on the table—and the envelope beside it. The envelope that apparently contained a letter with her name on it. In two quick strides, she was at the other end of the table, grabbing hold of both.

But a hand smacked down on hers. It was the woman, on her feet again on the other side of the table. Acting on instinct, Ridley set her magic free as her thoughts turned to fire. In an instant, flames engulfed her body. The woman yelled and snatched her hand away, sending cutlery and two side plates clattering to the floor as Ridley reminded herself not to panic. *I'm not burning. I'm not in pain. I'm not covered in fire, I* am *fire.*

Archer tackled the woman, but the masked man yelled at him to get out of the way. He seemed to be doing two conjurations at once: with one hand, he kept the other bodyguard at a distance, while the other hand performed a series of complex, intricate finger movements. Archer launched away from the woman, and the masked man swung both arms up and then outward, pointing at each bodyguard. Then he clenched both hands tightly into fists.

Both the man and woman halted. Their hands clawed at their throats, and they appeared to be trying desperately to breathe. Ridley looked away, not wanting to watch. Remembering she still held the flash drive and envelope in her burning hand, she let her body return to normal. Both items were fine—things she held onto when becoming the elements always seemed to return to normal—so she zipped the envelope up inside her jacket and pushed the flash drive into a pocket.

And that's when both bodyguards fell to the floor. Had they suffocated? Ridley didn't want to know. The unknown man—in the mask that looked both ridiculous and oddly familiar—lowered his hands to his sides. Behind him, the trellis shook, and Ridley became aware of people shouting on the other side of it. The masked man jumped over the fallen bodies and shouted, "Get us out of here!" as he reached Ridley.

And that voice—*that voice!*

"Archer!" the man yelled, reaching behind him with his hand. "Quickly!"

Archer launched over the bodies and grabbed the man's arm. "The flash drive?" he asked, looking around.

"I've got it," Ridley answered. And as the trellis rattled harder and cracked down the middle, she let her magic swirl around them and become the air. A breeze lifted them, and they spun away over the top of the glass pane.

CHAPTER 31

RIDLEY'S MAGIC SET THE three of them down in a quiet street several blocks away from Brex Tower. She checked for passing drones, then pulled her magic back inside herself. The moment they were visible again, she reached for the masquerade mask—the mask that had looked so strangely familiar—and pulled it free, taking the beanie with it. At the sight of those blue eyes she knew almost as well as her own, her heart leaped. "Dad!" She dropped the mask and beanie and flung both arms around him. "You're okay," she whispered as tears stung her eyes.

He hugged her tightly. "We're both okay. Everything's okay."

"Not yet," Archer said from behind them. "I need to get to the mayor's house. Lawrence's computer needs to be destroyed."

"Already done," Dad said, pulling away from Ridley and looking at Archer.

"What?" she asked. "You ... what were you doing there?"

"Looking for you. I overhead the mayor's wife on her

commscreen. Fortunately, Lawrence gave away enough information for me to know I needed to destroy his computer. And just before the call went dead, I heard him say your name. So I used a conjuration to crush the computer and all its component bits and pieces, then went straight to Brex Tower."

Archer exhaled, his shoulders relaxing. "Thank you, Mr. Kayne. That's a relief."

"But you still need to leave," Dad added. "Make sure you're seen somewhere else as soon as possible." He looked back in the direction of Brex Tower. "You definitely don't want to be linked to the murder of the mayor's son."

"Right. Of course not. You said you have the flash drive?" Archer asked Ridley. She nodded as she removed it from her pocket and handed it to him. He dropped it onto the sidewalk and ground his heel back and forth into it until it broke apart into numerous tiny pieces. Dad crouched down and did a quick conjuration—*a conjuration!* Her father was using *magic!*—that lit the remains of the flash drive on fire.

"And the envelope?" Archer asked as Dad straightened. "Because if that's still up there, we should go back for it. It might contain sensitive information."

Ridley paused for a fraction of a second before shaking her head. "It burned up."

"Oh. Are you sure?"

"Yes. I managed to get hold of the flash drive, so it was protected when I became fire, but the envelope was on the table and it burned right through. It was nothing but ashes." She couldn't quite explain why she kept the truth from him.

Perhaps it was that she still didn't fully trust Archer, or perhaps it was because he already knew too much about her. But whatever was inside her letter, she wanted to be the first to know it.

"Okay. Well, that's good. No one else can get hold of it." He looked over his shoulder, then back at her. "I guess I need to go make sure my face is seen somewhere far from Brex Tower."

"Yeah, just make sure you clean the blood up first," Ridley said. "And maybe get yourself into a bar fight as soon as possible so you have an explanation for your swollen nose. Actually—" She stepped closer to him. "Just come here. I'll fix it quickly." And for the second time that day, Ridley weaved her hands through the air in the conjuration that caused magic to fix broken bones. "I hope it's a broken bone," she muttered. "If it's something else—the cartilage?—then this probably won't help." She lowered her hands and stepped back when she was done, and only then did she think to look around to see if there was a drone nearby or a person looking out of a window. What was wrong with her? She was usually so careful.

"It's okay," Dad said. "I didn't see anyone."

"Thanks," Archer said, gesturing to his nose. "And thanks for helping me get the flash drive back. And I'm glad you're okay, Mr. Kayne." He glanced at Ridley's father, then back at Ridley. "I'm glad you're both okay." His eyes lingered on her face for several more moments before he turned and jogged away.

When he'd disappeared around the corner, Ridley took

her father's hands and held them tight. "Dad, you were using magic. You were *fighting* with magic. Which means ... you don't actually have an AI2?"

Dad pulled his wedding ring off and showed her where an extra piece of metal had been fused to the inside. "That's my AI2. I had it removed from my skin a few months after it was first put in. I just ..." He inhaled deeply and shook his head. "I needed to know I could protect you if something ever happened. So yes, I know how to use certain offensive conjurations. Some that probably haven't been used in decades. I hoped I would never have reason to use them, but today I did."

Ridley nodded slowly. "Is that what helped you get away from Lawrence's guys? The ones who came to our apartment?"

"Yes. And now you're okay and I'm okay, and anyone who knows what you can do is gone."

"Gone?" She swallowed, not sure if she wanted to know exactly what her father was capable of. "So those guys who were in our house ..."

"It was me or them, Riddles."

She nodded slowly, trying not to think of the blood on the floor. "And the man and woman on the balcony ... did you kill them?"

"They weren't planning to let us get away. They wanted to kill *you*. I did what I had to do."

Something in his words made her remember Shen, and the tears that filled her eyes were unstoppable. She shook her head, sucked in a deep breath and managed to say, "It was—him. Dad, it was Shen. He really did—kill that—man." She sniffed and tried to steady her voice, but it was impossible. "The man in—the alley. Shen killed him."

Dad's hands moved up to her shoulders as his frown deepened. "No, I think you're confused."

She shook her head vigorously and took in another deep breath. "I'm not confused. He was there now on the balcony. He wanted to kill Lawrence and Archer. Last week in the alley—he was trying to hit Archer. But he hit the other guy by accident. And tonight, *he* was the one who shot Lawrence. And then he just *jumped.* Over the edge and onto a drone. A big drone. Like he knew it was going to be there."

Dad stared at her for what seemed like ages. Eventually, he pulled her into a hug. "I don't know what to say. I'm sorry, Riddles. I'm just ... I don't know what to say."

They stood like that for some time, until eventually Ridley's tears had stopped falling and her shoulders had stopped shuddering. She stared down at the embellished blue mask sitting on the sidewalk and said, "The masquerade mask? Really?"

"I was in a rush," Dad said. "I grabbed the first thing I thought of that would cover my face."

Ridley nodded against his shoulder. "Whatever works, I guess."

"Yep." Dad let out a long sigh, then said, "Let's go home, okay? You can have a shower. Maybe eat something. We can talk about Shen after that."

∞

They returned home, and after they'd tidied the living room as best they could, Ridley headed to the shower. She spent far longer than normal beneath the cascade of hot water, letting it ease the numerous aches she'd gathered throughout the day. Her brain replayed everything way too many times, reminding her that she didn't know nearly as much about the people in her life as she'd always believed: her best friend didn't lead an innocent, simple life; her father wasn't the gentle, law-abiding man she needed to take care of; and Archer wasn't the self-absorbed heir who hated magic as much as the rest of his family. And perhaps *she* wasn't the person she thought she was either.

From what I'm hearing, this is more about bitterness and revenge than about justice. Archer's words whispered in her mind, and this time, she didn't shove them away. This time, she recognized that he might be right. Her crimes had definitely helped people, but she'd taken far too much pleasure in stealing from those who'd rejected her and Dad after the Cataclysm. Where did this leave her though? Would she stop stealing? Would she stop trying to help people? Or would she continue doing exactly as she'd always done, but with the knowledge that her motives weren't as pure as she might like them to be?

As the water began to lose its heat, she turned it off, pushing aside her guilty thoughts to deal with later. Stepping out of the shower, she heard music from the direction of the living room. One of Mom's favorite old bands. Ridley almost managed a smile as she wrapped herself in a towel and stood with her eyes closed for a while, listening to the strumming of a guitar and a warm voice singing the words Mom used to sing along with whenever they drove long distances outside the city.

Ridley thought of the day she'd lost Mom, and she imagined what it would have been like if she'd lost Dad today. She banished the thought immediately because the ache in her chest made it almost impossible to breathe. She pulled the towel tighter around herself and headed for her bedroom.

Once she was in her pajamas, she sat cross-legged on her bed and pulled the yellow envelope out from beneath her pillow. Part of her was afraid to know what was inside here; part of her wondered if maybe it was a silly, small thing she would end up rolling her eyes at. There was only one way to know.

She opened the envelope and tipped it upside down. Numerous folded white pages fell out, none with a name on the outside, though each did have a drawing of a tree. She thought the tree design seemed familiar, but it was possible she was imagining that. What had Lawrence said about the names? He'd only noticed them on the letters later on. They'd appeared as if by magic.

Patches of glowing blue color rose to the surface of Ridley's skin as she moved her hand over the letters spread in front of her. Slowly, names materialized on each one. Her heart raced a little faster as she spotted hers. She picked it up, remembering how she'd snuck through the mayor's house and through Lawrence's bedroom using magic. Was that why the names had appeared on these letters then? Had she come close enough to this envelope that her magic had touched it?

With fingers that shook the tiniest bit, she opened her letter.

Dear <u>Ridley</u>,

We're writing to you in case you don't know what you are. In case you've never known there are others like you. In case you don't know that your kind has been in danger for centuries.

You are an elemental. The same magic that exists in the elements exists inside you. It has always been feared by some, and so there have always been those who want to hunt down and kill your kind. An organization has existed for centuries. The Shadow Society. Its reach has extended into every country, every city, every sphere of life. You can't go to the authorities. You can't trust any of them. Their purpose is to rid the world of us.

We've quietly been keeping track of every elemental we know of, but that information has been stolen. The society has some of it now—and they will soon have the rest. They don't know yet exactly who you are or where you live, but they know how many of you there are in your city. And now that they know, they won't stop searching for you. It's only a matter of time before they discover you. You need to get out. If they catch you, they'll kill you.

Alfie Biyela, Heng Wu, Serena Adams, Mary Wood-

stock. These are just a few of the elementals who've been discovered and killed in recent years. If you know of any of them, you may have heard their deaths were accidental. They were not.

If you stay where you are, you won't be safe. You'll be hunted and killed, as they were. Make your way into the wastelands. Look for the signs. Listen to the elements. You will find us.

Your brothers and sisters

Ridley read the letter four times before finally lowering it. Her skin was covered in goosebumps, and her breath was quick and shallow. So she was an *elemental*, and there were others just like her. She wasn't alone. *She. Was. Not. Alone!* The truth pounded on the inside of her brain, begging to be screamed from the rooftops. Random thoughts bombarded her mind, suddenly making sense in the light of everything she'd just read. Of course the Madsons had an air freshener filled with arxium particles. They knew there were other people like her, and they were protecting themselves. They must be part of this Shadow Society. This organization that wanted to wipe out everyone like Ridley.

And the information that was stolen? The information that the author of this letter was worried would soon wind up in the society's possession? That must have been the information on the flash drive. Serena Adams, another elemental, was supposed to fetch it after Archer hid it inside the figurine. She was supposed to keep it from the Shadow Society. Ridley's guess—that it contained details about the underworld of regular magic-users beneath Lumina City—had been wrong.

And Archer had let her believe her own assumption.

He knew about these elementals. He knew she wasn't the only one and he *lied* to her when she asked! And the tree—the tree! Ridley crumpled the edge of the letter in her hand as the memory surfaced abruptly: The tree carving on Dad's little wooden box that Mom had given him years ago. It looked just like this one. That couldn't be a coincidence, could it? No. Her father knew what she was. He knew there were others like her.

And he'd never told her a thing.

She climbed off the bed, her face flushed and her hands shaking. She walked to the living room and stood in the doorway, the letter clutched in her hand. Dad was sitting in one of the armchairs, and she waited for him to look up at her before she said, "No more secrets."

His brow drew lower. "What are you talking about?"

She held the letter up so he could see the drawing of the tree. "We need to talk."

She expected surprise, at the very least, but Dad's expression didn't change. He looked across the room at the person sitting on the couch, partially concealed in shadows. The person Ridley hadn't noticed until this moment. "Yes," Dad said. "I think we do."

Author's Note & Acknowledgments

Do you ever watch those nature documentaries? You know, like *Blue Planet* or *Planet Earth* or the ones made by National Geographic? They're not the kind of thing I ever watch on my own, but my husband and I enjoy watching them together (and we both agree that falling asleep on the couch on a Sunday afternoon to the sound of David Attenborough's voice is one of the best things).

I'm always amazed and awed by the incredible beauty of our world that I see in these documentaries. But many of them end on a sobering note. They highlight a gorgeous part of our world, and then they show the viewer how that portion of our world is being destroyed because of the effect humans are having on it.

And it's just so darn sad.

I didn't start out the Ridley Kayne Chronicles by wanting to highlight some important issue in the real world. I don't ever start stories that way. For me, stories start with characters and everything else is built upon that layer by layer. At the end of the day, all I really want is for you to *feel all the feels*, and come away having had a satisfying escape into another world.

But I wasn't too far into Ridley's story when I realized that the history of her world—the broken, damaged planet with its magic that humans took advantage of for too long—mirrored what we, in real life, are doing to our planet.

This *isn't* a story about saving the environment, and this note isn't meant to make you depressed. It's just a small reminder to not take for granted the glorious creation we live in. Enjoy it! Appreciate it! (And maybe think twice next time you're about to use a plastic straw. ;-))

Thank you: to God for our beautiful world; to Kimberly Belden for editing notes; to my early readers for leaving reviews and spreading the word about this book; to Kyle for supporting my writing career no matter how many, *many* hours I spend lost in my fictional worlds; and *you*, for taking a chance on this first book in a new series!

xx Rachel

© Gavin van Haght

Rachel Morgan spent a good deal of her childhood living in a fantasy land of her own making, crafting endless stories of make-believe and occasionally writing some of them down. After completing a degree in genetics and discovering she still wasn't grown-up enough for a 'real' job, she decided to return to those story worlds still spinning around her imagination. These days she spends much of her time immersed in fantasy land once more, writing fiction for young adults and those young at heart.

www.rachel-morgan.com

22764698R00184

Printed in Great Britain
by Amazon